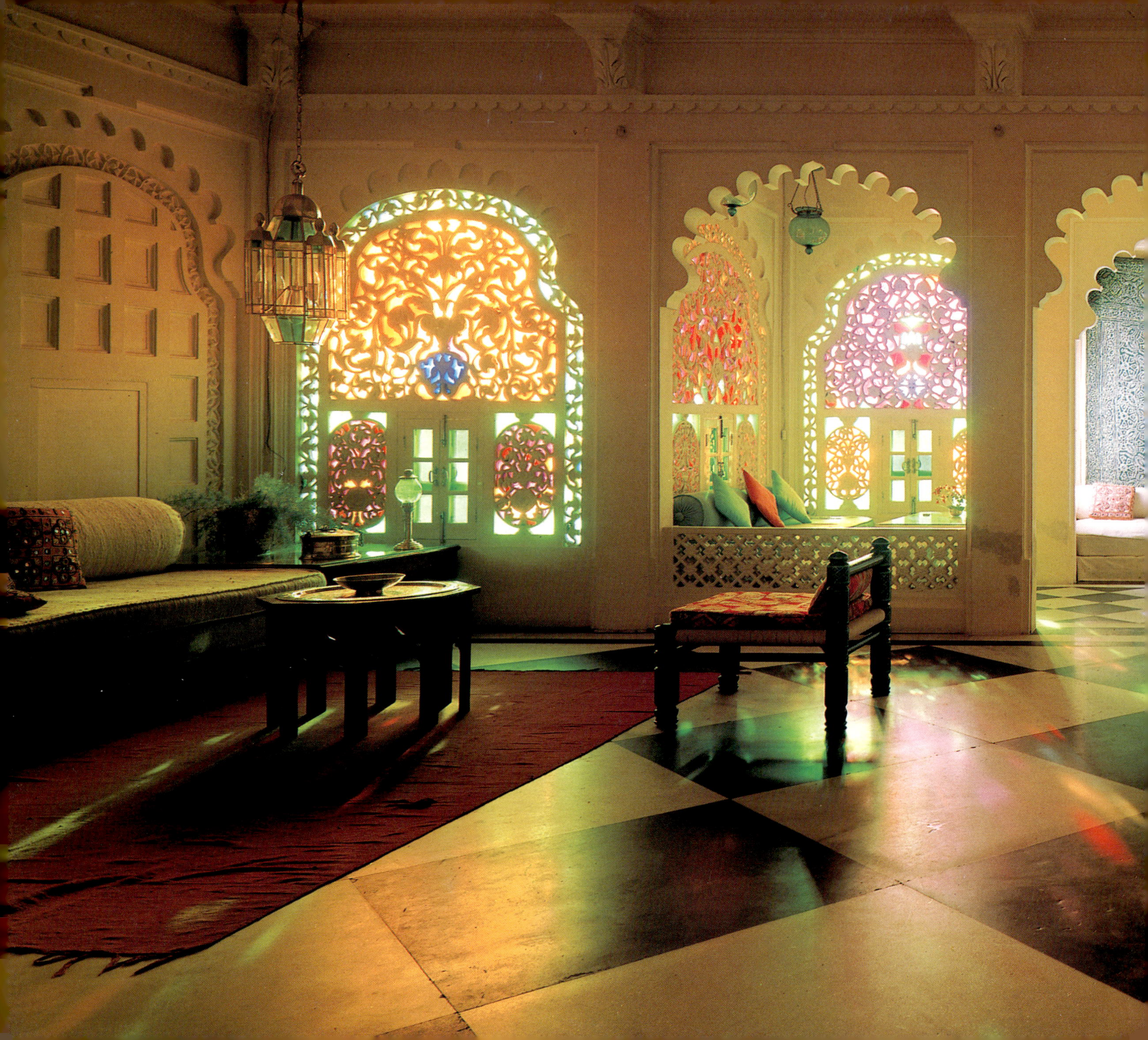

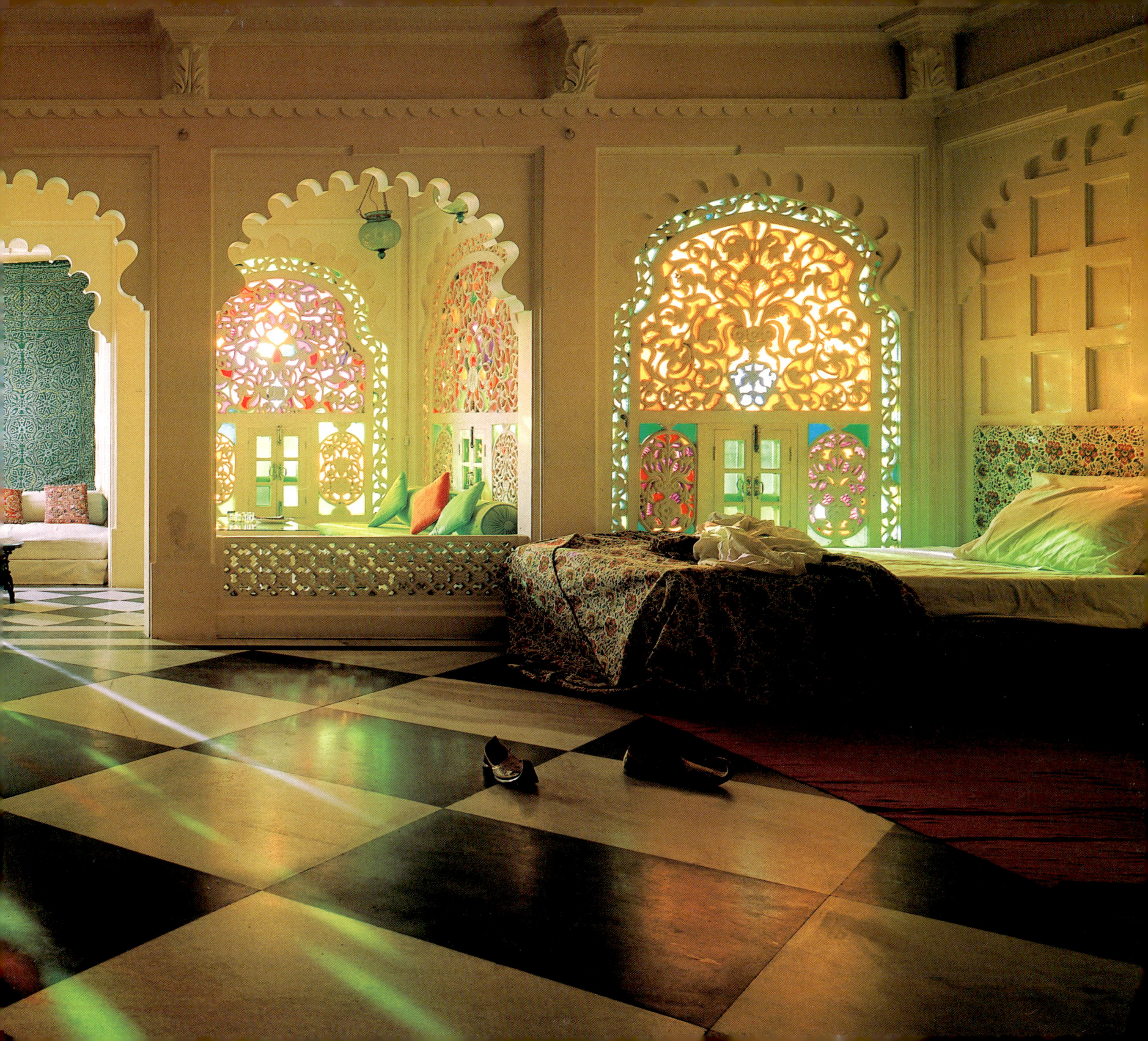

Executive Editor/Seiji Horibuchi
Translator/Yuji Oniki
Art Direction/Shinji Horibuchi
Publisher/Keizo Inoue

Originally published as *Hotel Rakuen* by Shogakukan, Inc. in Japan
Editor/Shuji Shimamoto
Art Direction/Yukimasa Okumura

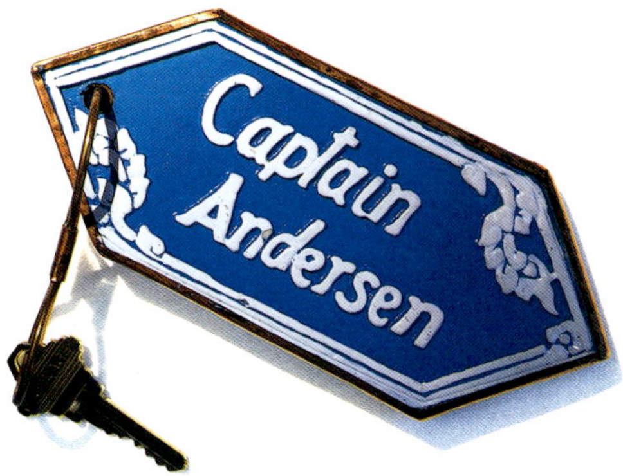

Printed in Japan

ISBN 1-56931-149-8

First printing, November 1996

Cadence Books
A division of Viz Communications, Inc.
A subsidiary of Shogakukan, Inc.
P.O. Box 77010, San Francisco, CA 94107

PREVIOUS PAGES/
LAKE PALACE HOTEL (UDAIPUR)

HOTEL PARADISE

A PHOTOGRAPHIC JOURNEY
TO THE WORLD'S MOST EXOTIC RESORT HOTELS

KAZUYOSHI MIYOSHI

CADENCE BOOKS

CONTENTS

INDIA

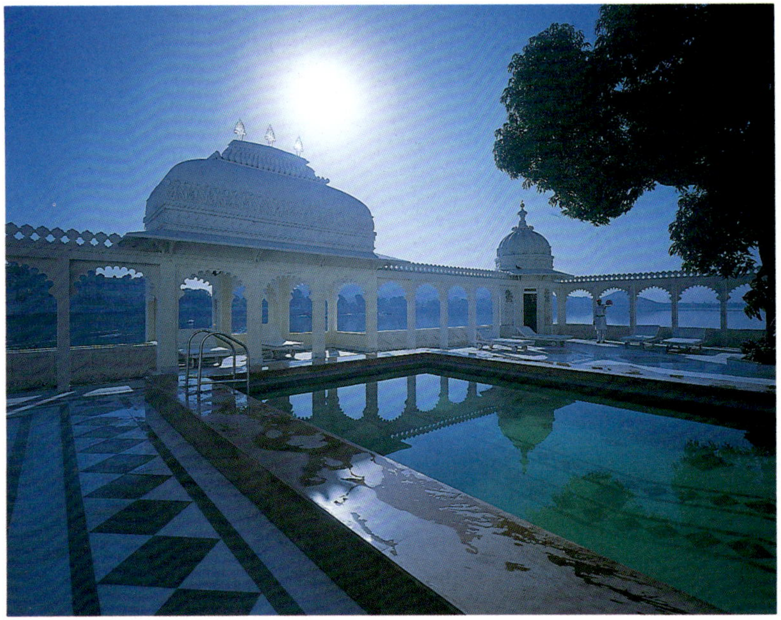

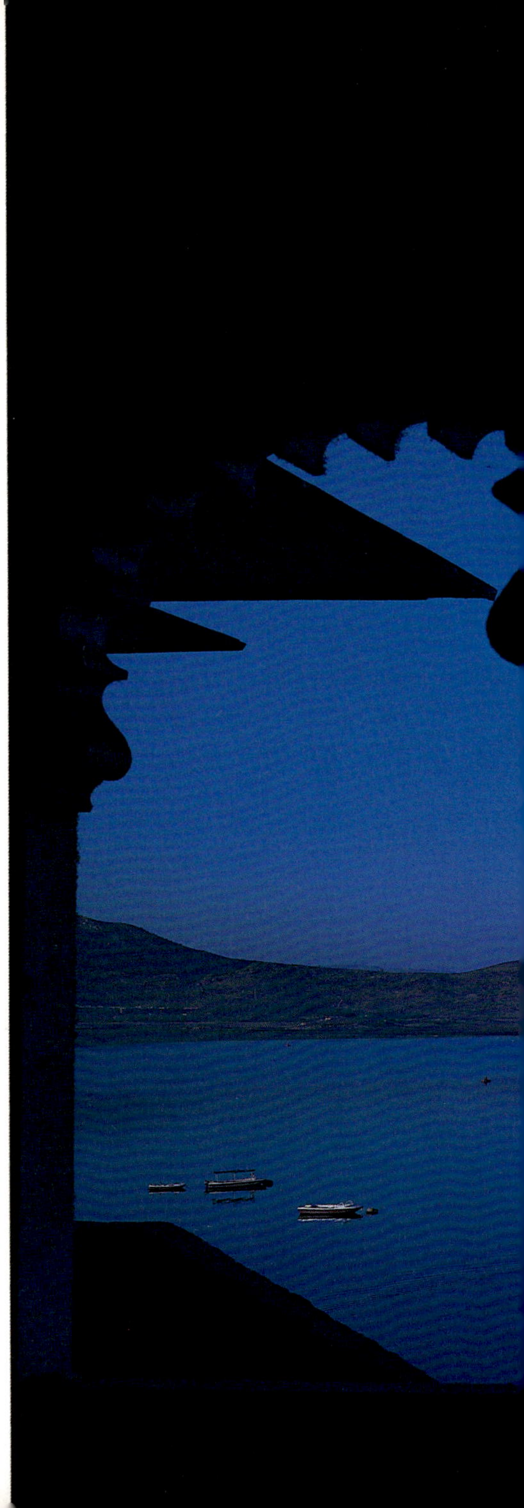

LAKE PALACE HOTEL (UDAIPUR)

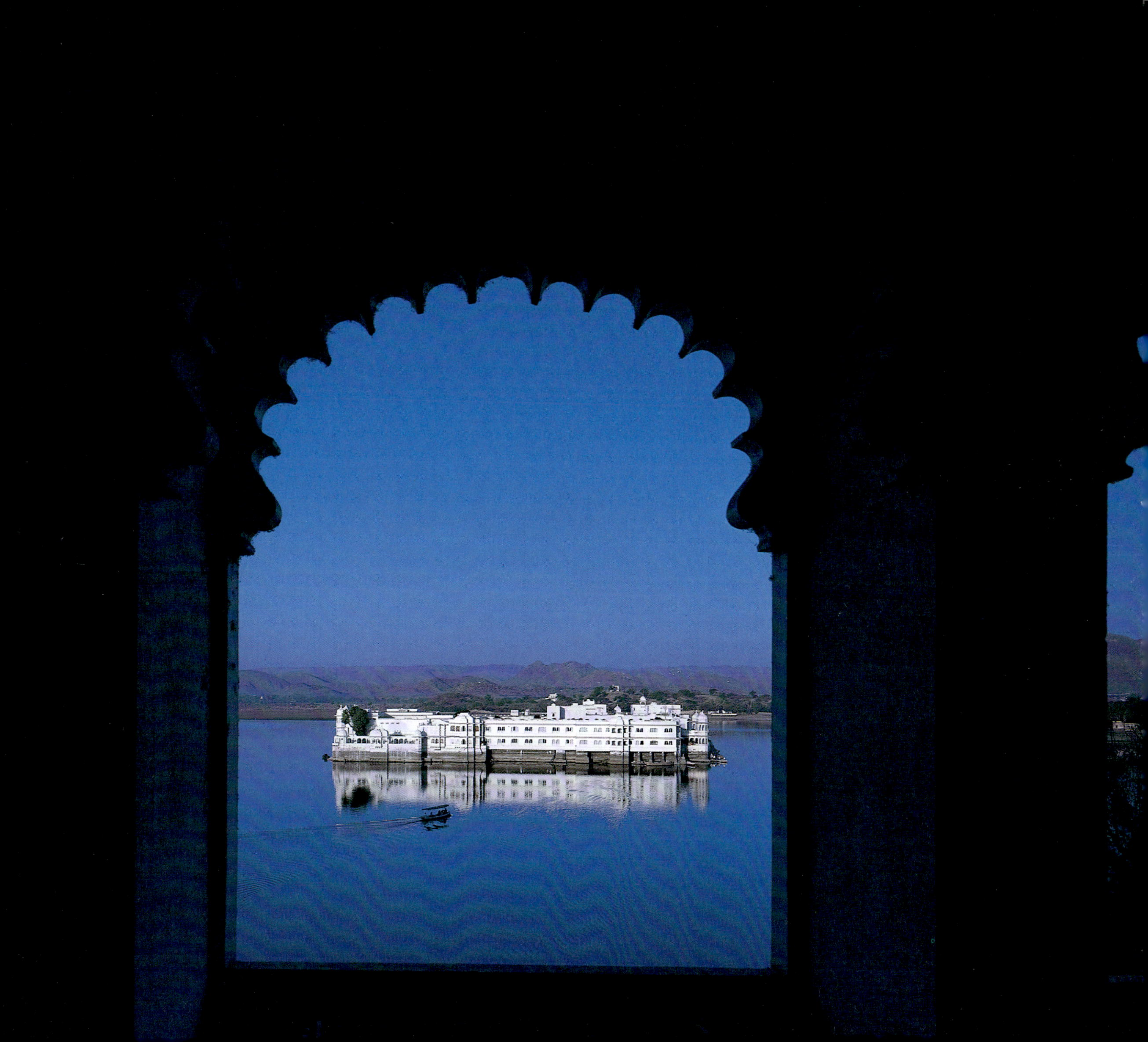

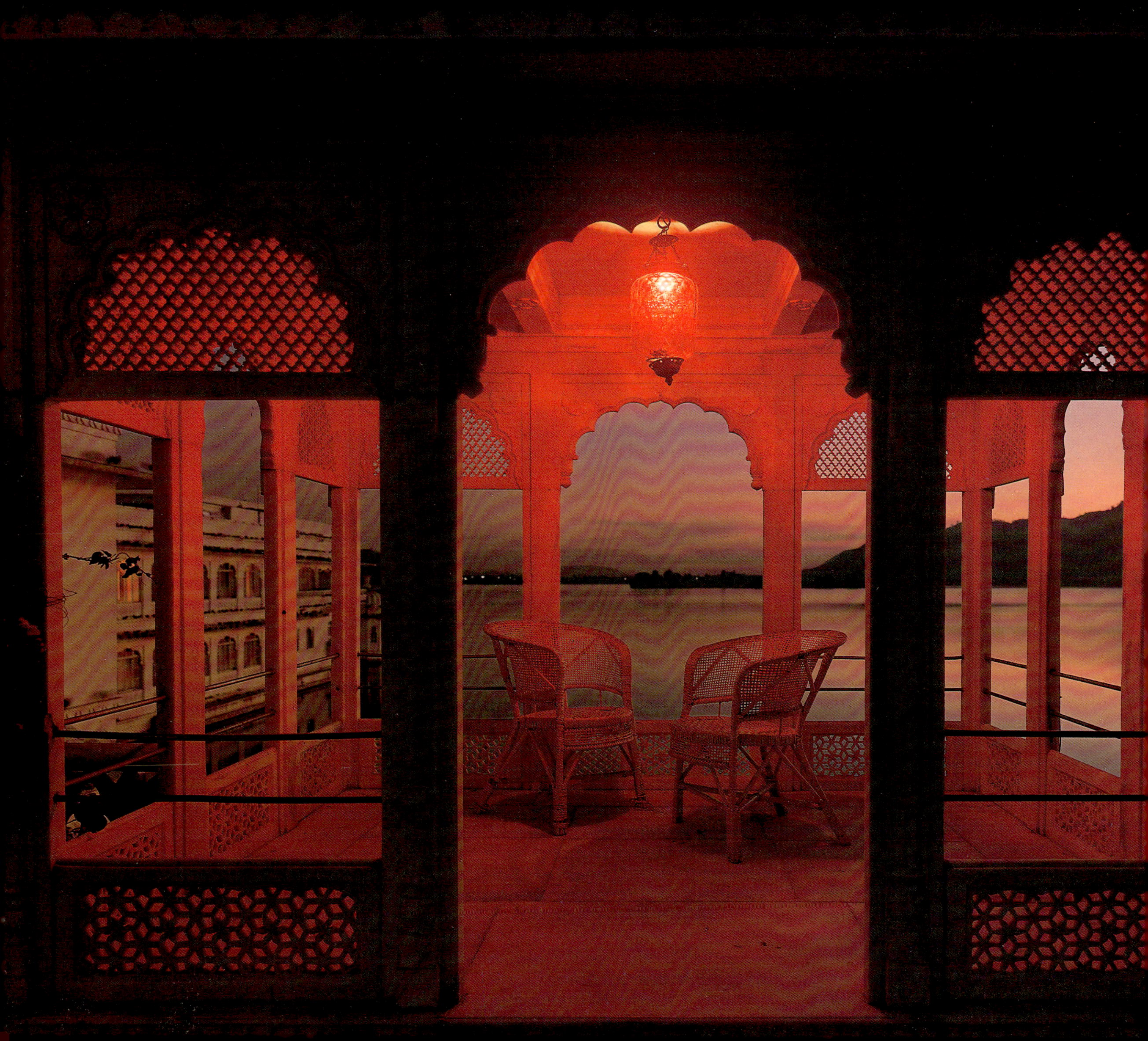

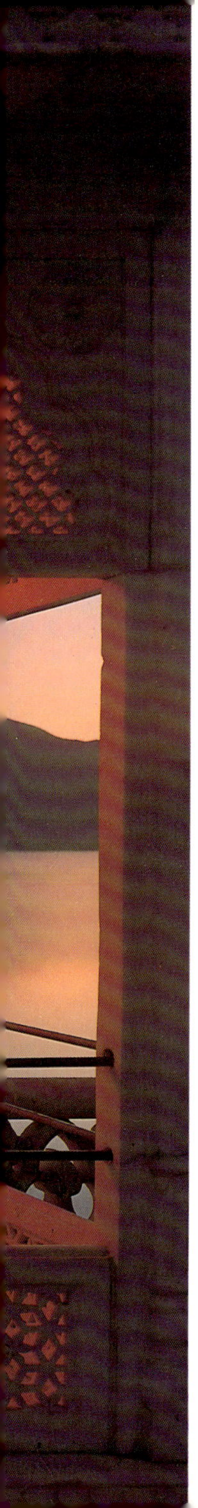

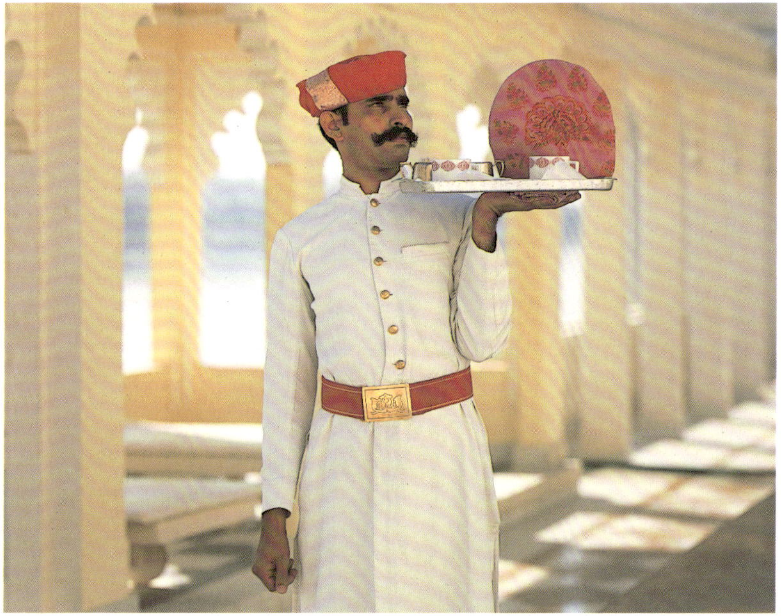

LAKE PALACE HOTEL (UDAIPUR)

14

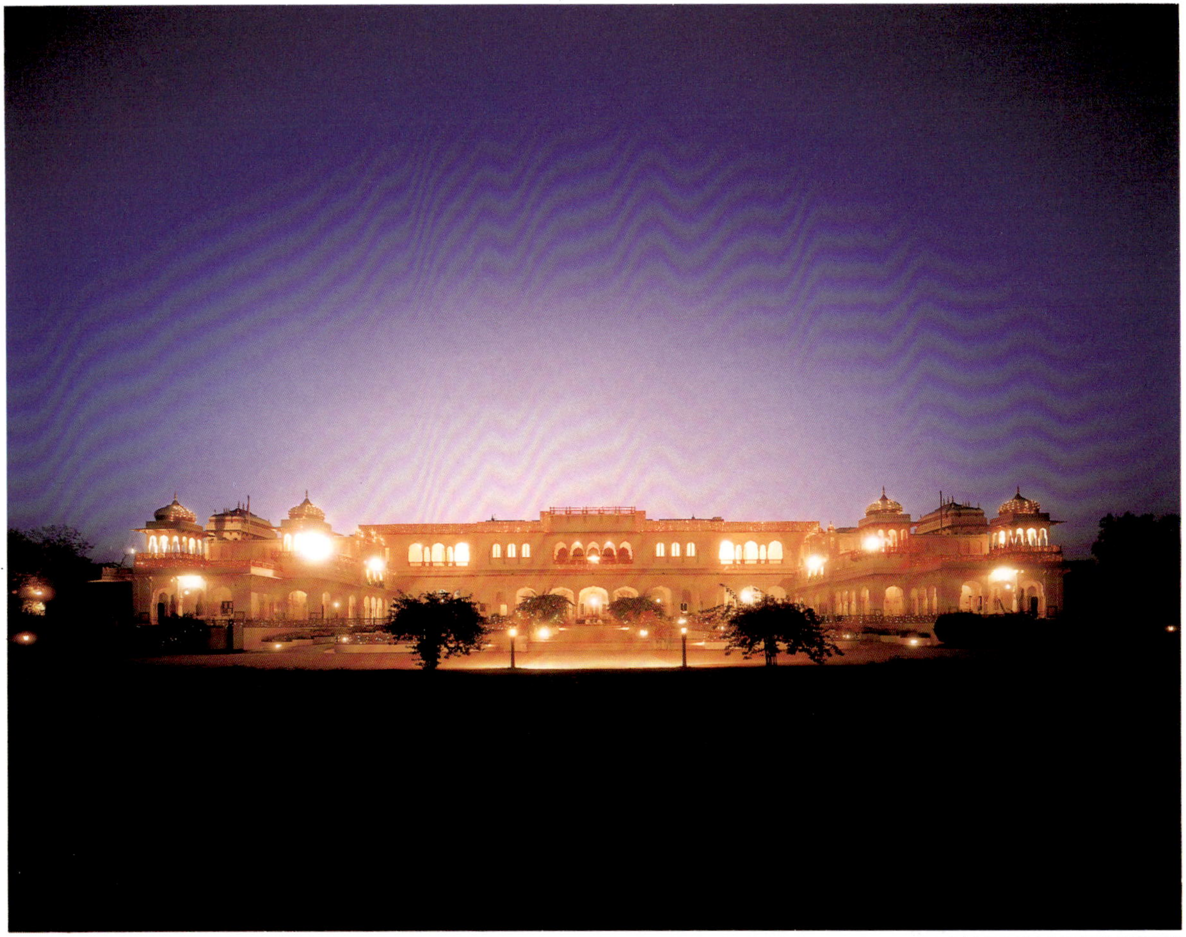

RAMBAGH PALACE (JAIPUR)

RAMBAGH PALACE (JAIPUR)

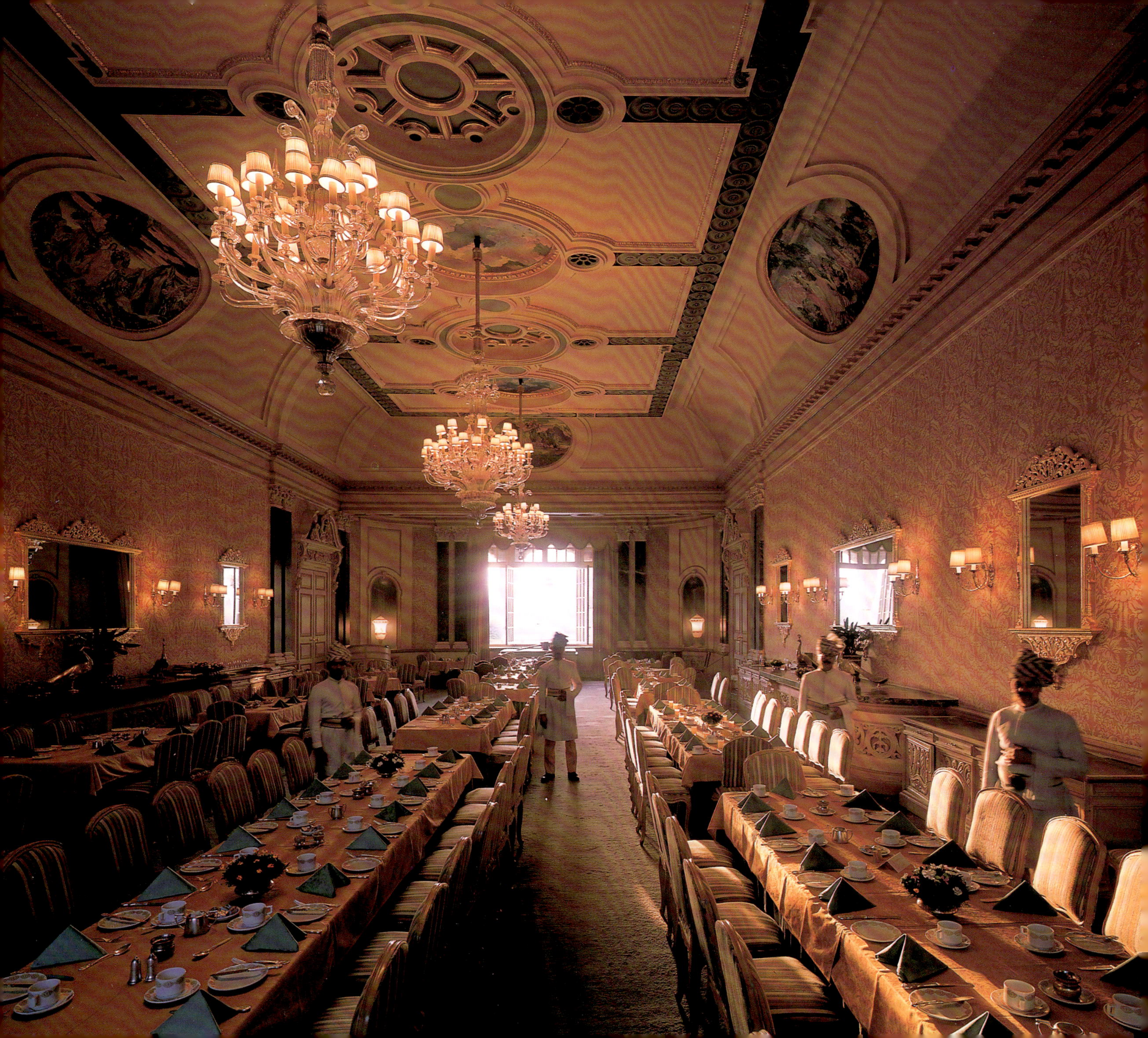

16

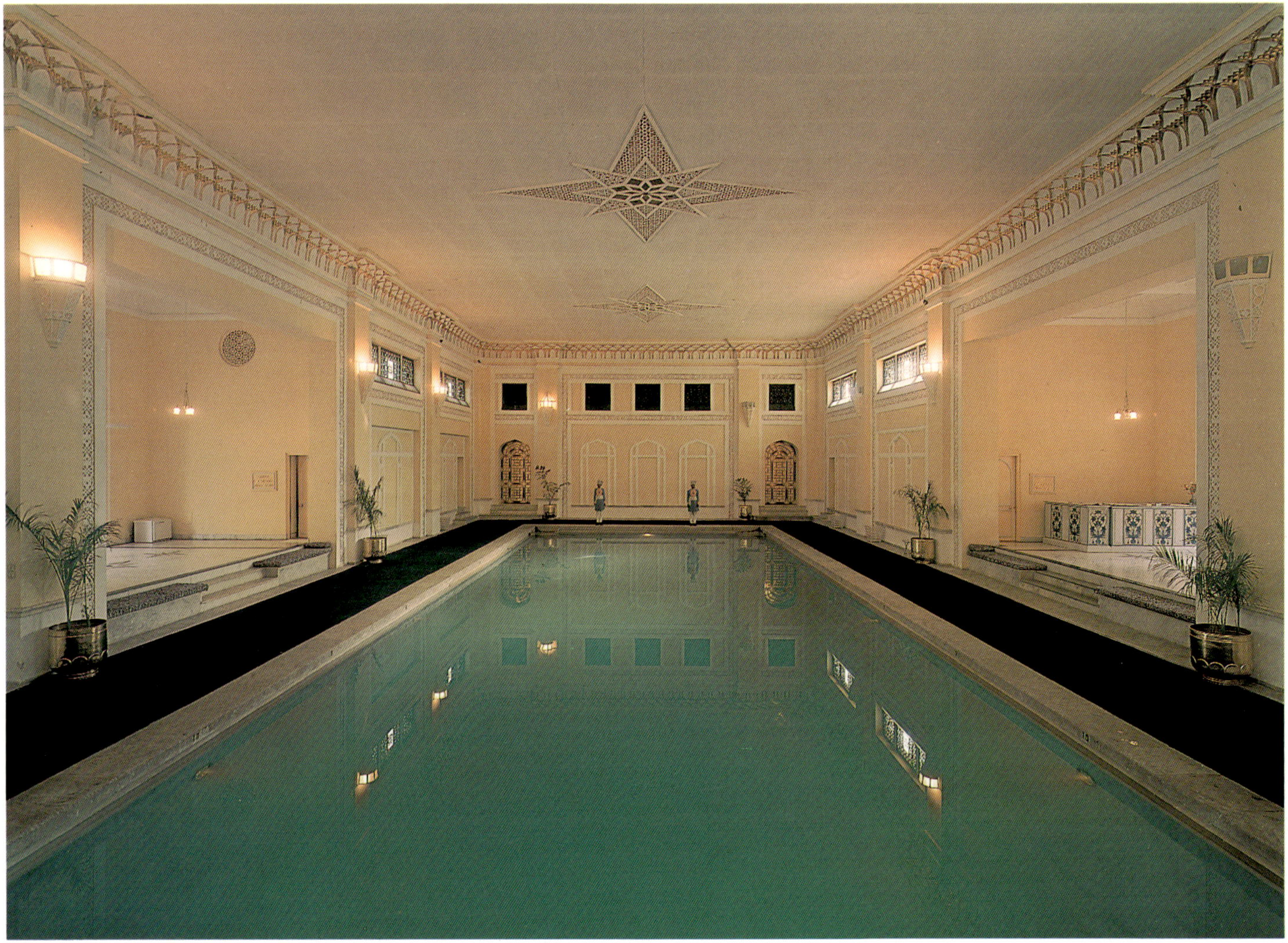

RAMBAGH PALACE (JAIPUR)

RAMBAGH PALACE (JAIPUR)

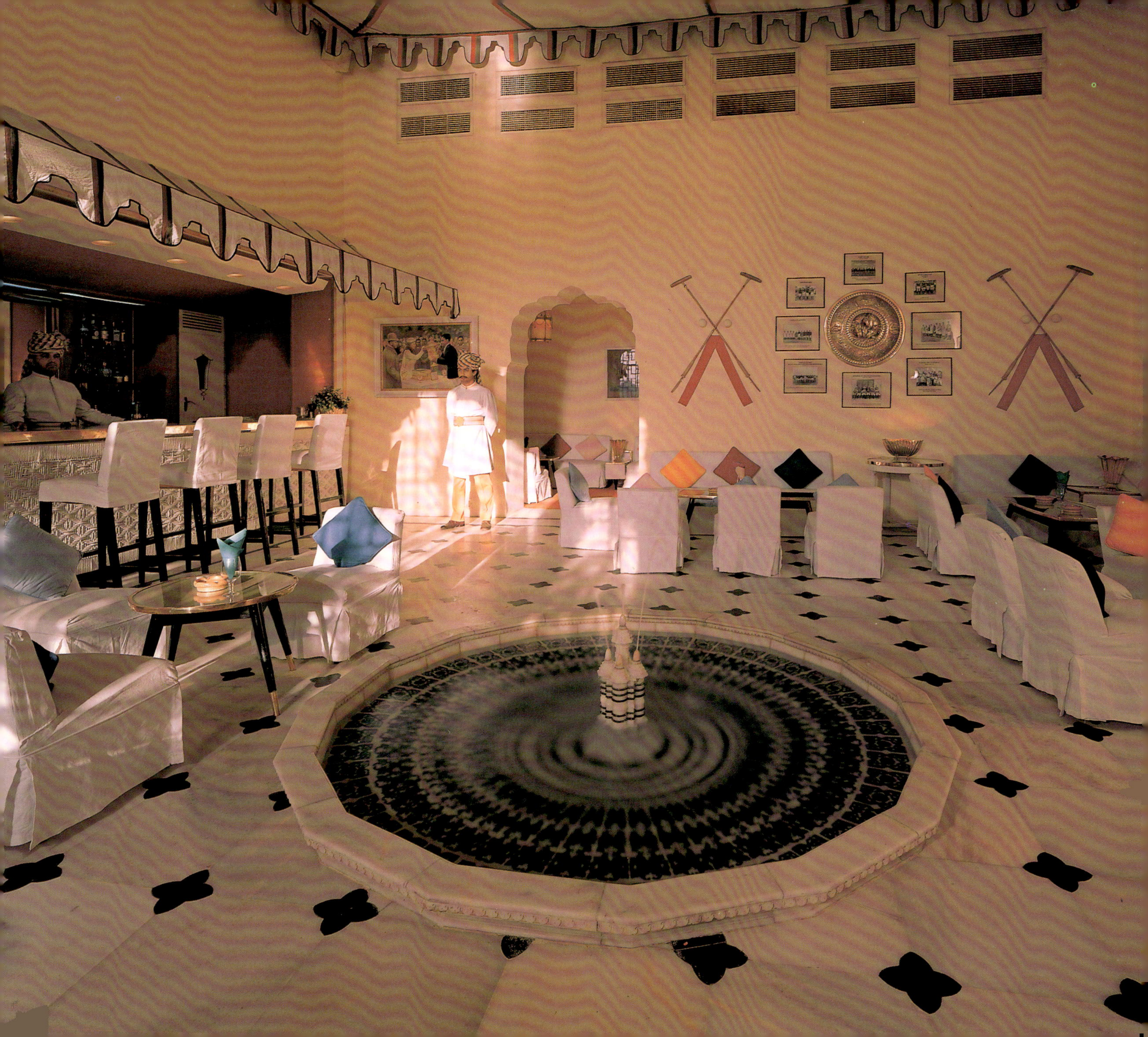

SRI LANKA

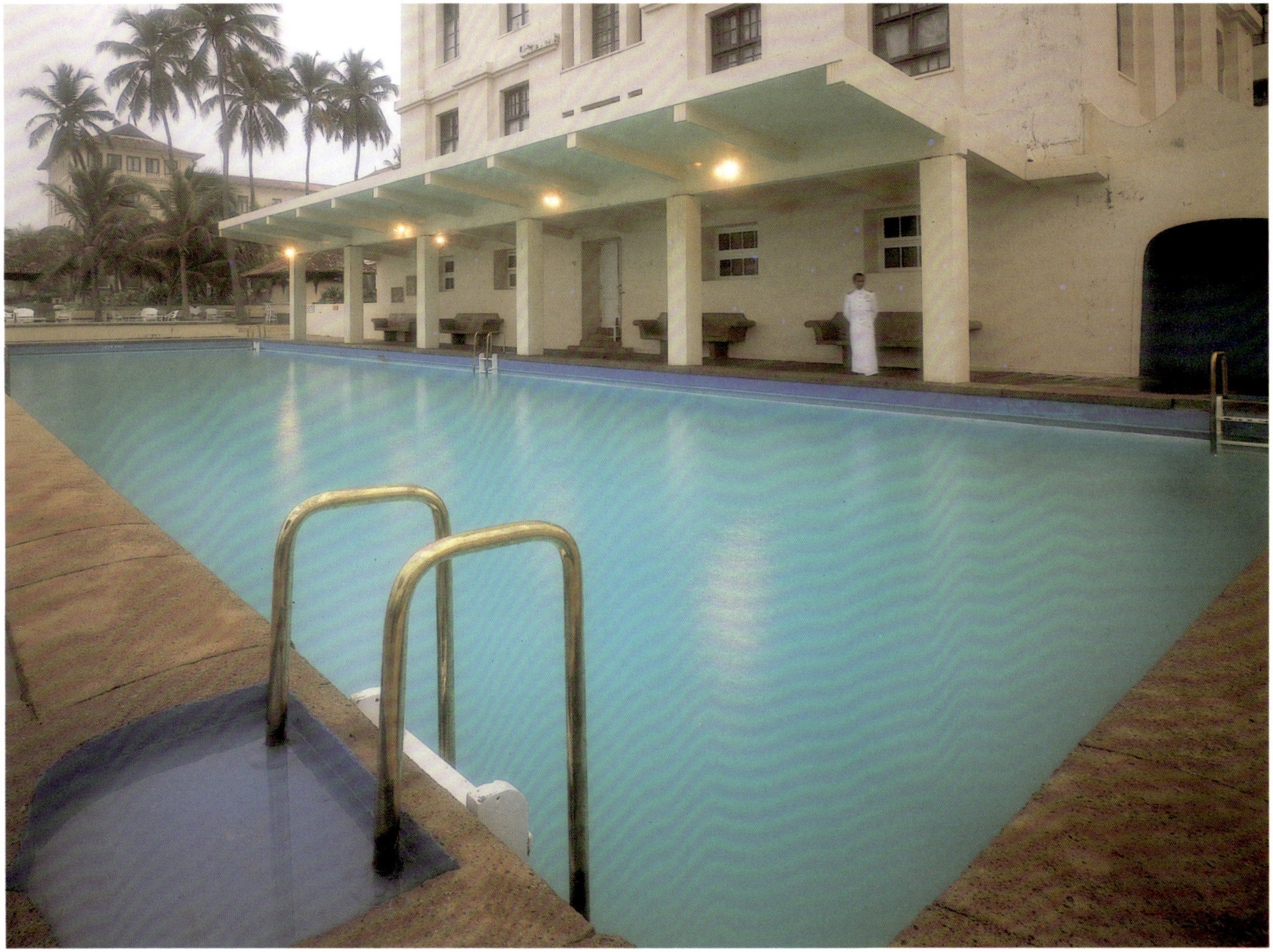

GALLE FACE HOTEL (COLOMBO)

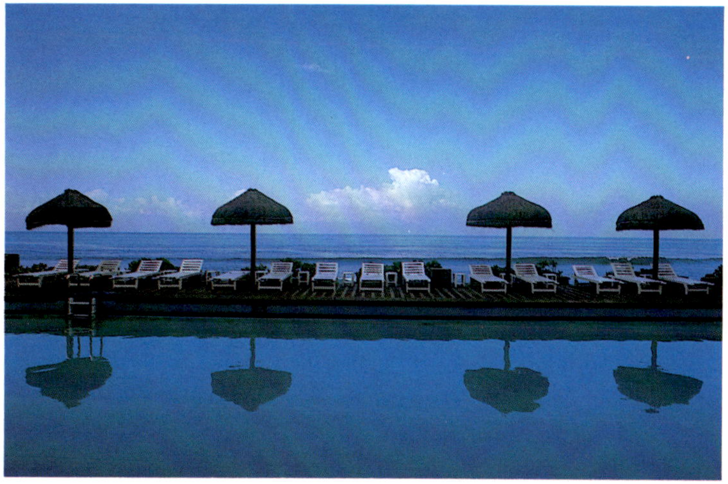

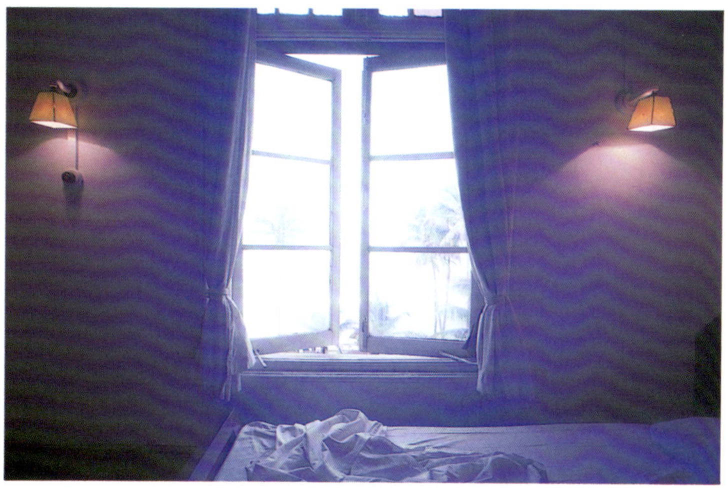

GALLE FACE HOTEL (COLOMBO)

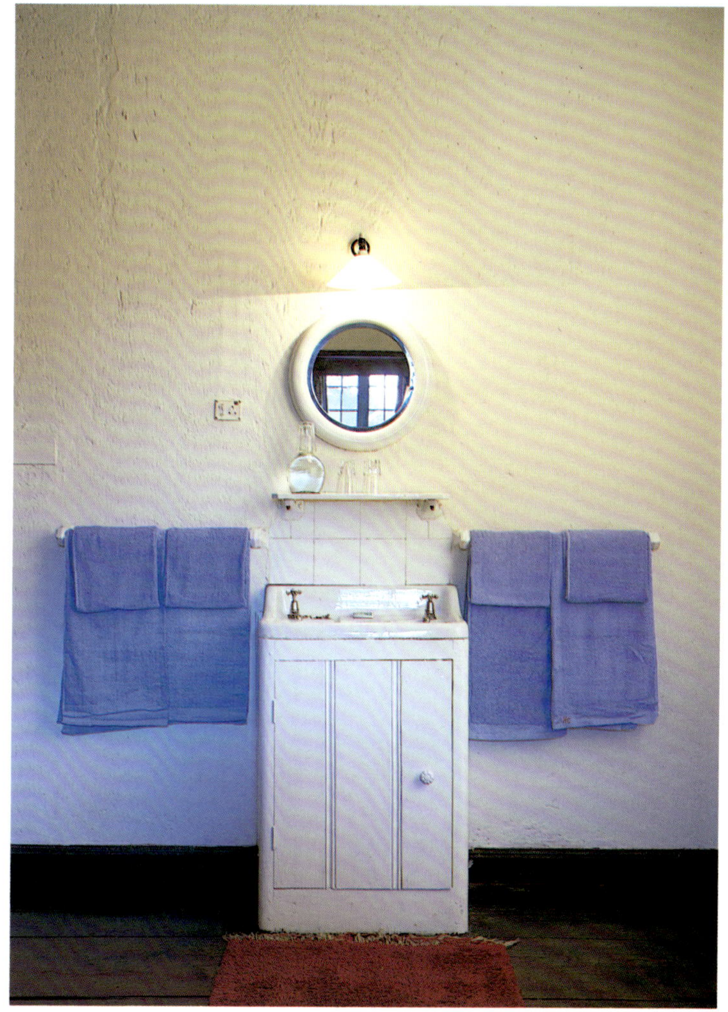

THE HILL CLUB (NUWARA ELIYA)

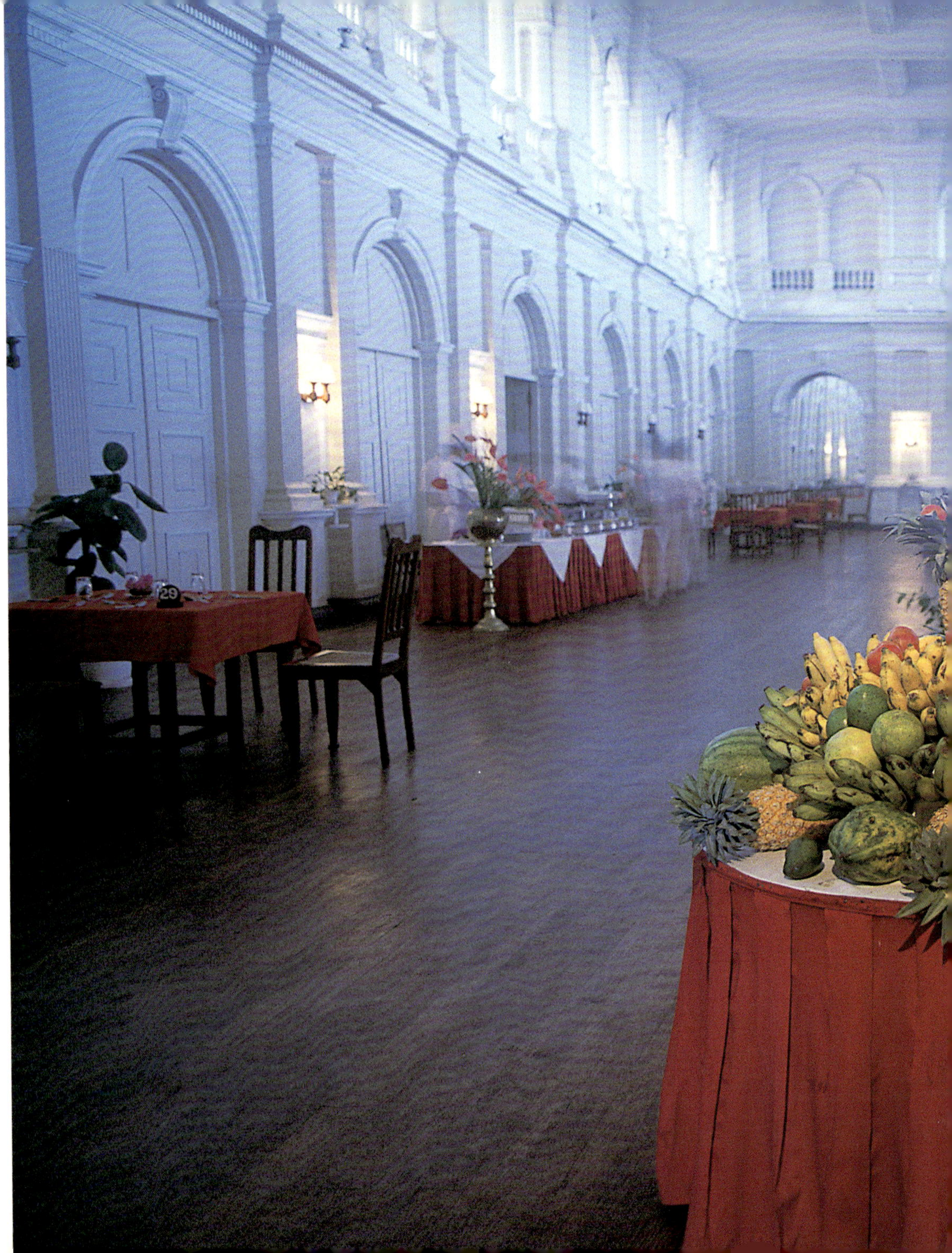

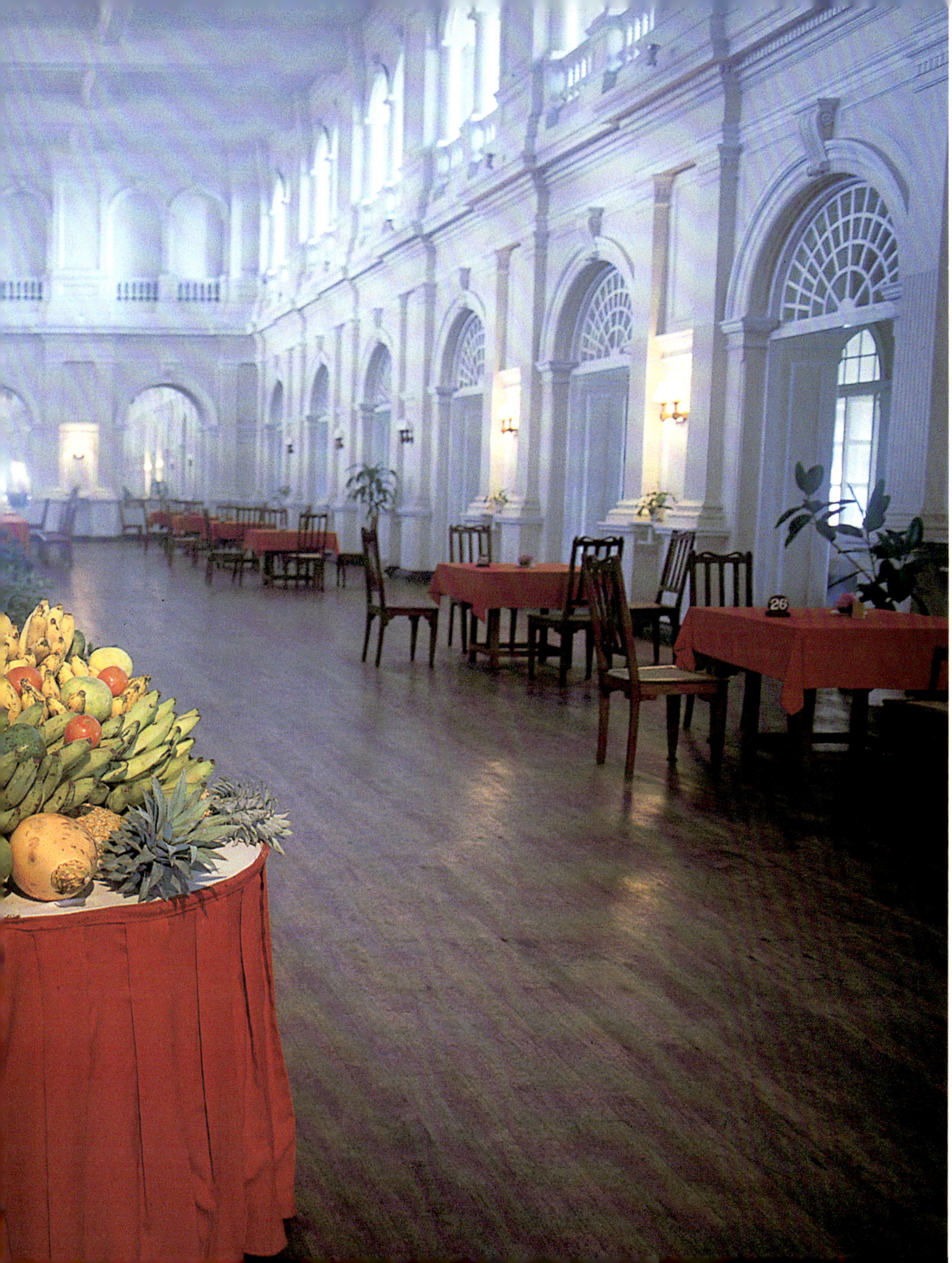

GALLE FACE HOTEL (COLOMBO)

MALDIVES

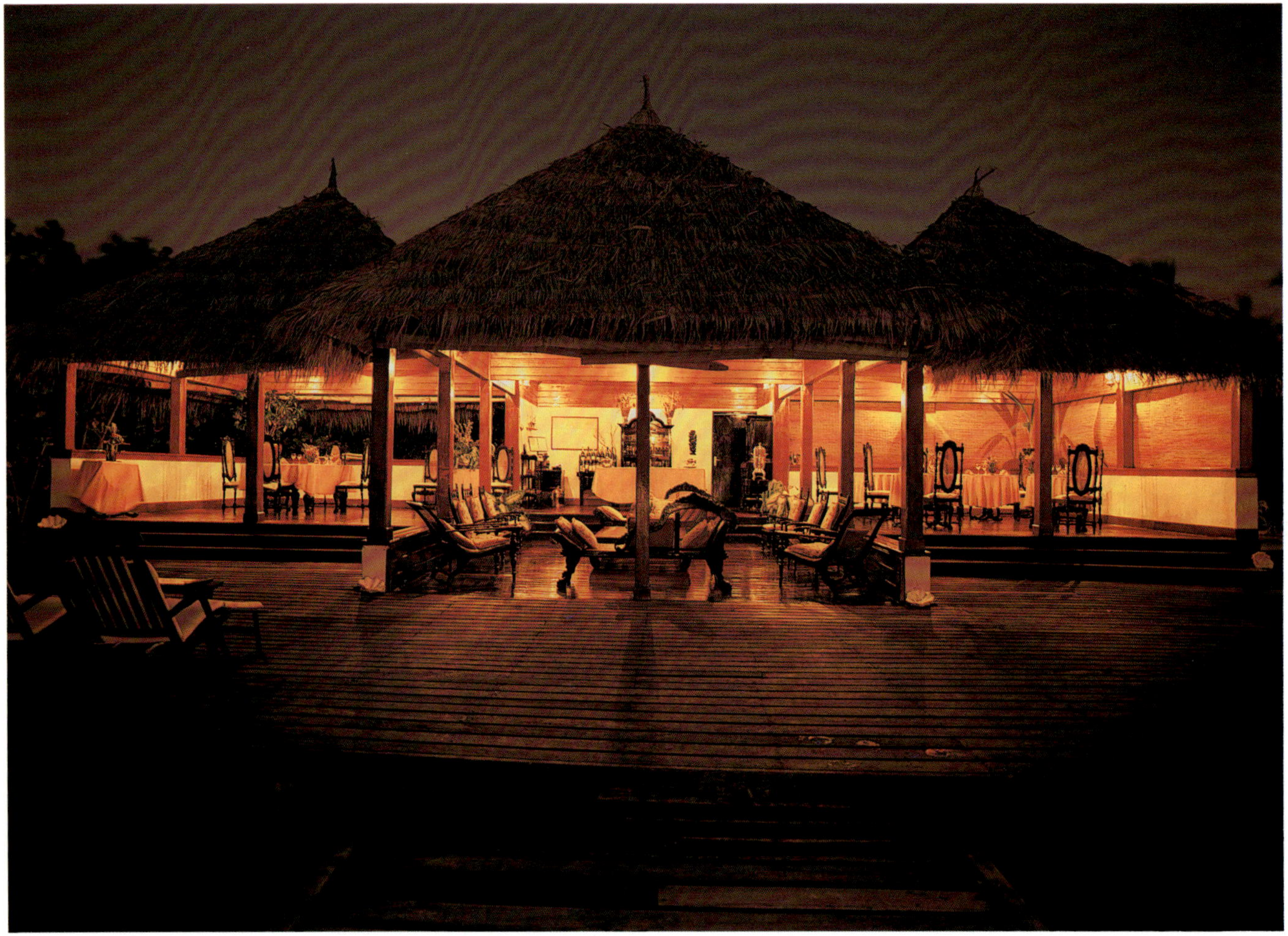

KUDAHITI TOURIST RESORT (NORTH MALE ATOLL)

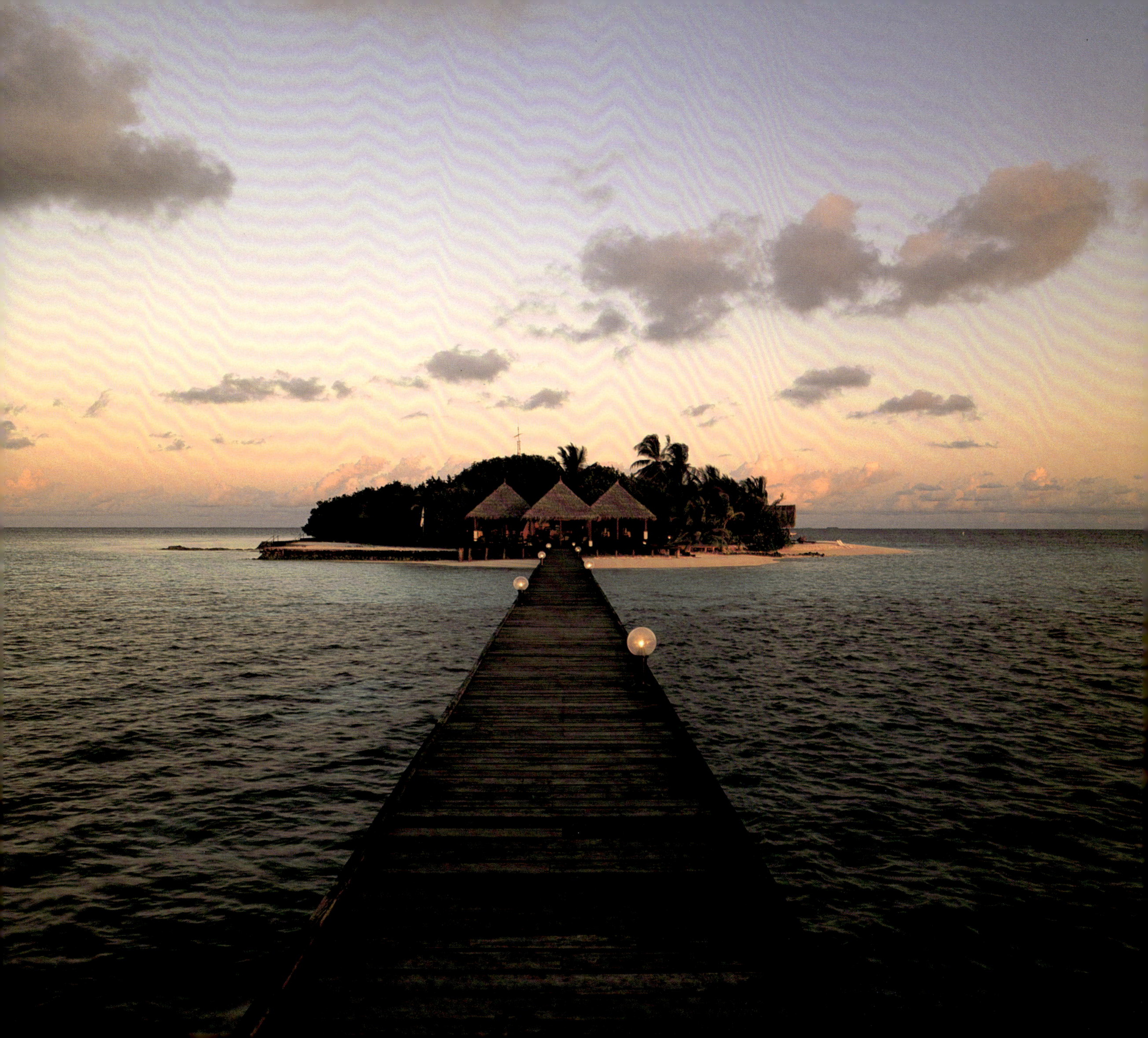

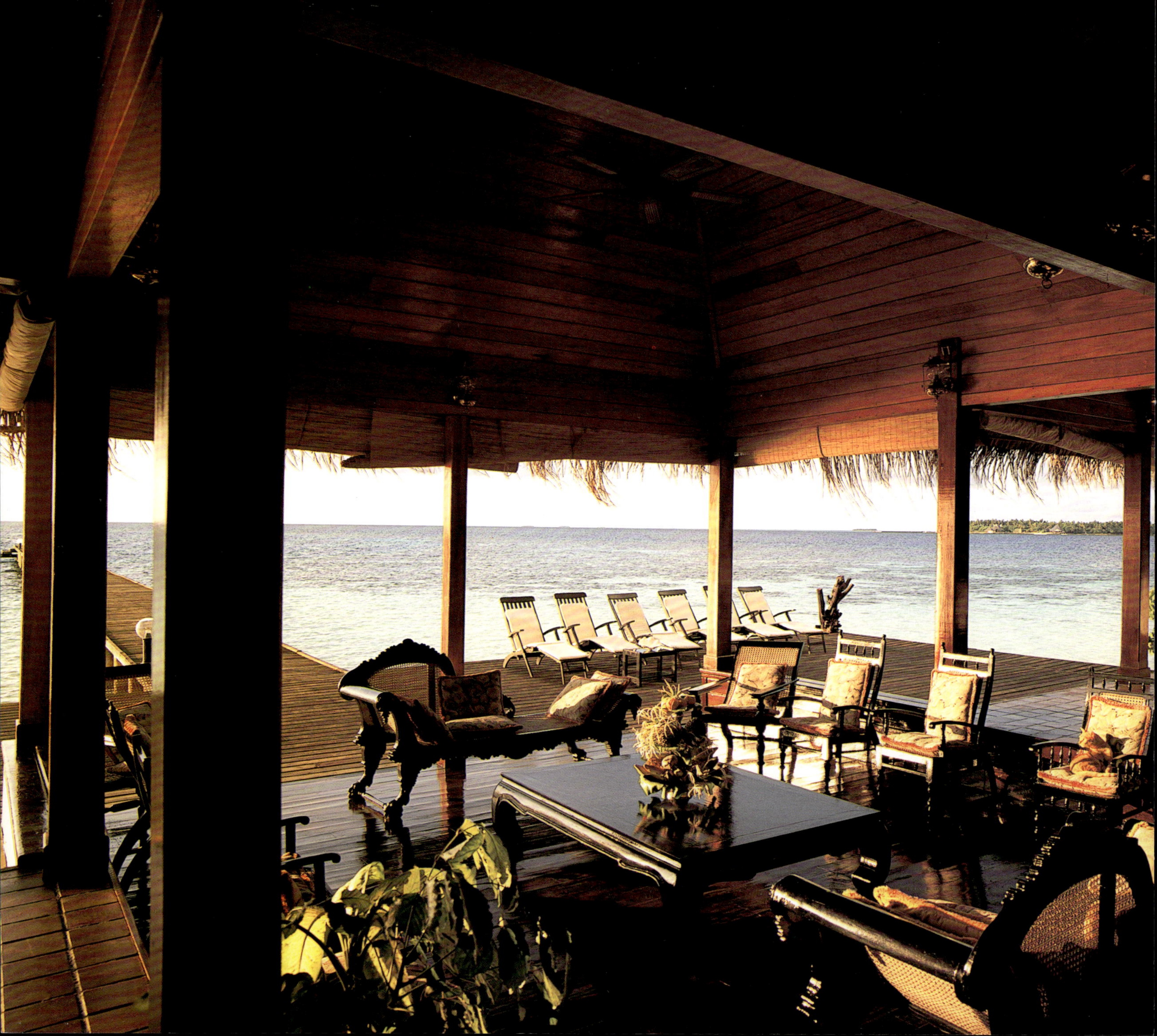

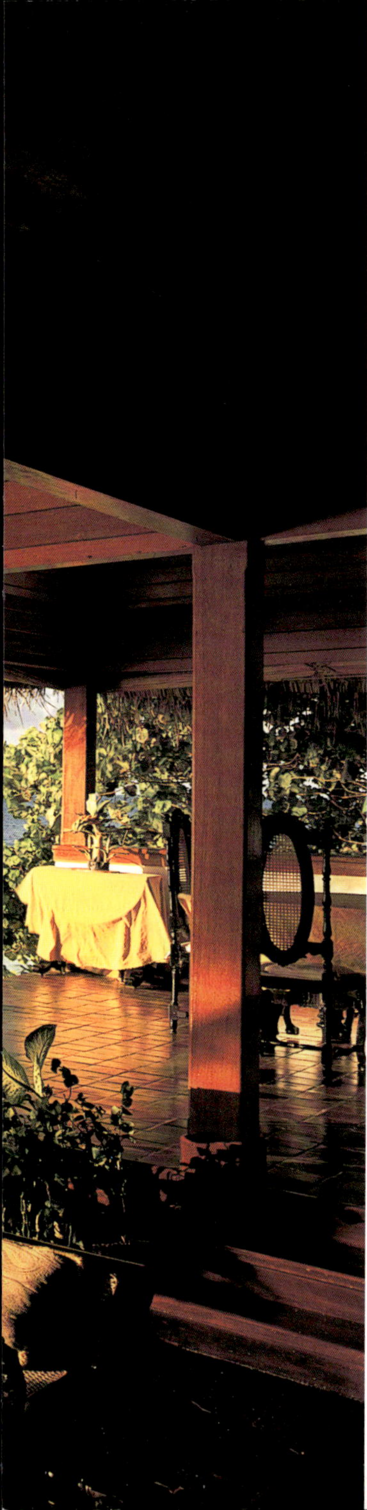

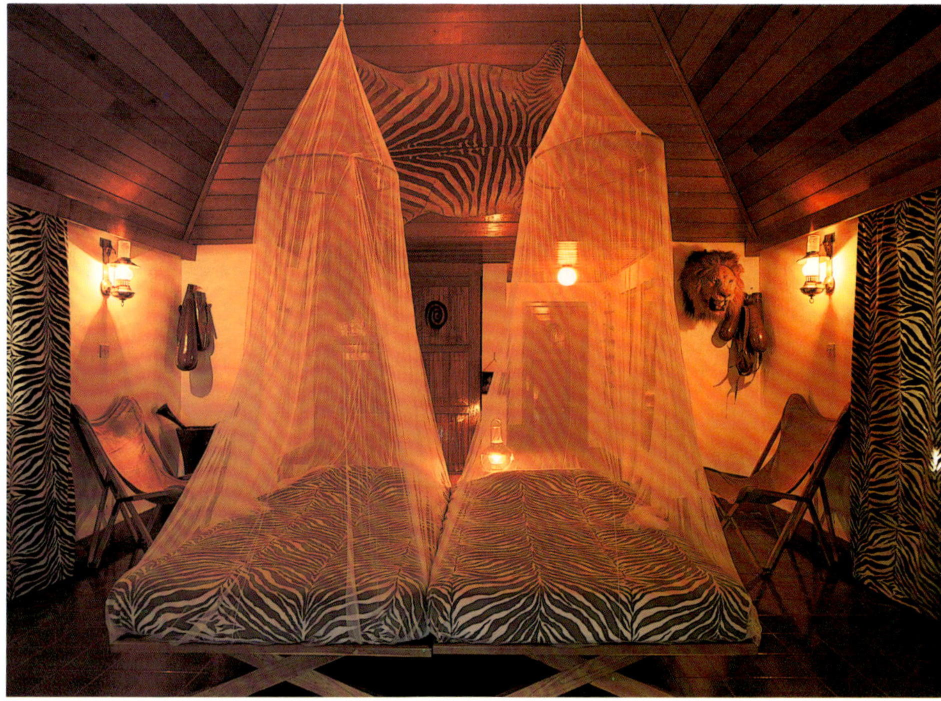

KUDAHITI TOURIST RESORT (NORTH MALE ATOLL)

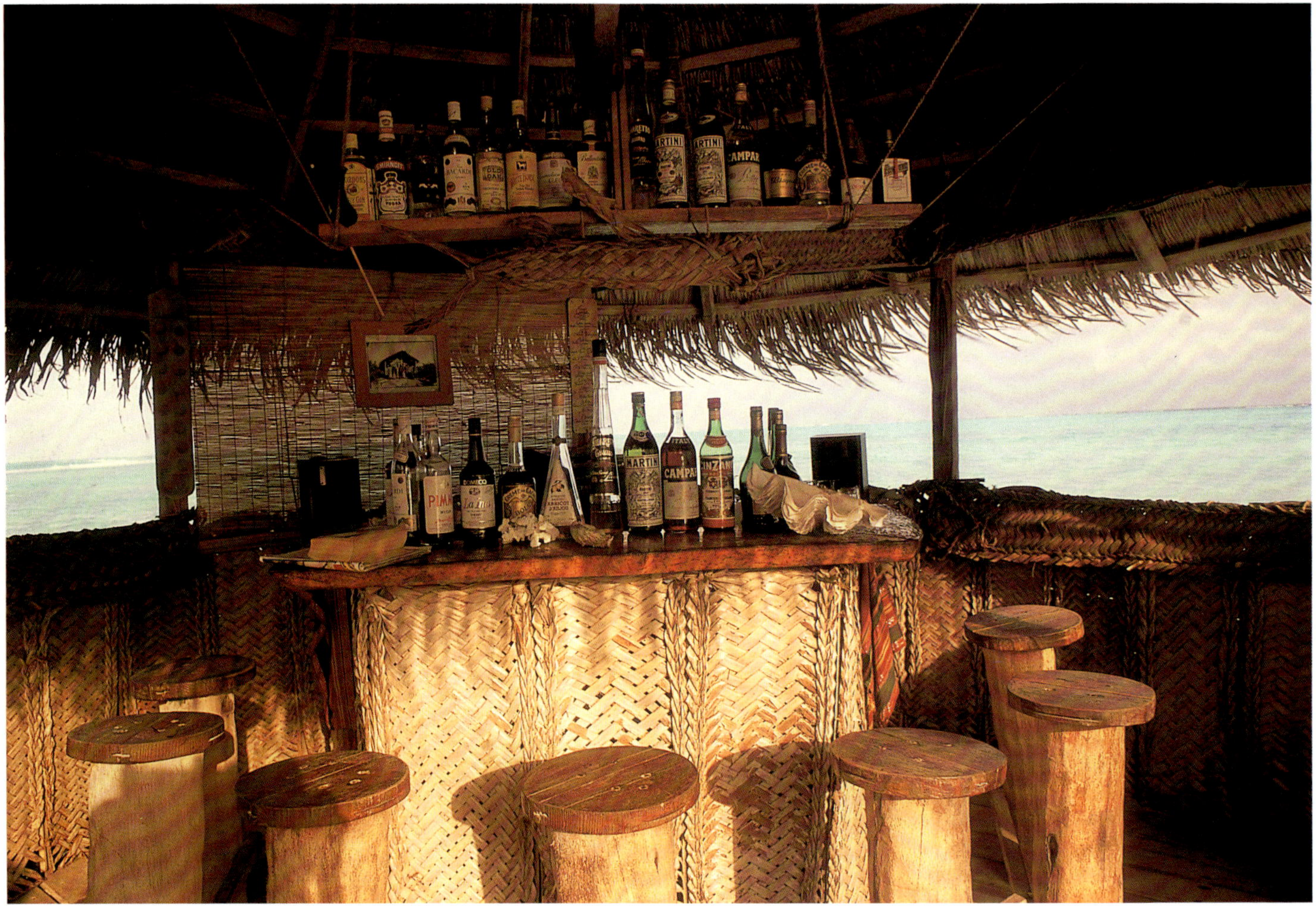

COCOA ISLAND (SOUTH MALE ATOLL)

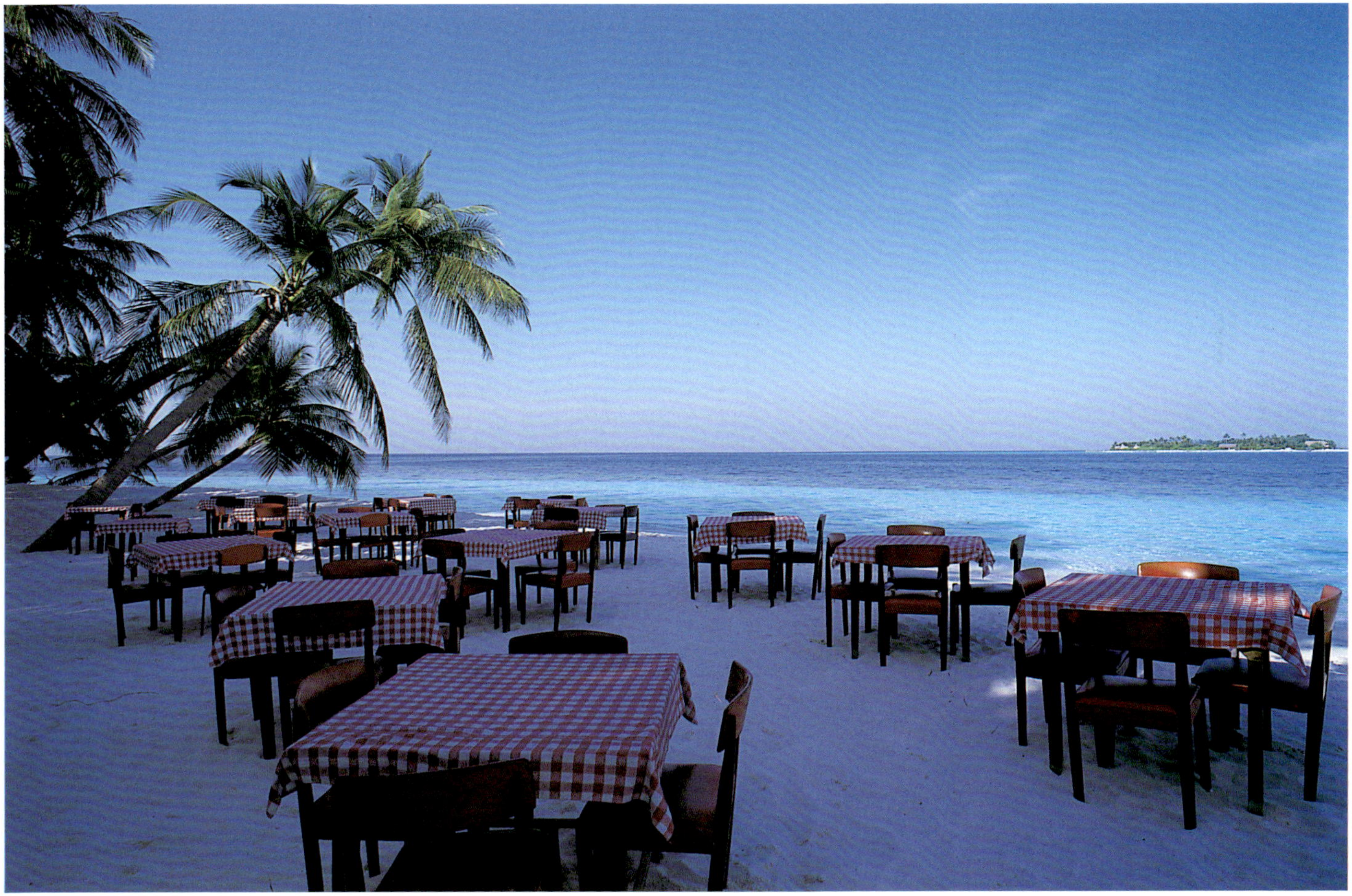

IHURU TOURIST RESORT (NORTH MALE ATOLL)

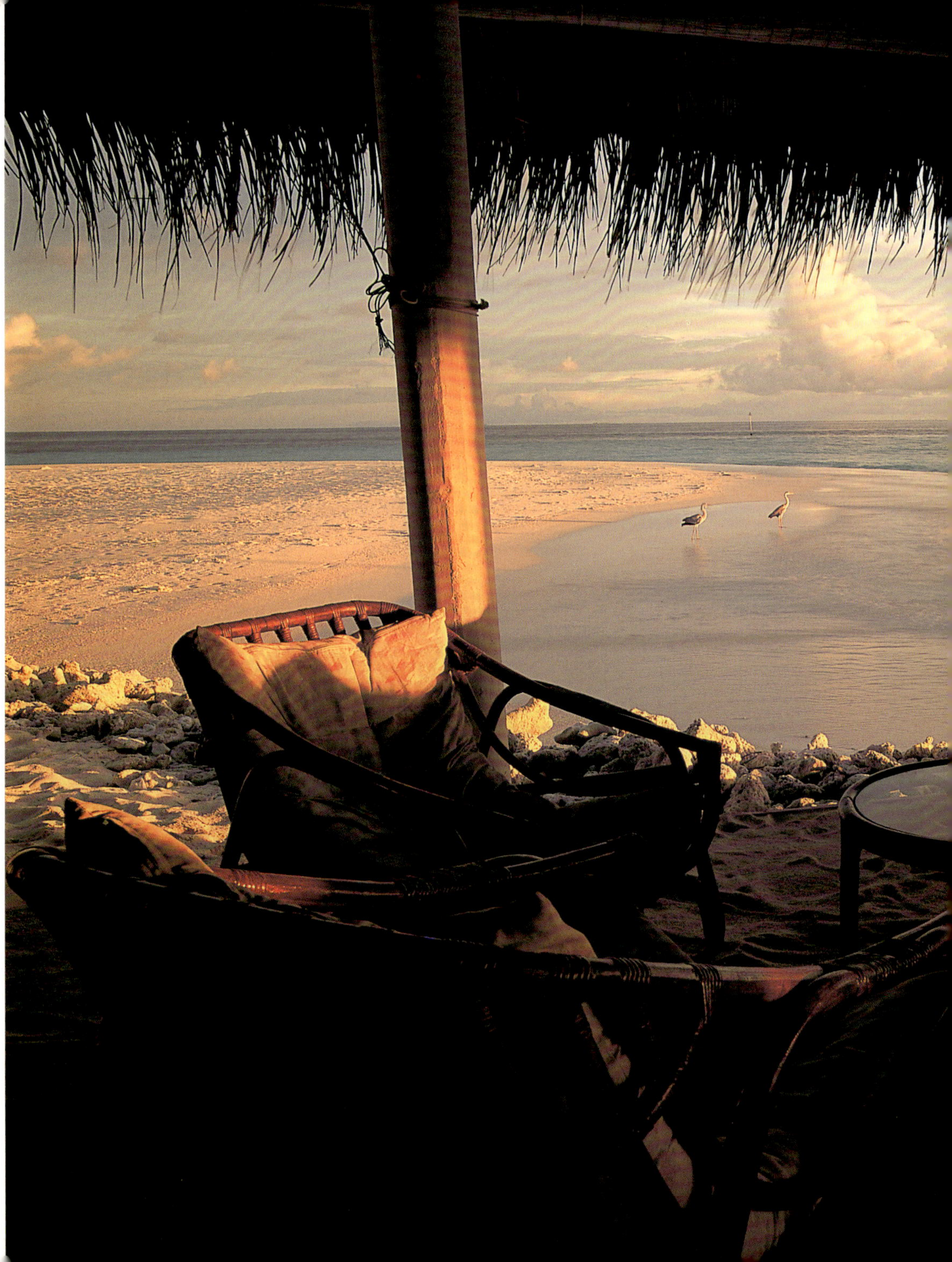

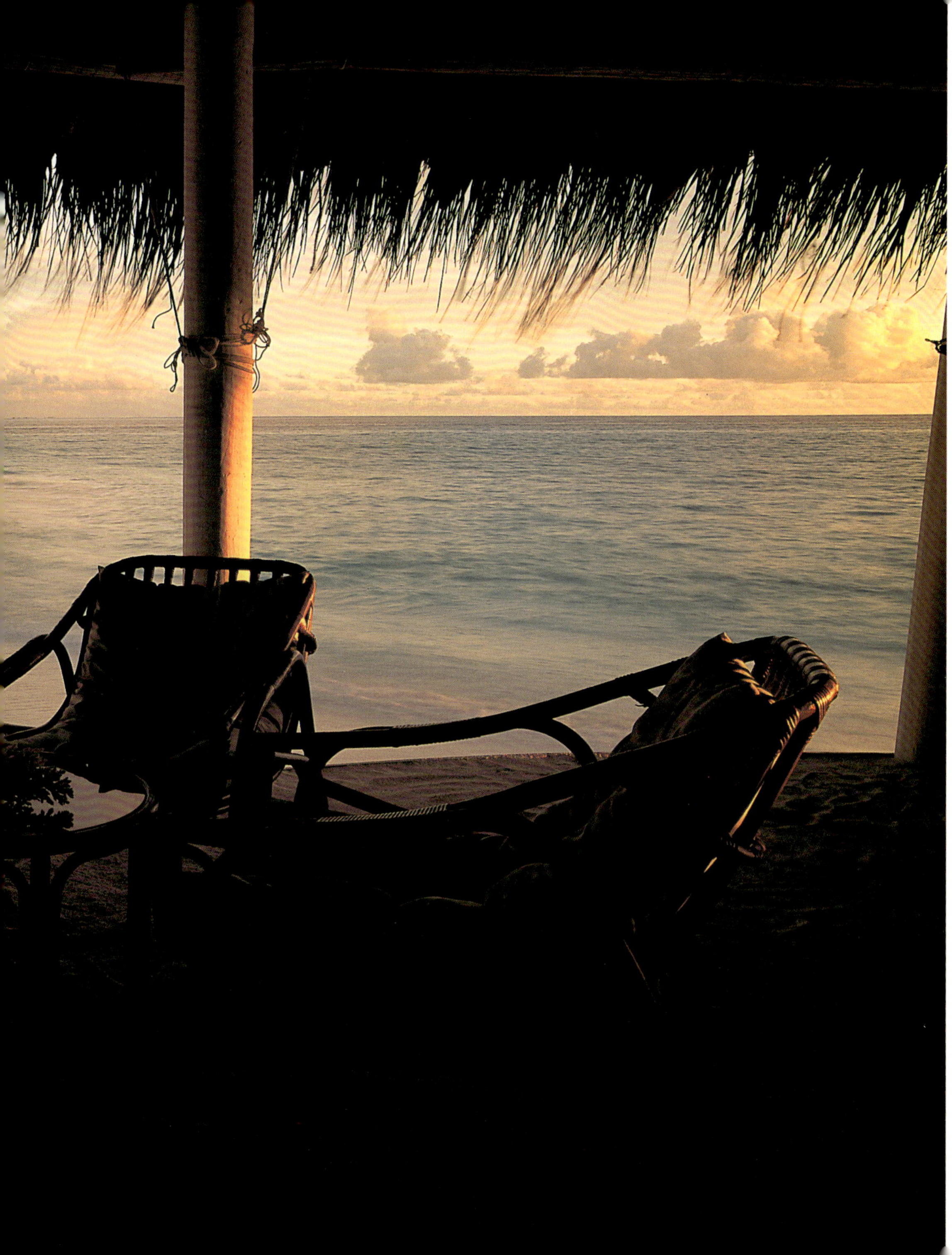

ANGAGA RESORT (ARI ATOLL)

NEPAL

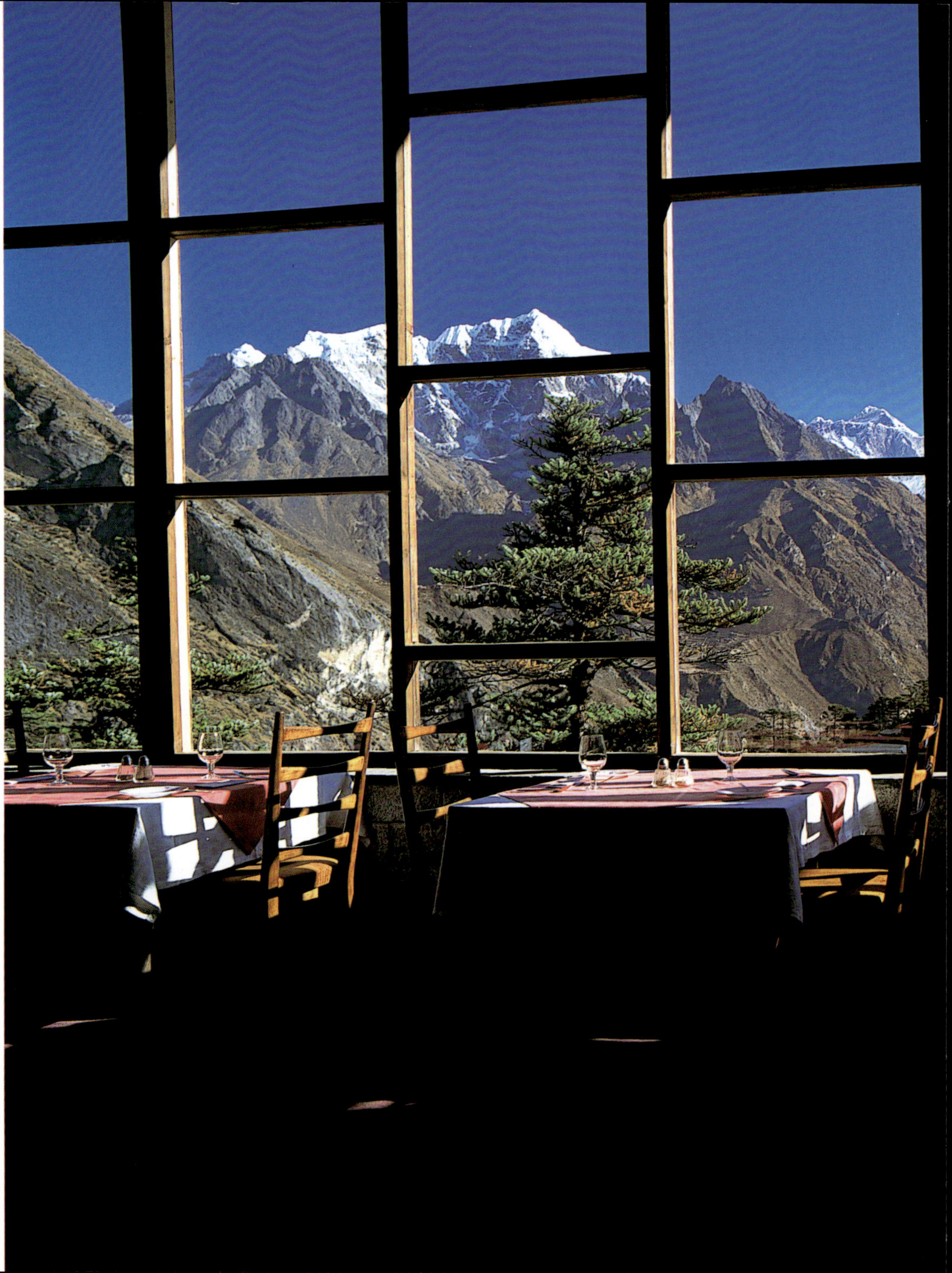

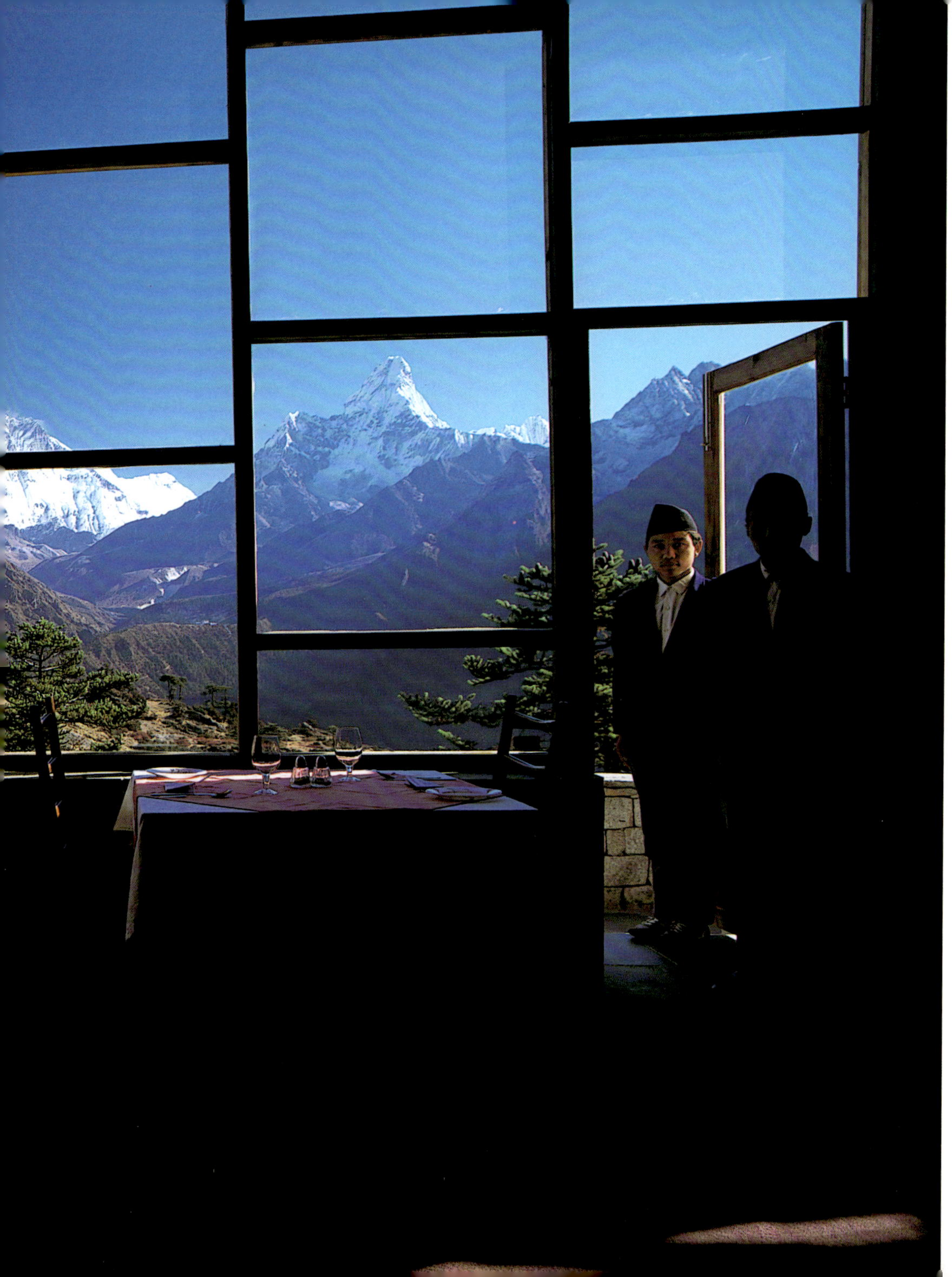

HOTEL EVEREST VIEW (SHYANGBOCHE)
ALSO FOLLOWING PAGES

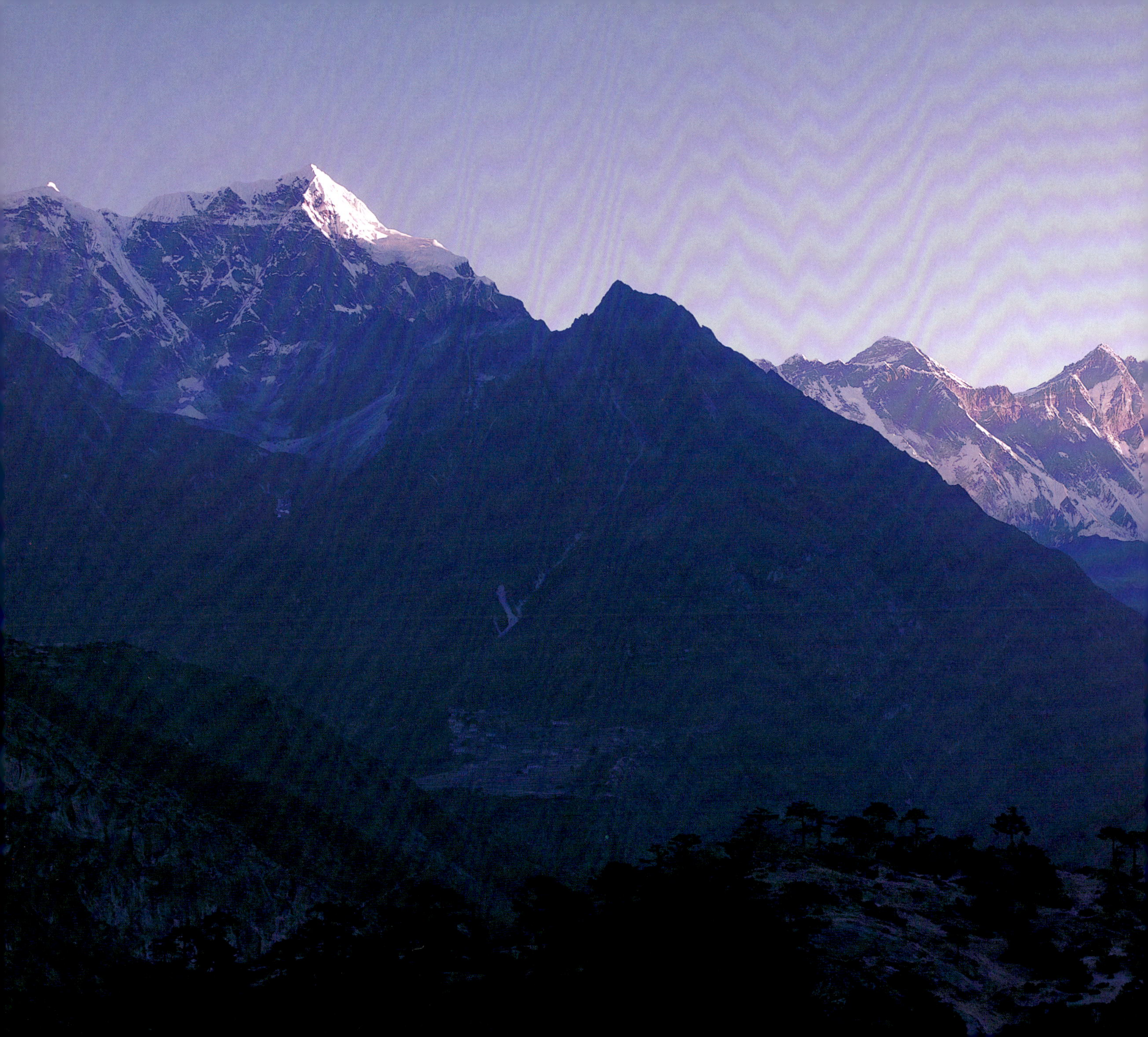

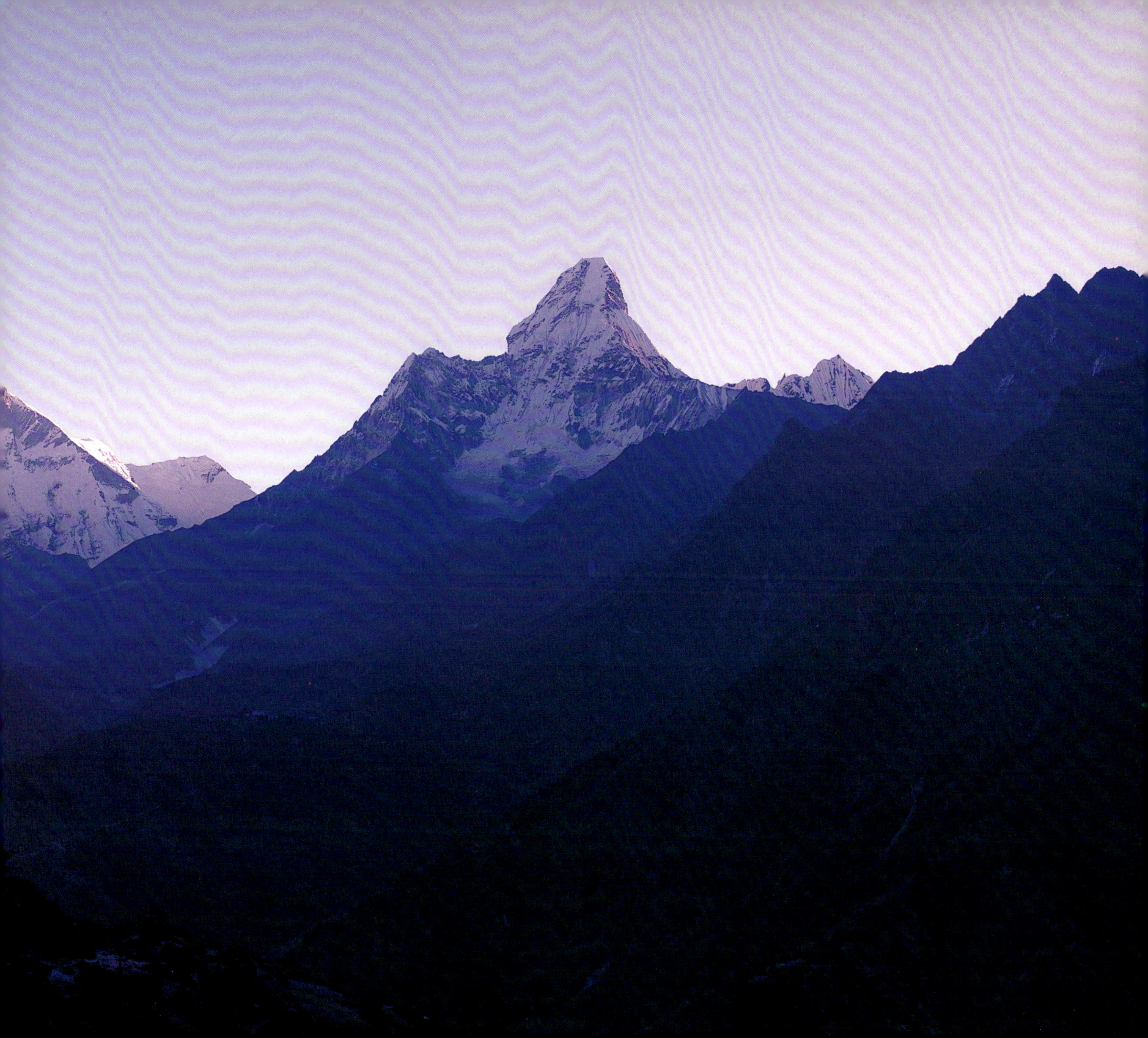

SINGAPORE

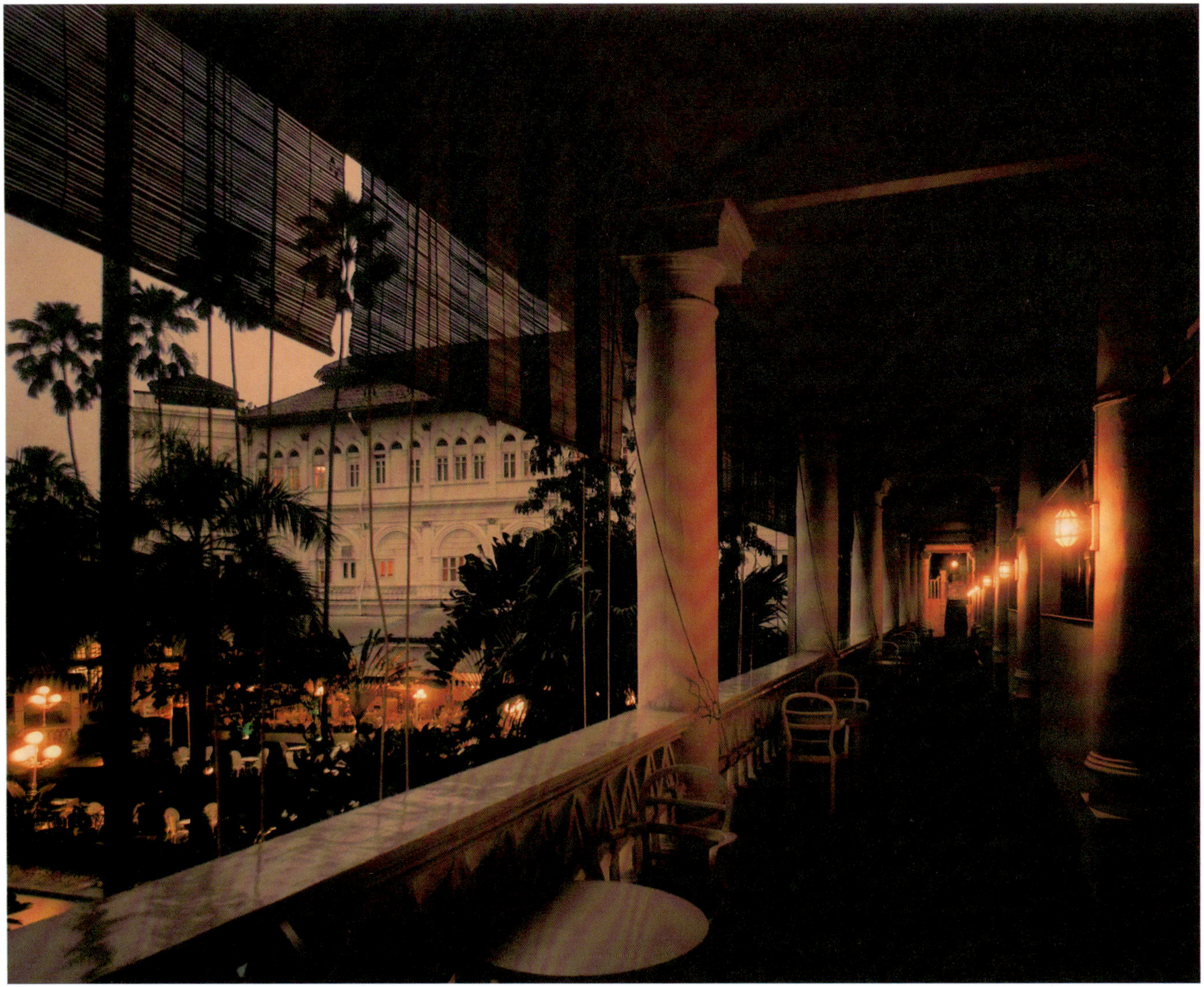

RAFFLES HOTEL (SINGAPORE)

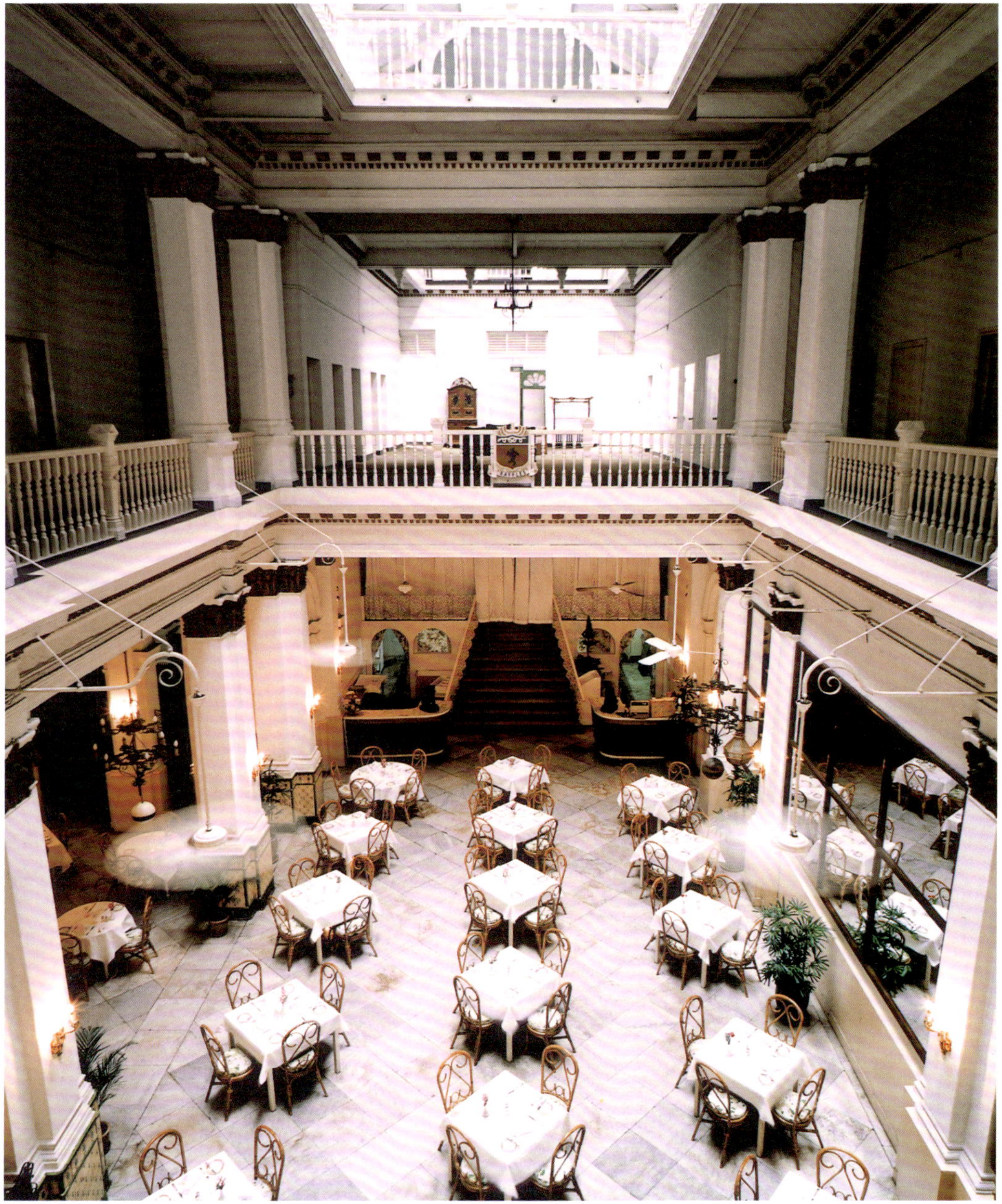

RAFFLES HOTEL (SINGAPORE)

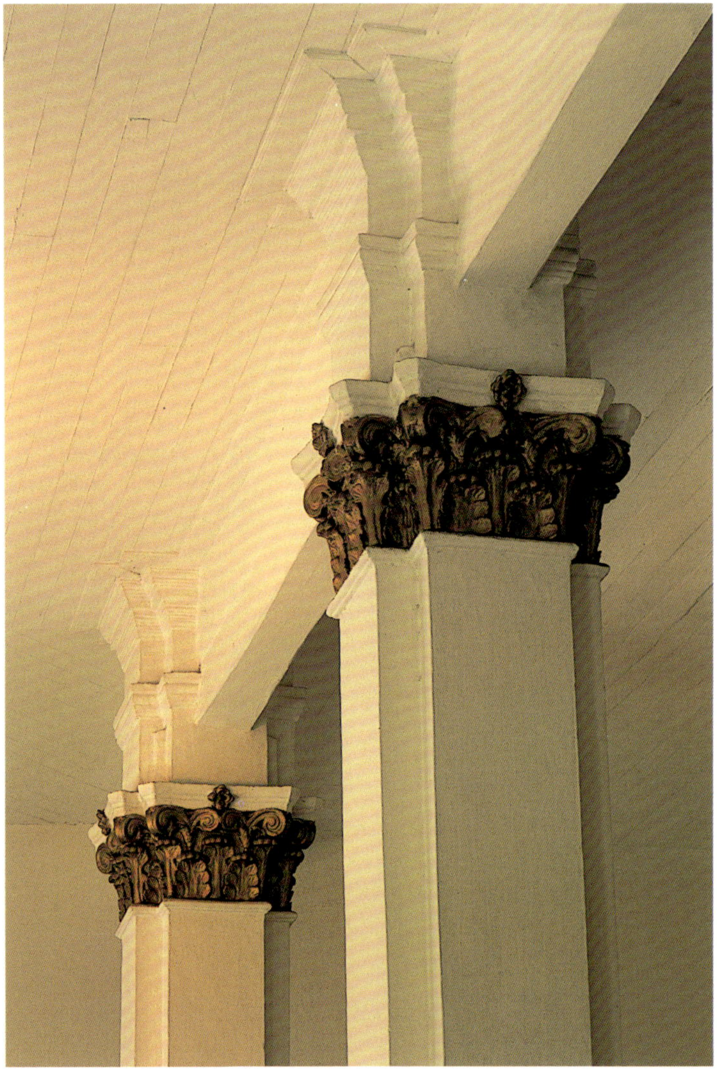

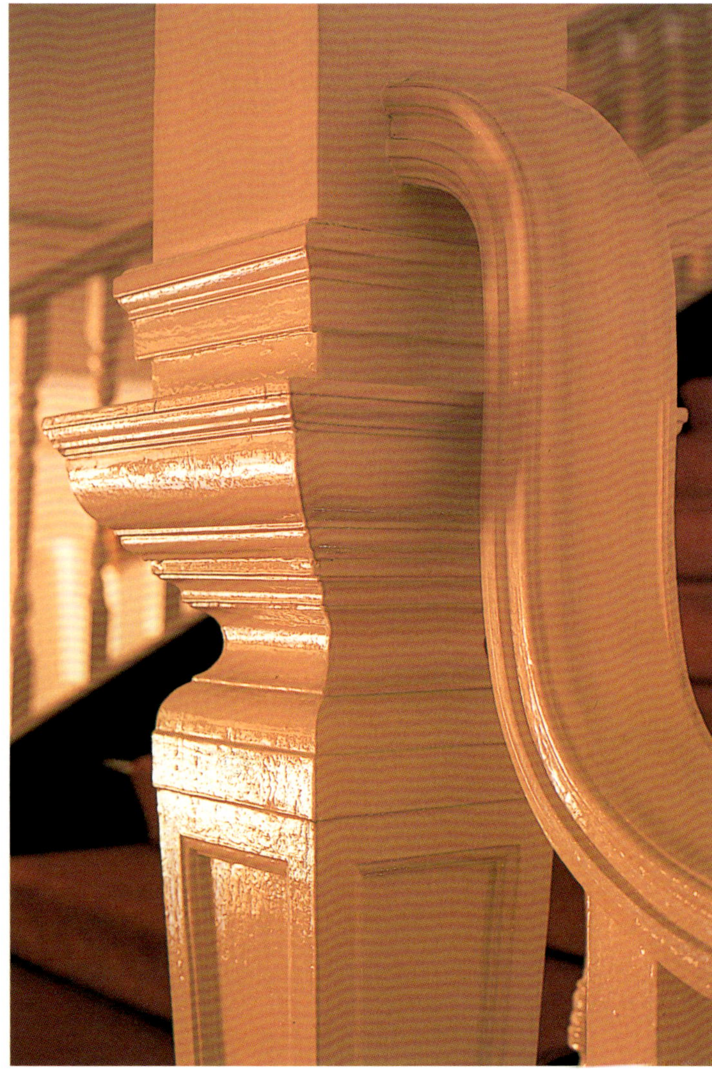

RAFFLES HOTEL (SINGAPORE)

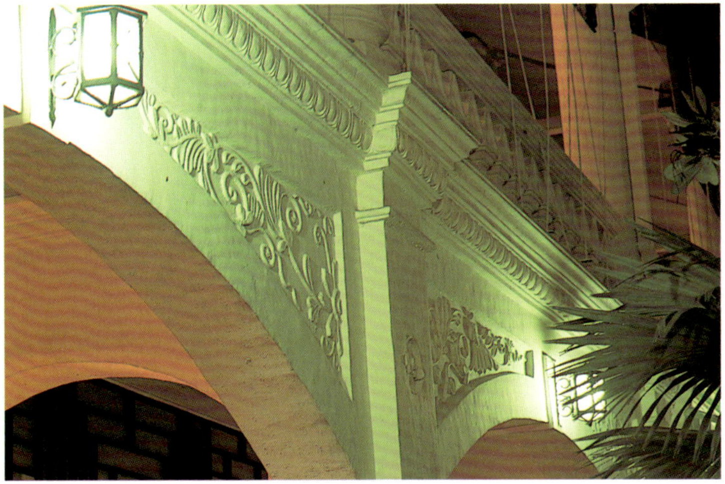

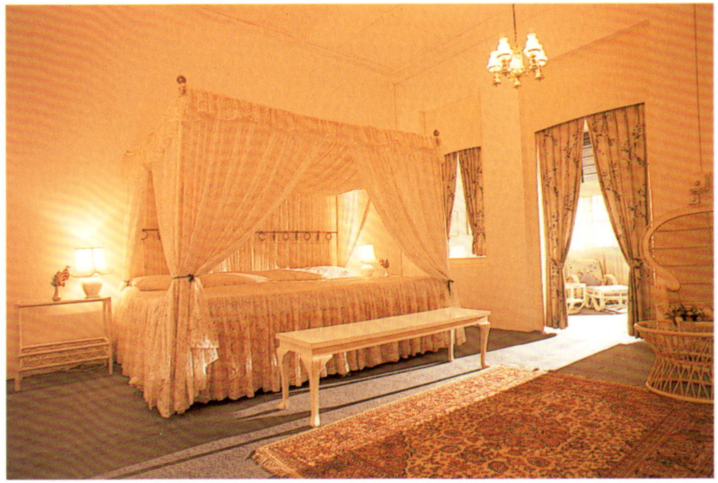

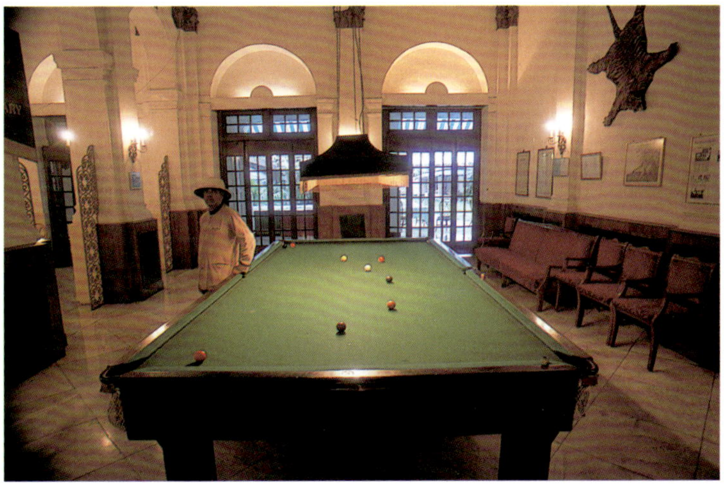

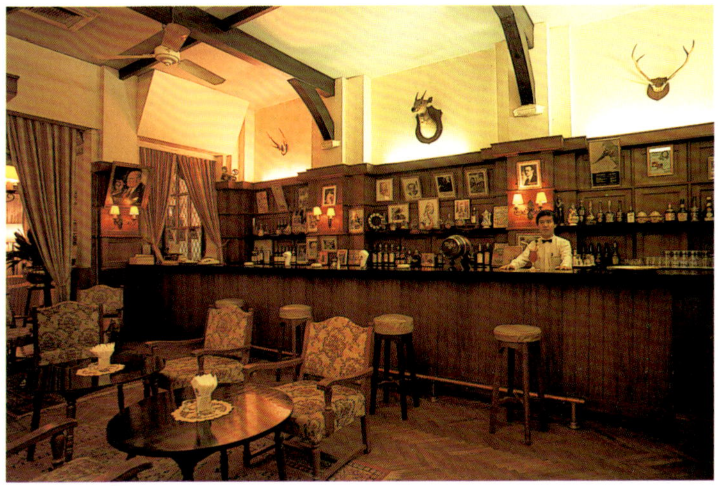

RAFFLES HOTEL (SINGAPORE)

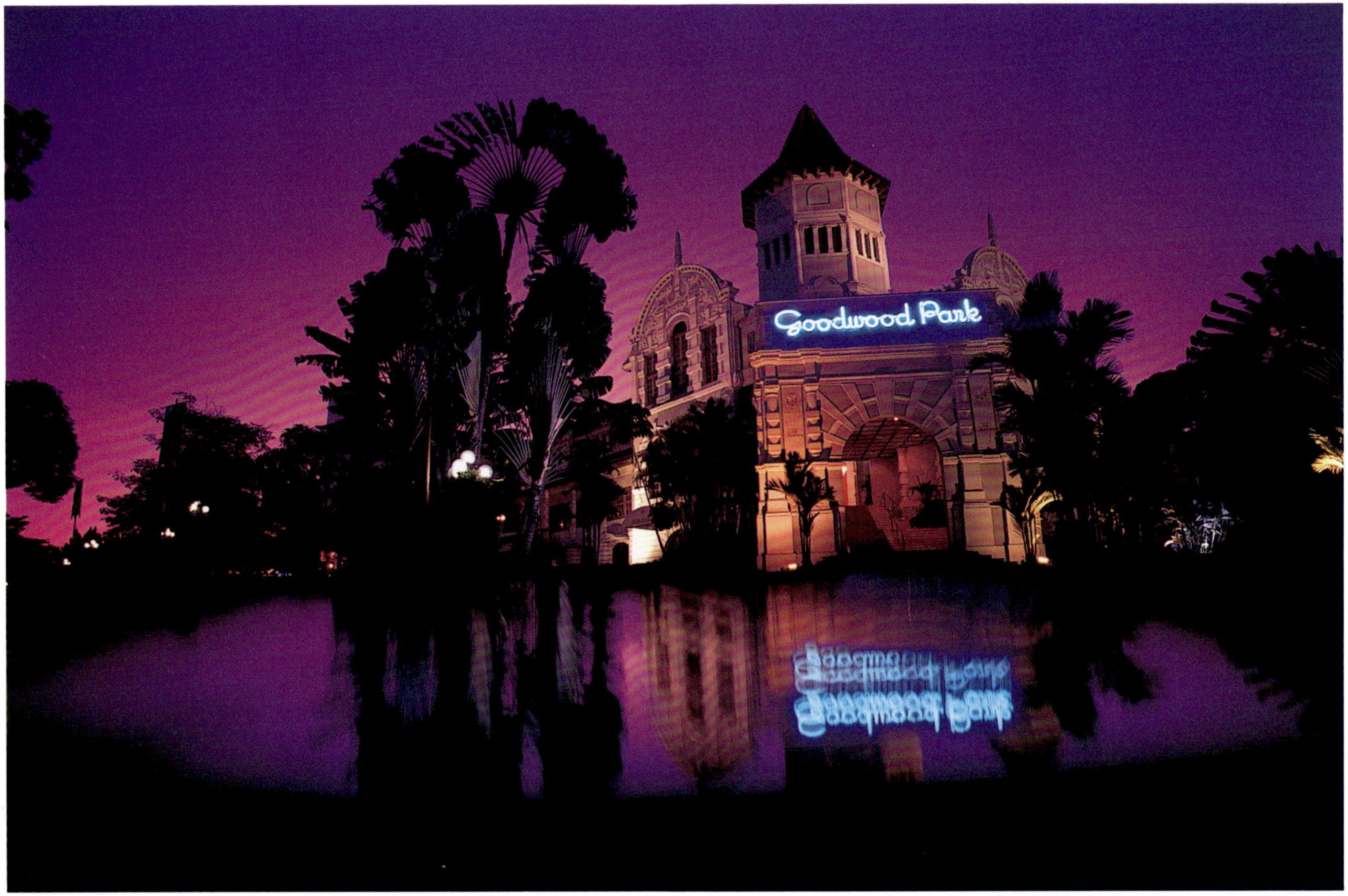

GOODWOOD PARK HOTEL (SINGAPORE)

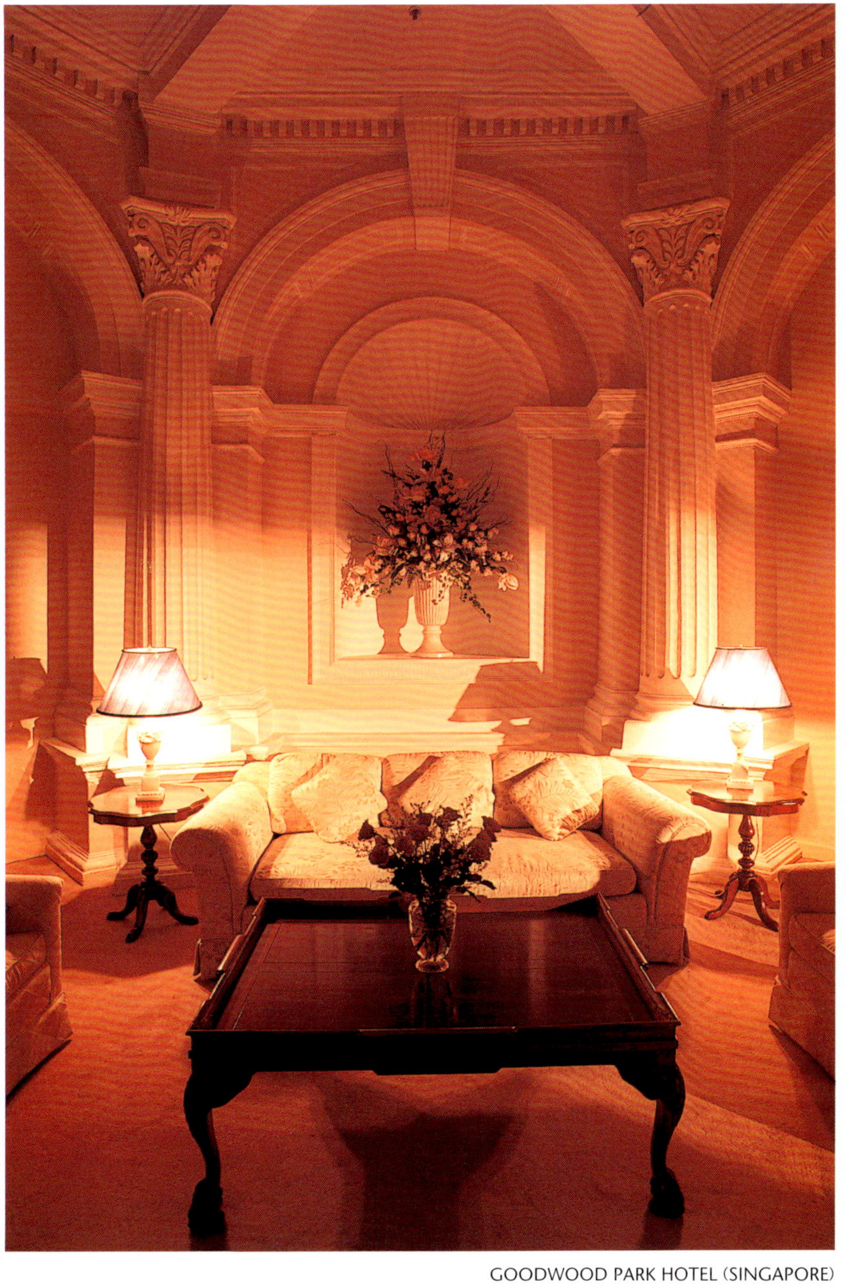

GOODWOOD PARK HOTEL (SINGAPORE)

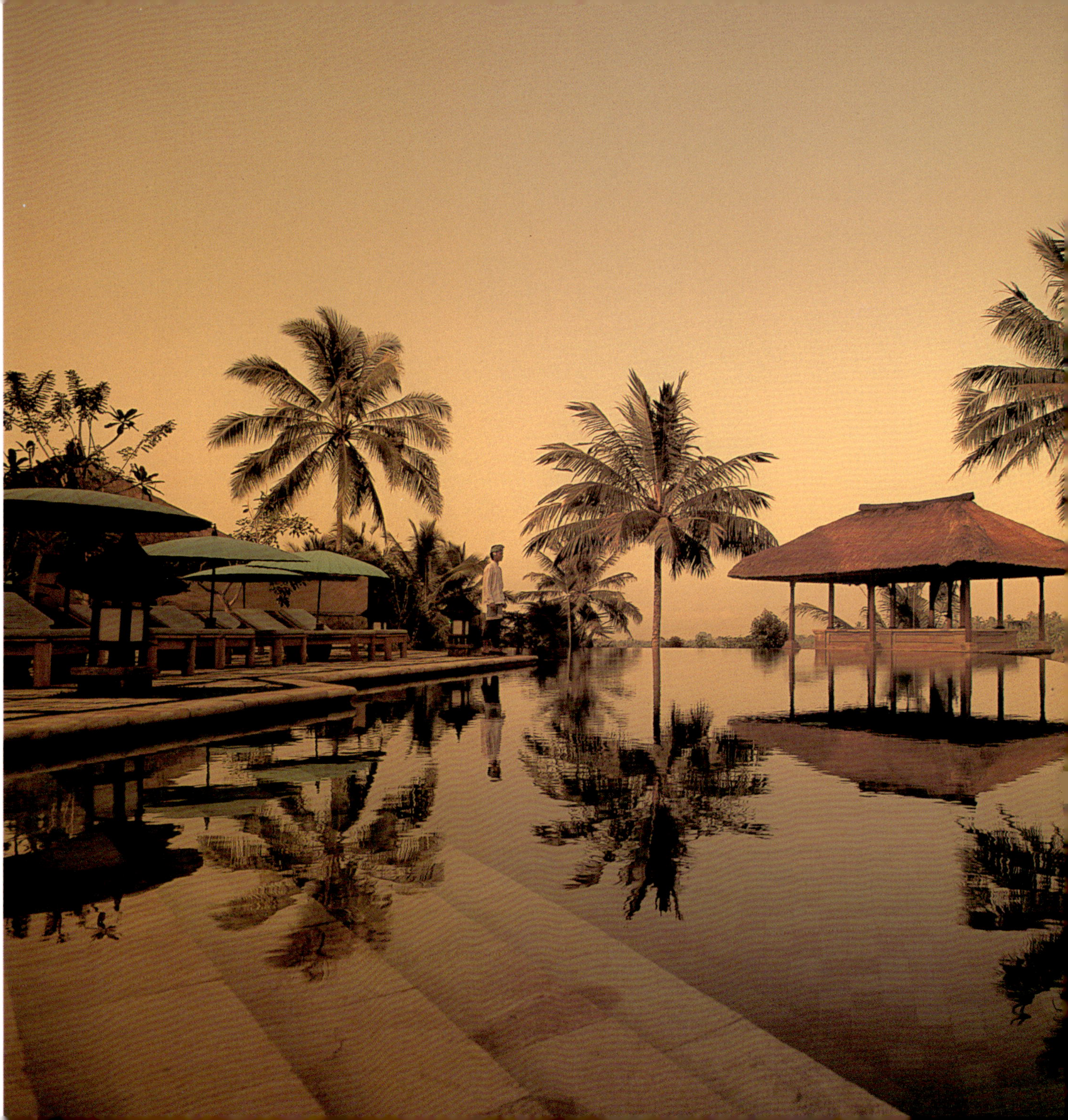

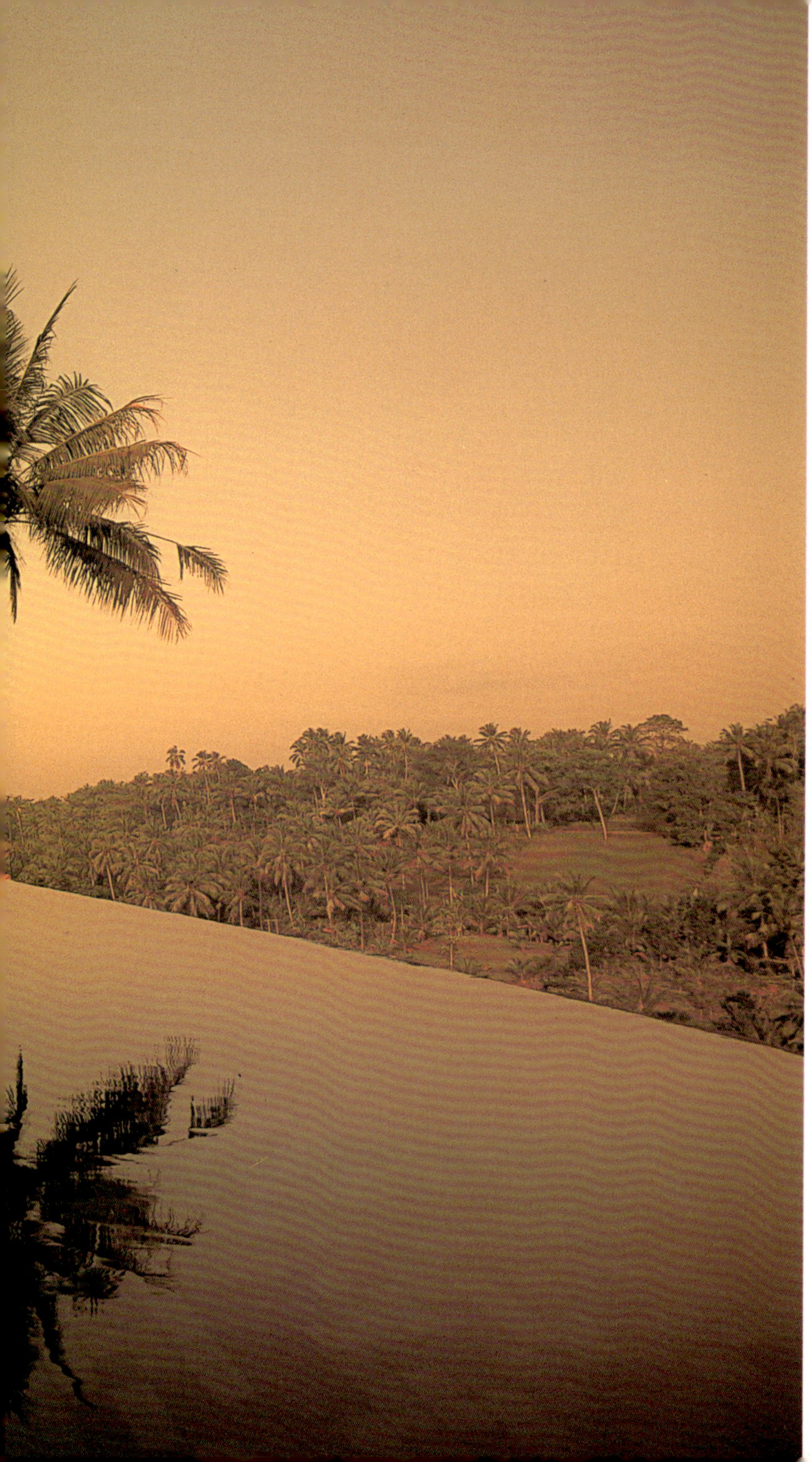

AMANDARI (UBUD)

BALI

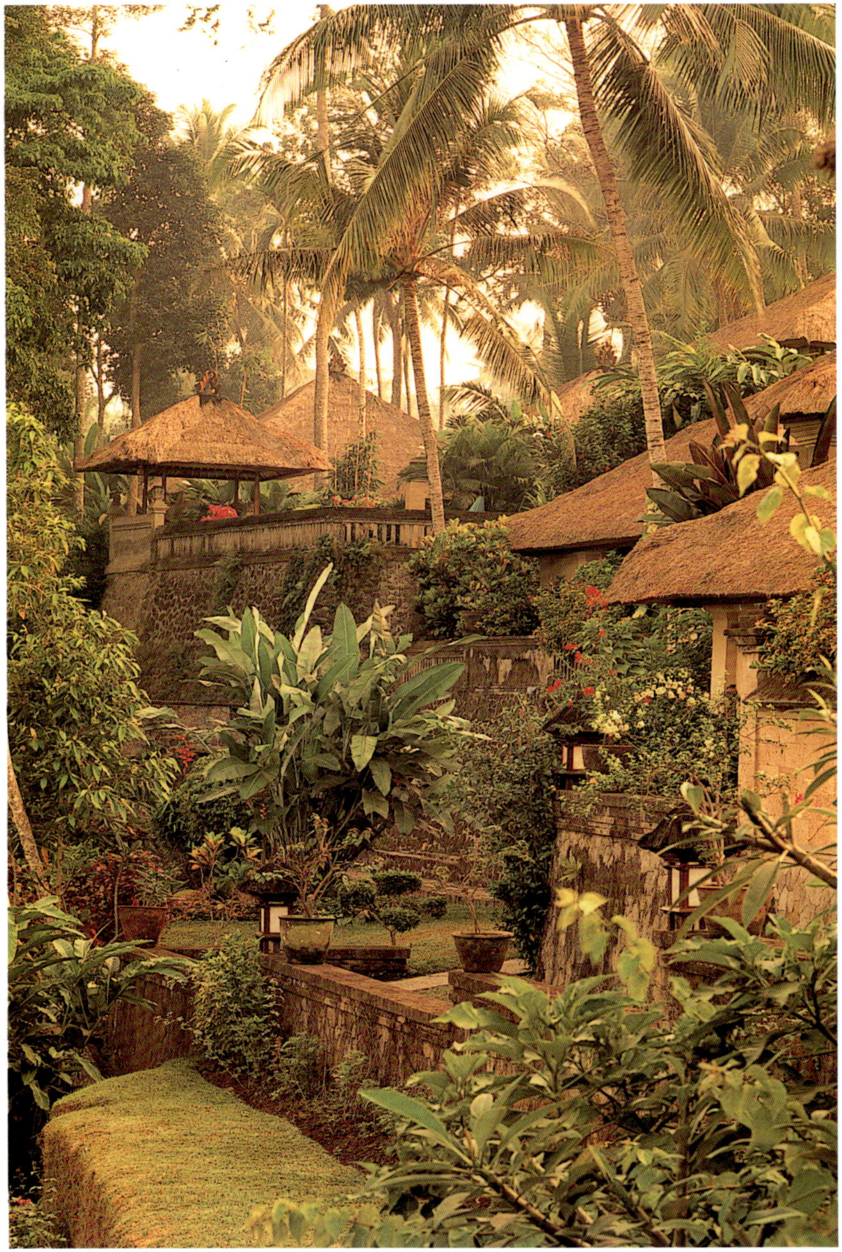

AMANDARI (UBUD)

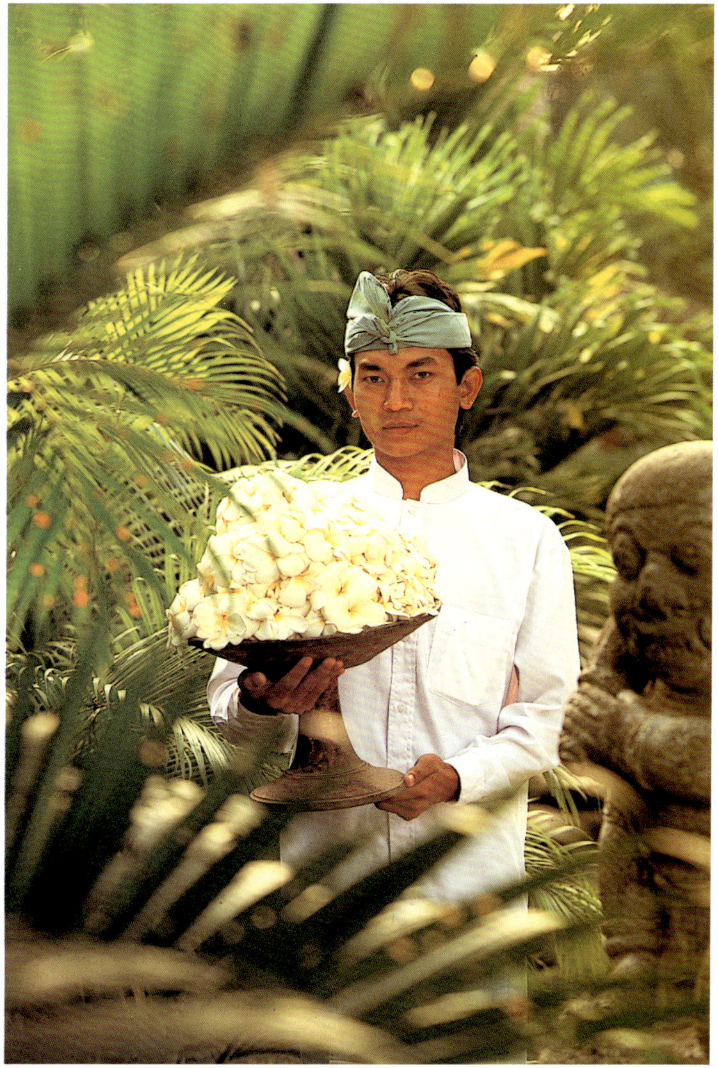

AMANDARI (UBUD)

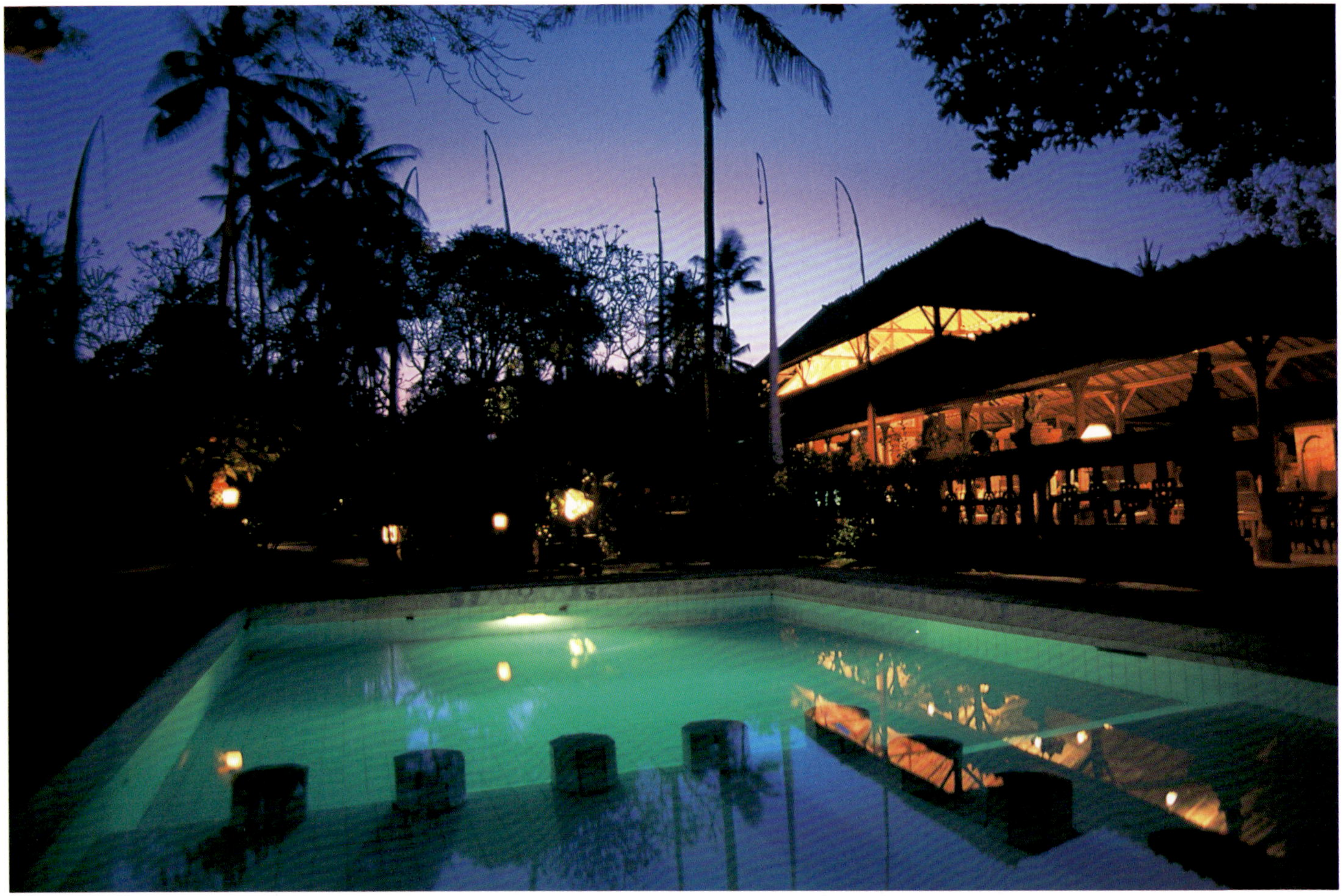

TANDJUNG SARI (SANUR)

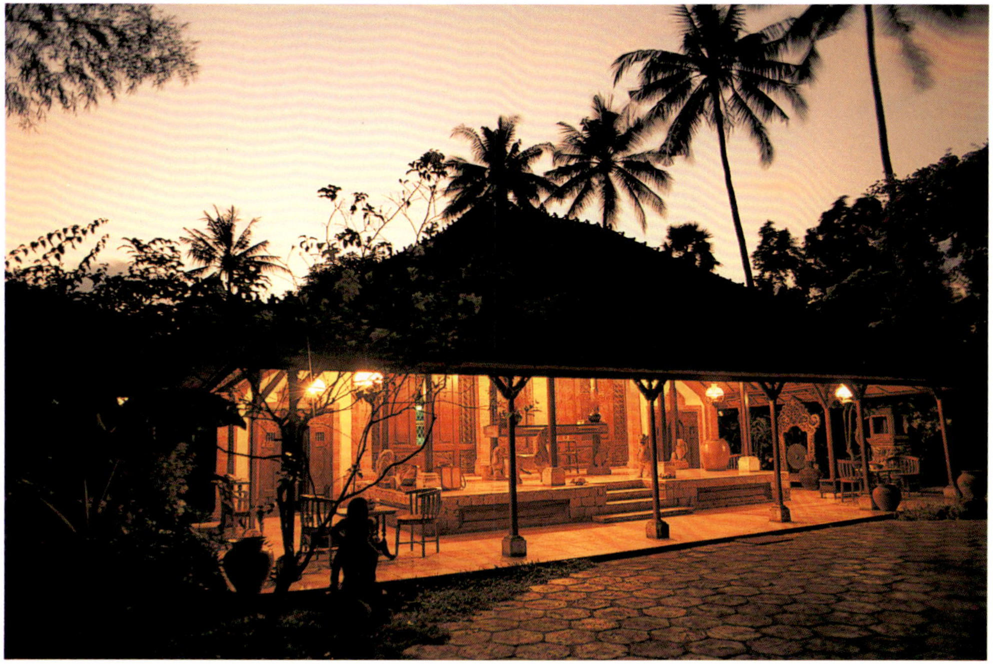

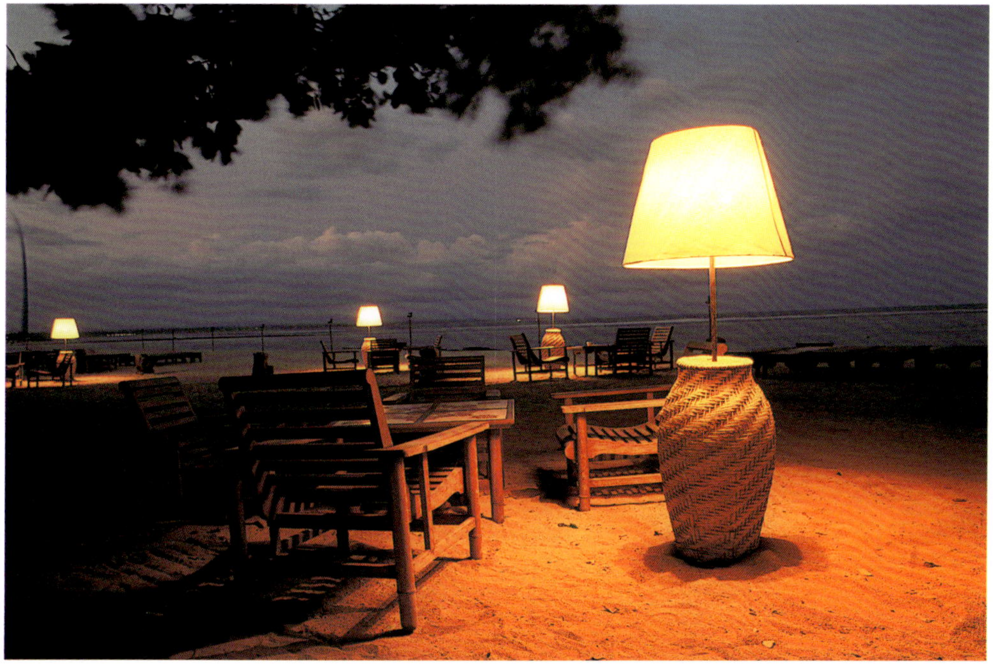

TANDJUNG SARI (SANUR)

THAILAND

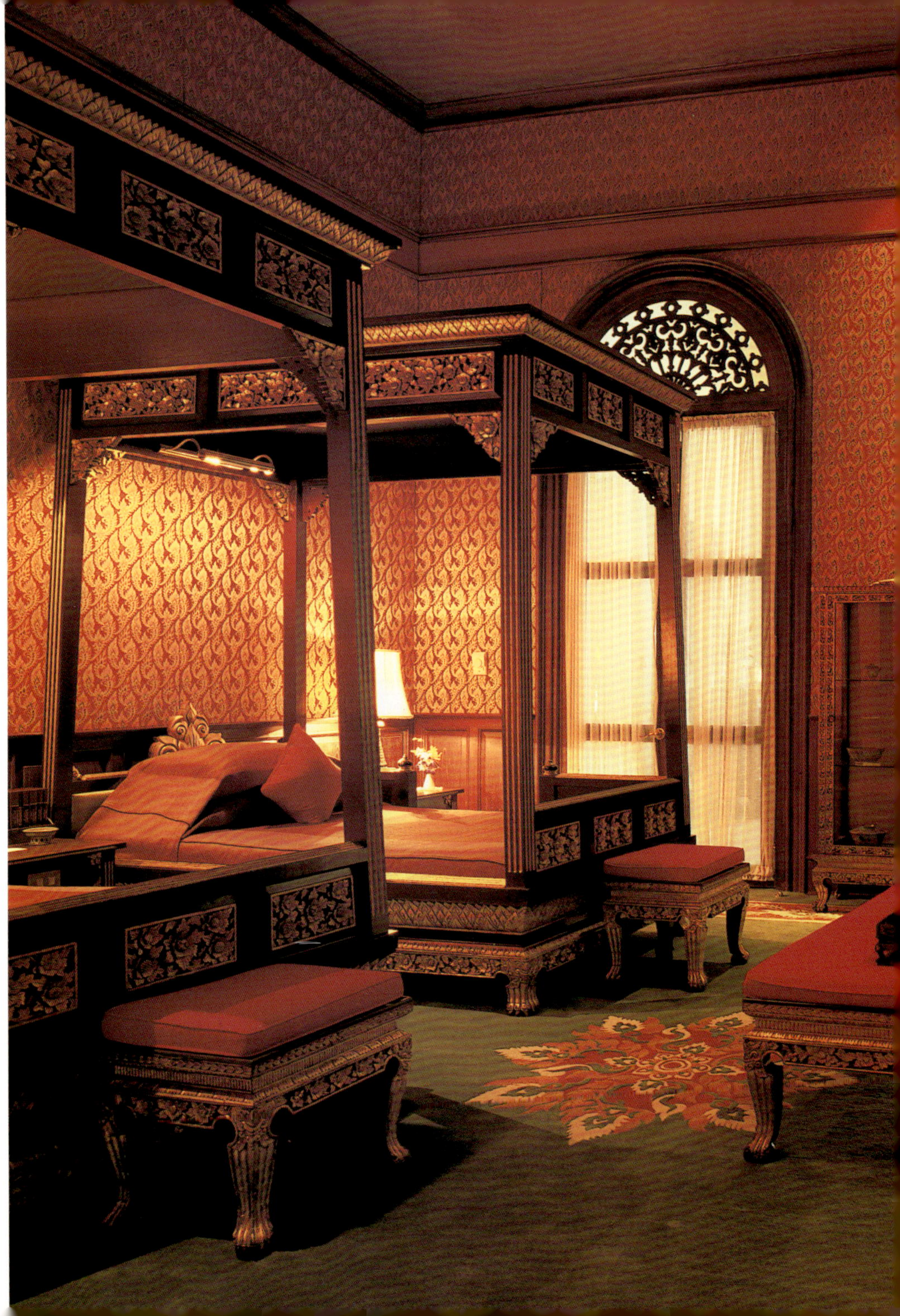

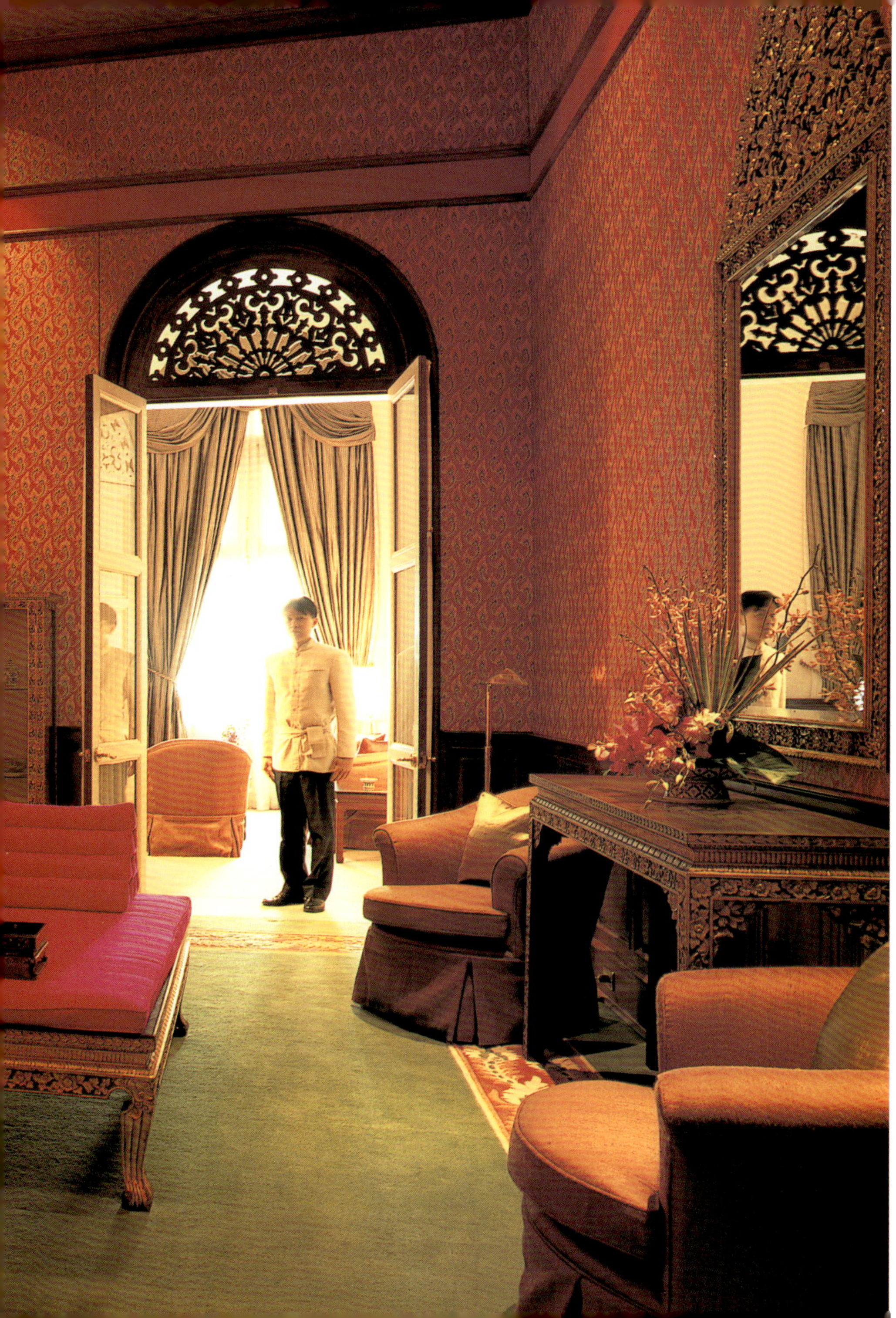

47

THE ORIENTAL BANGKOK (BANGKOK)

48

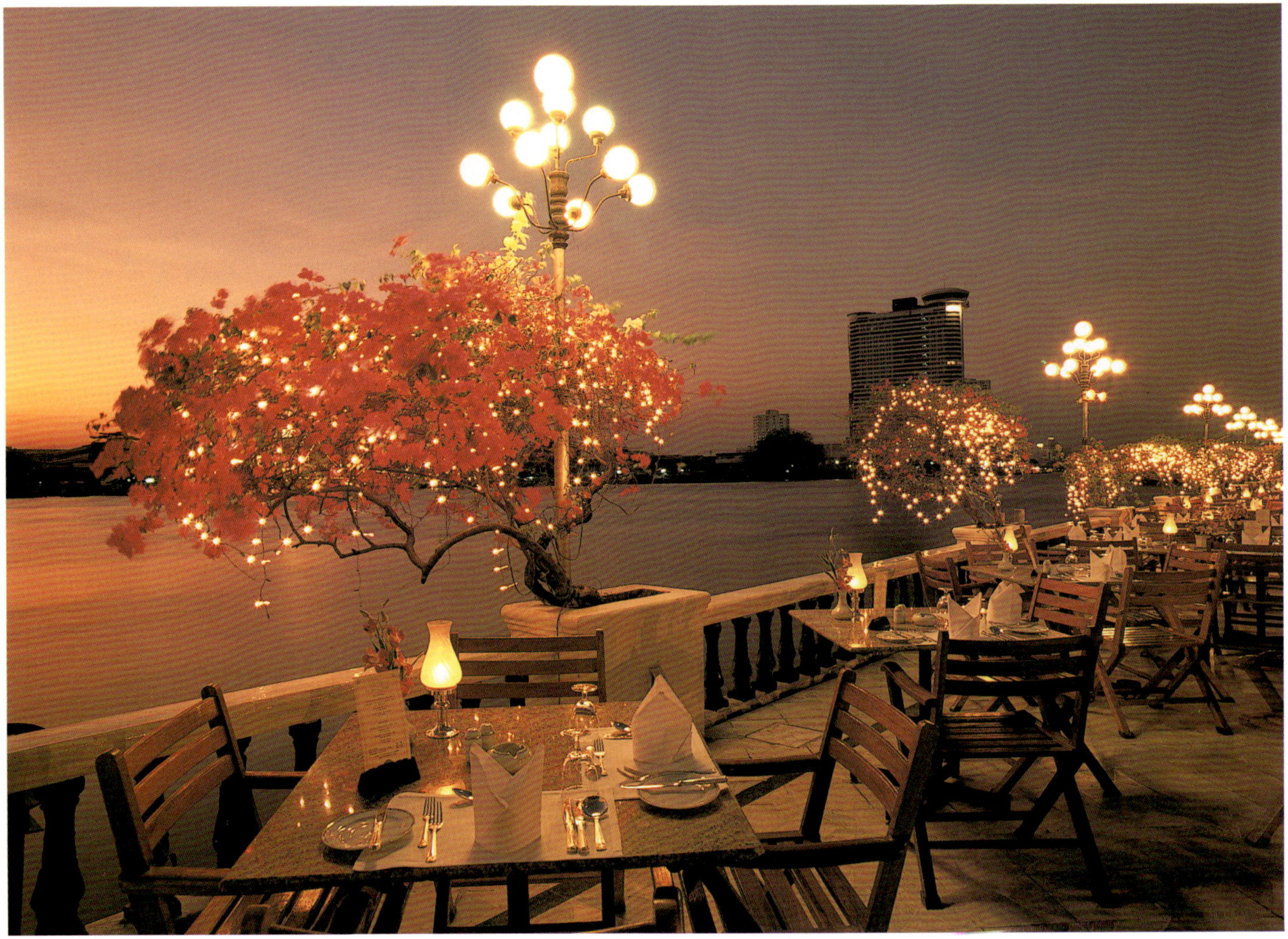

THE ORIENTAL BANGKOK (BANGKOK)

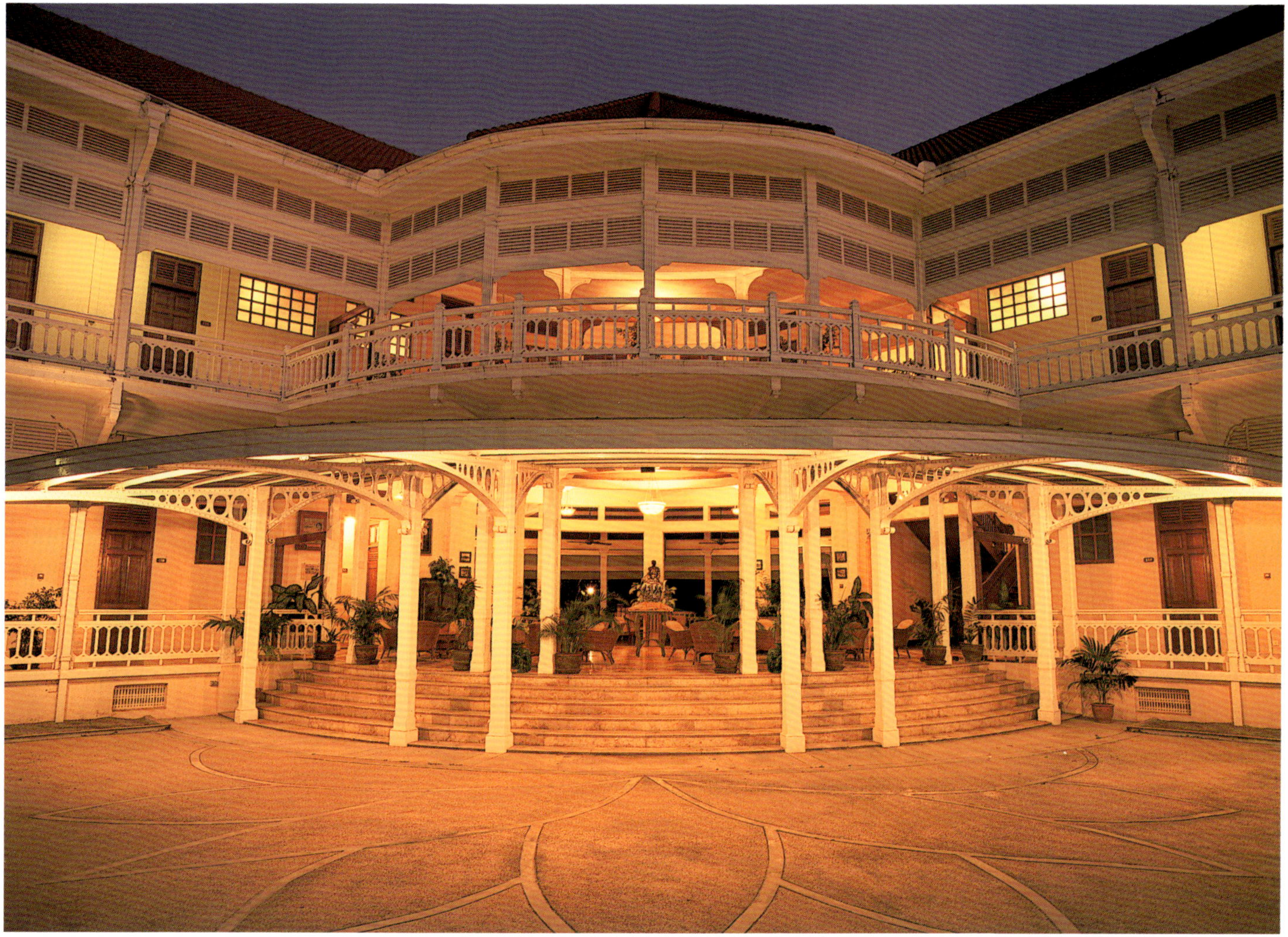

HOTEL SOFITEL CENTRAL HUA-HIN (HUA-HIN)

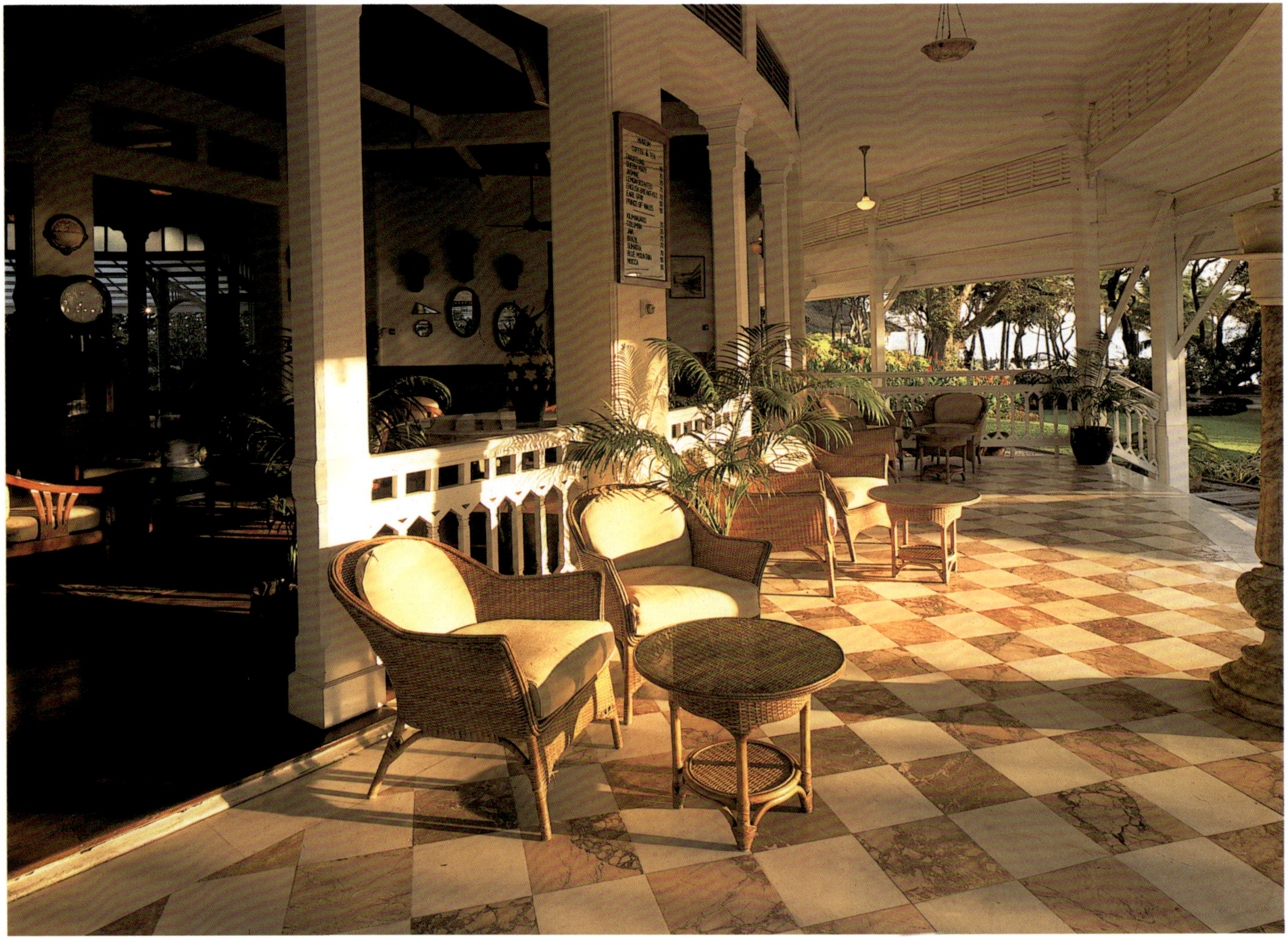

HOTEL SOFITEL CENTRAL HUA-HIN (HUA-HIN)

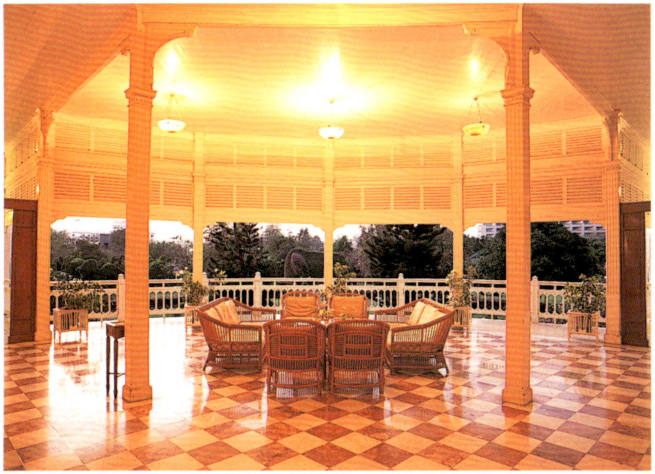

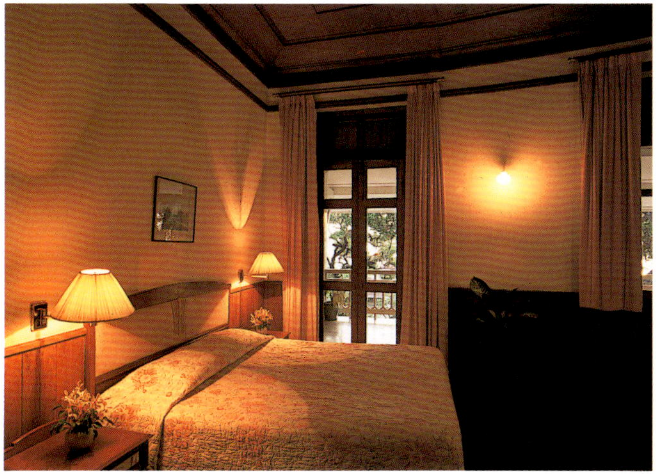

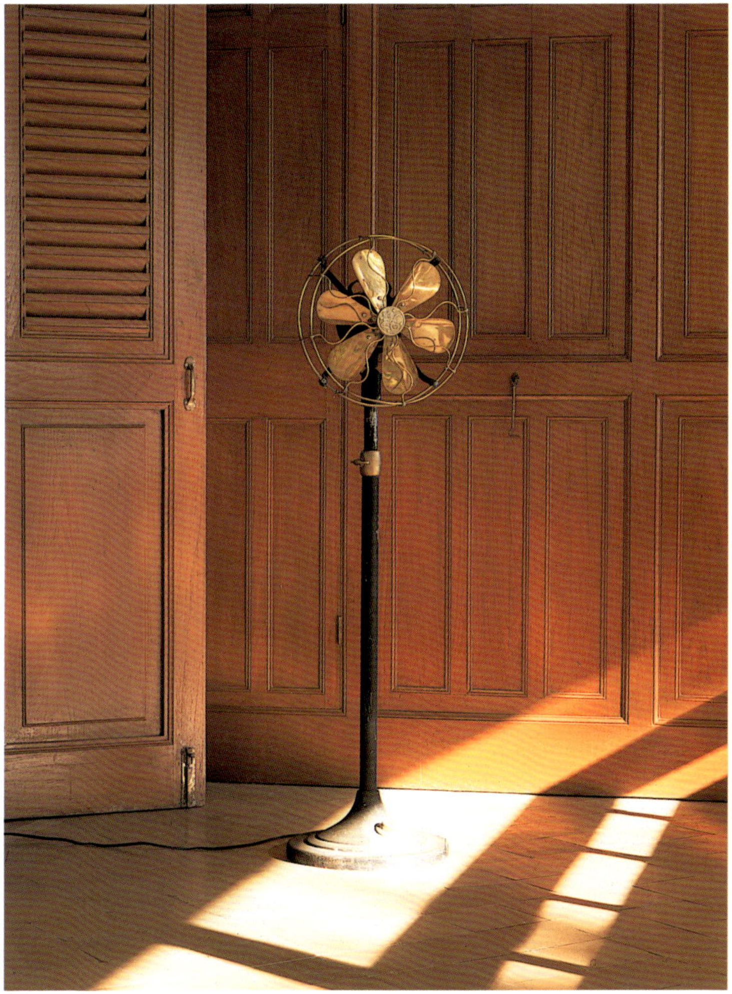

HOTEL SOFITEL CENTRAL HUA-HIN (HUA-HIN)

U.S. VIRGIN ISLANDS

52

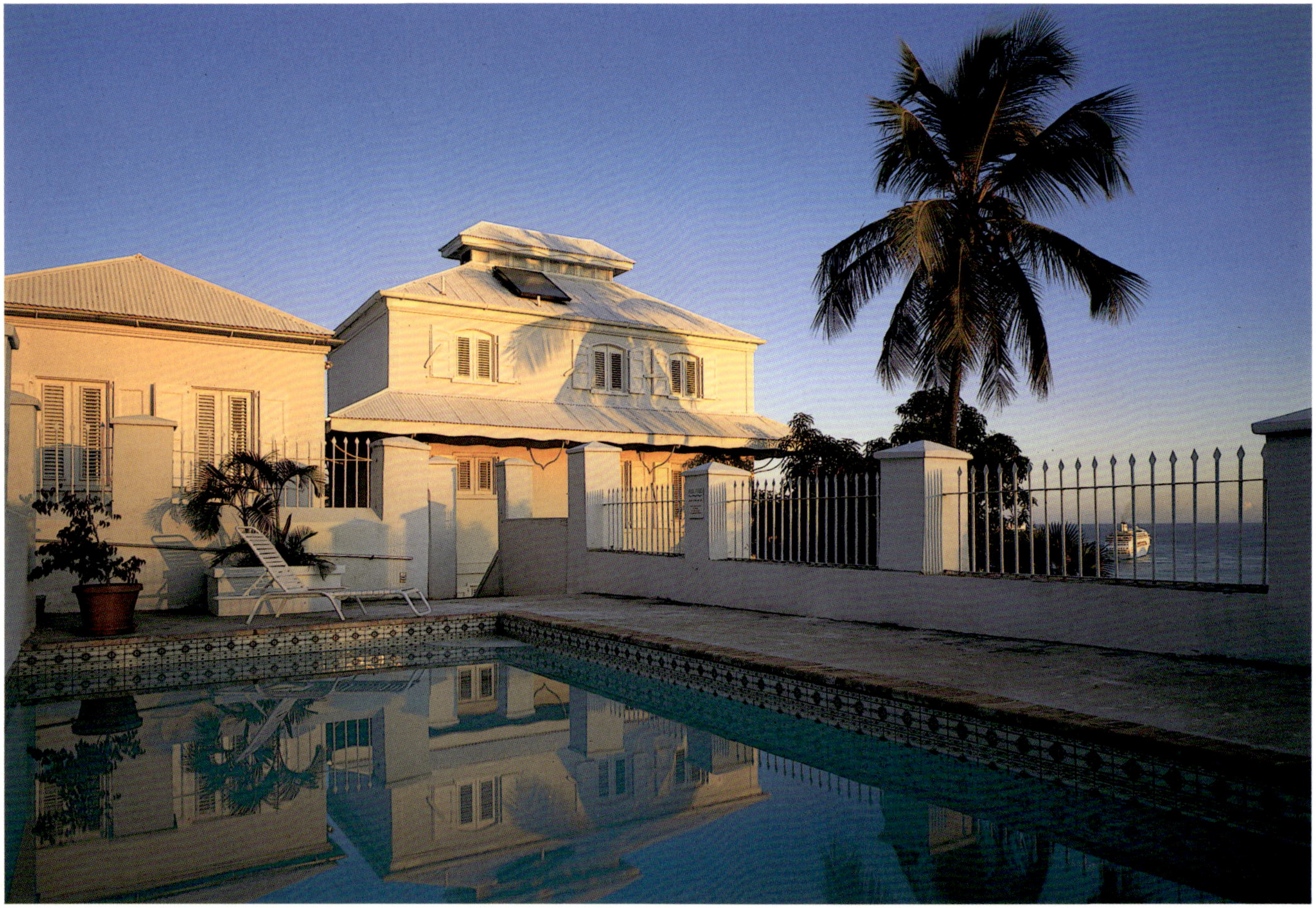

VILLA SANTANA (ST. THOMAS)

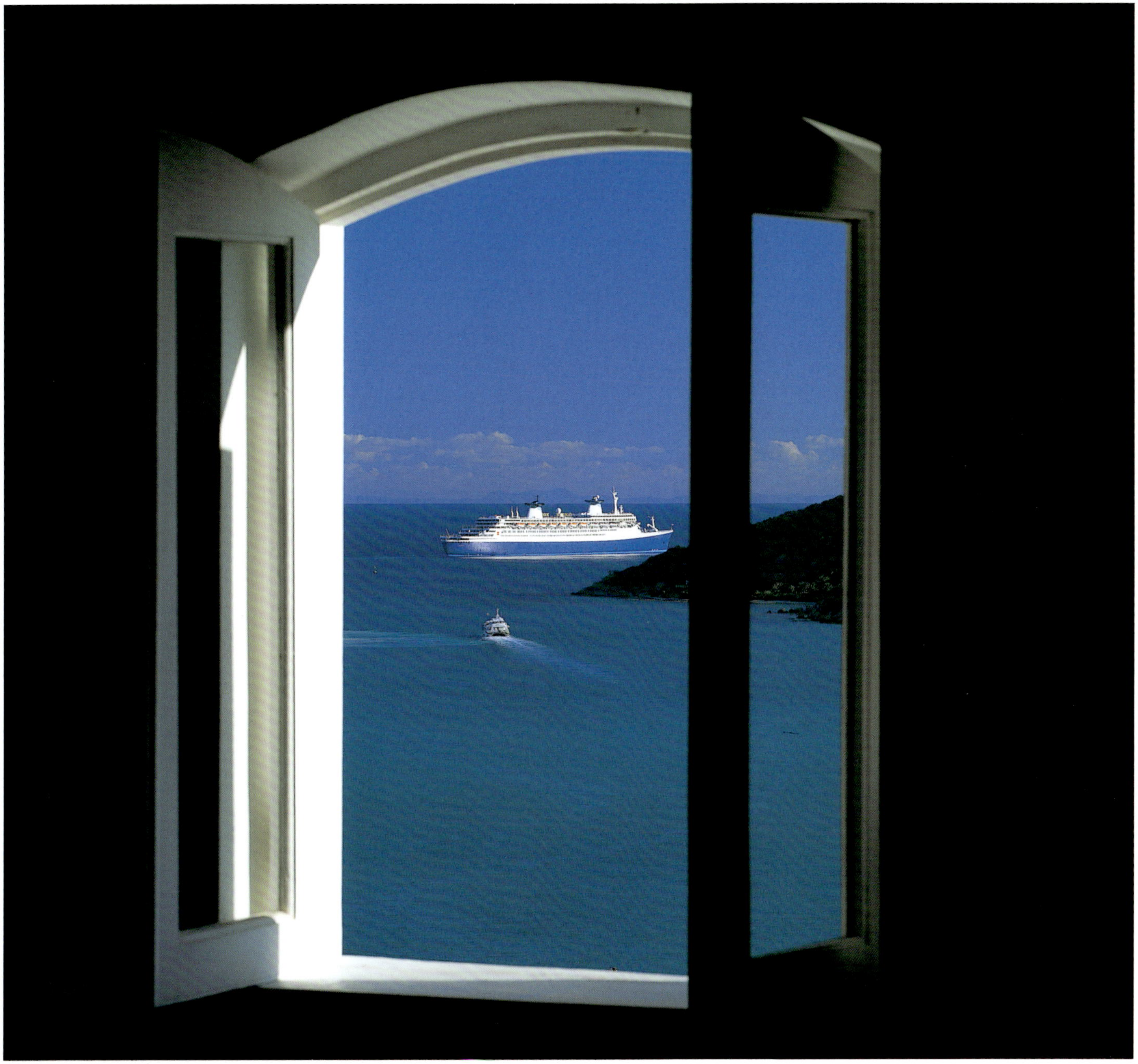

53

VILLA SANTANA (ST. THOMAS)

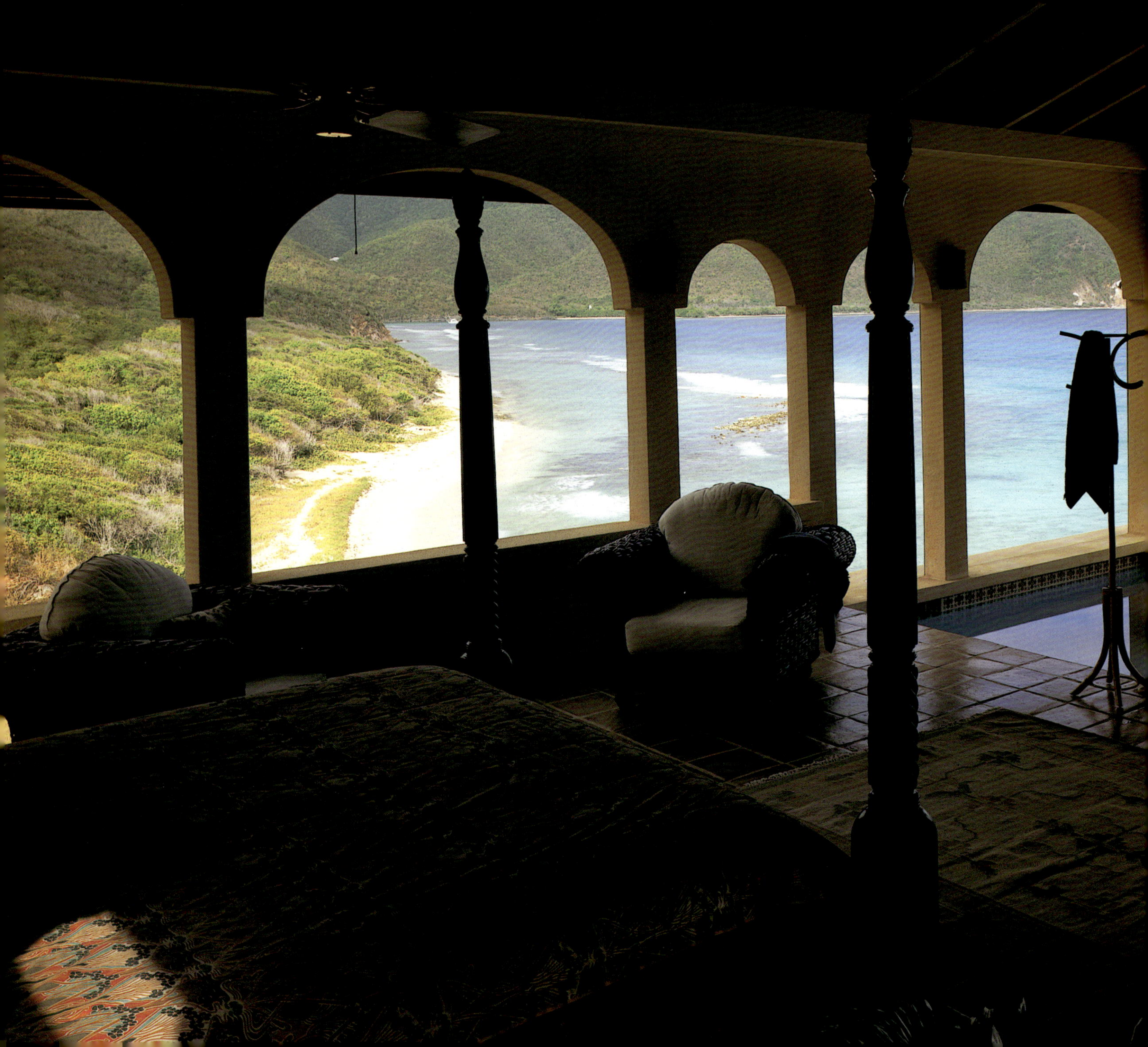

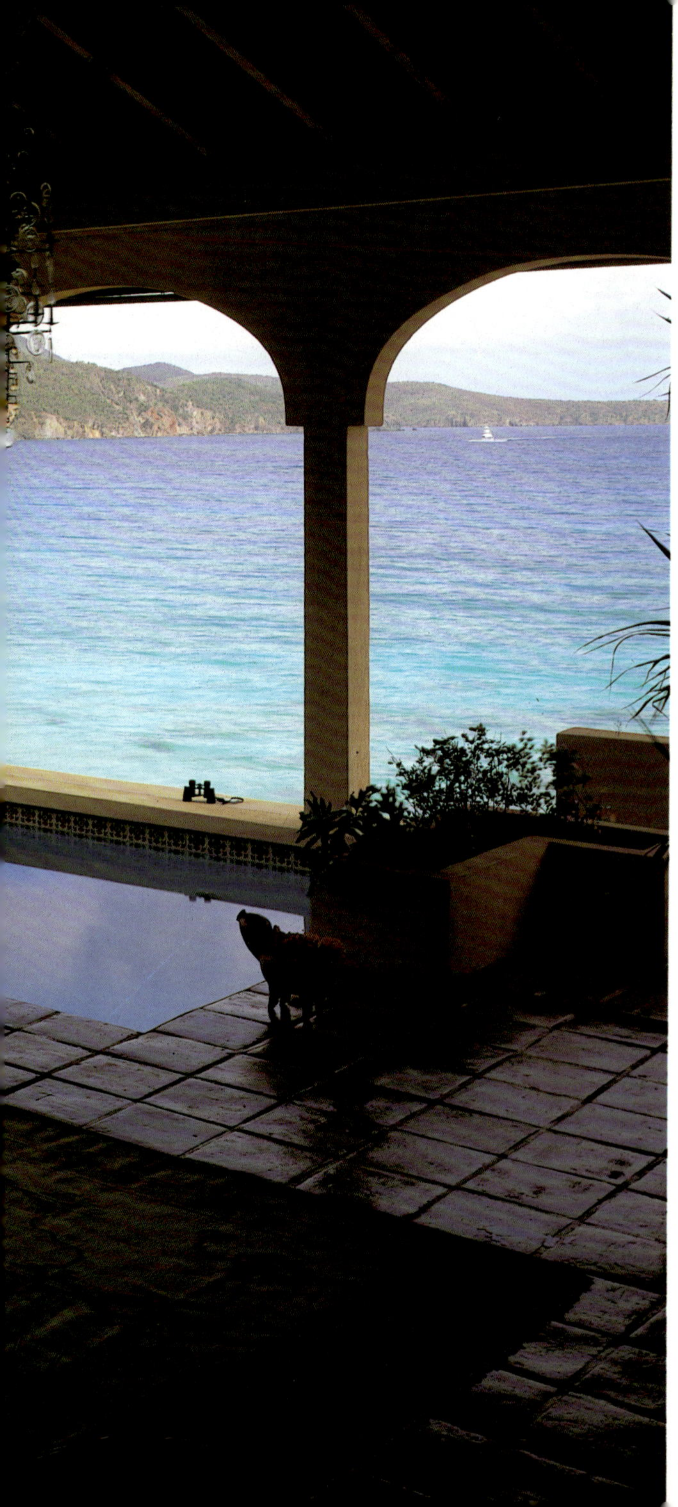

SAFARI (ST. JOHN)

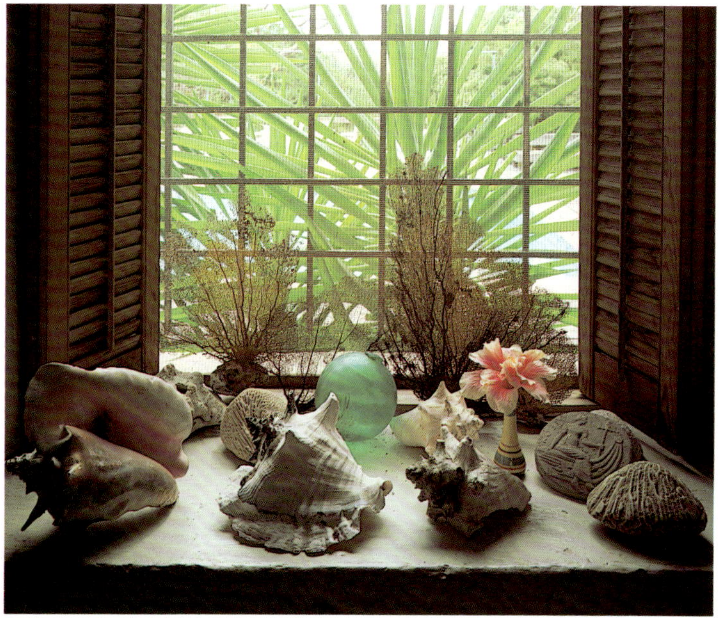

HILTY HOUSE INN (ST. CROIX)

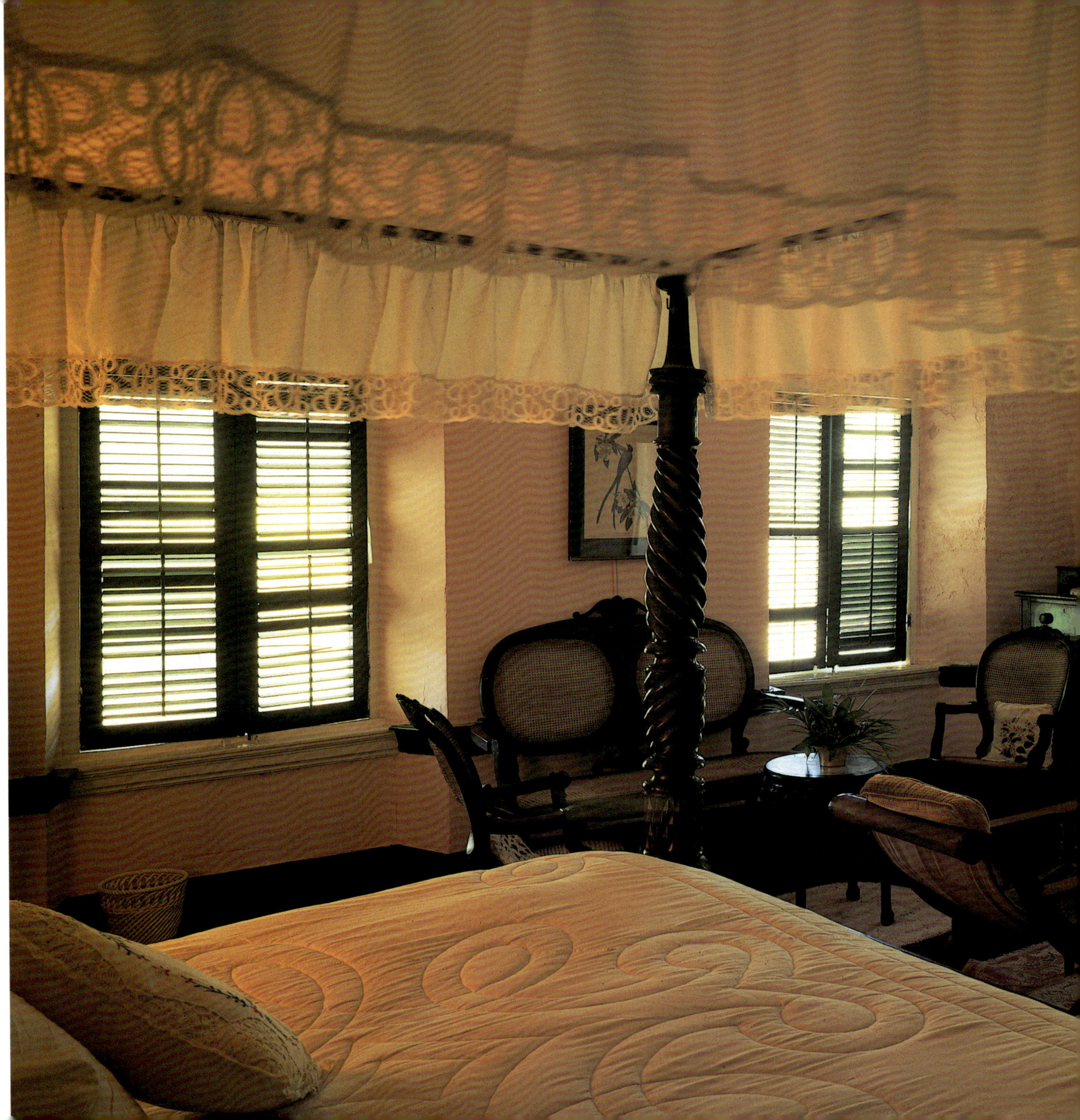

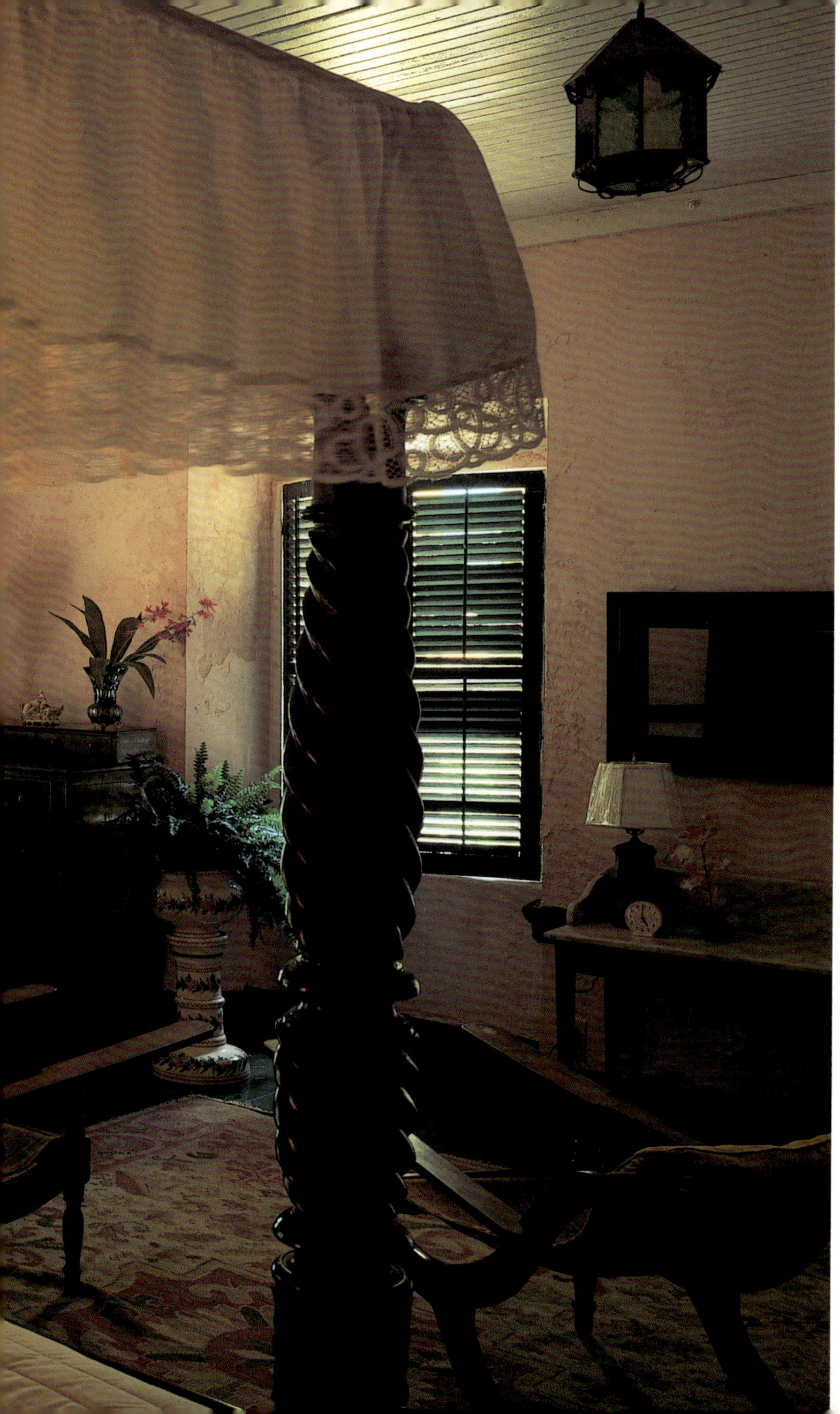

57

SPRAT HALL PLANTATION (ST. CROIX)

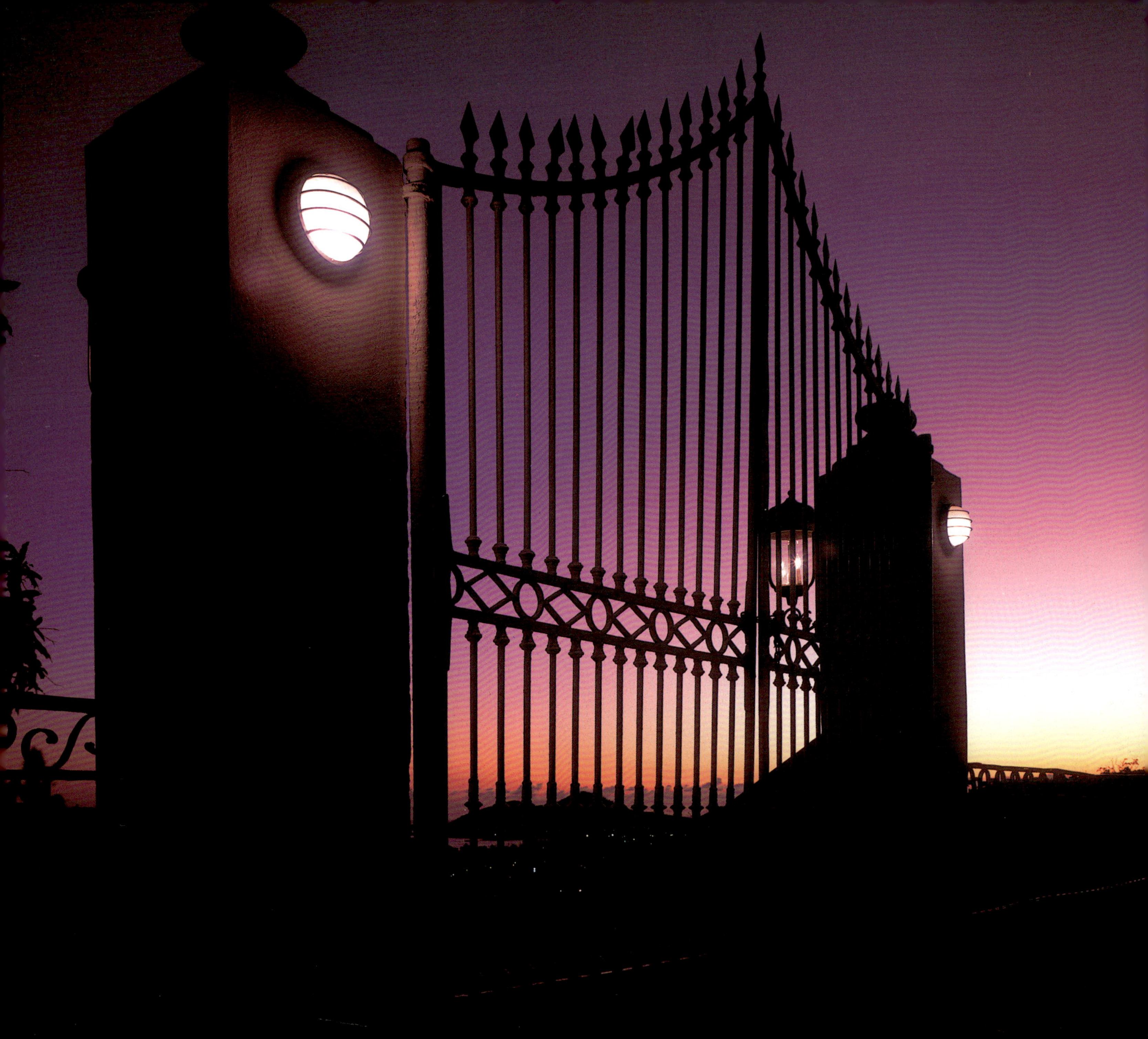

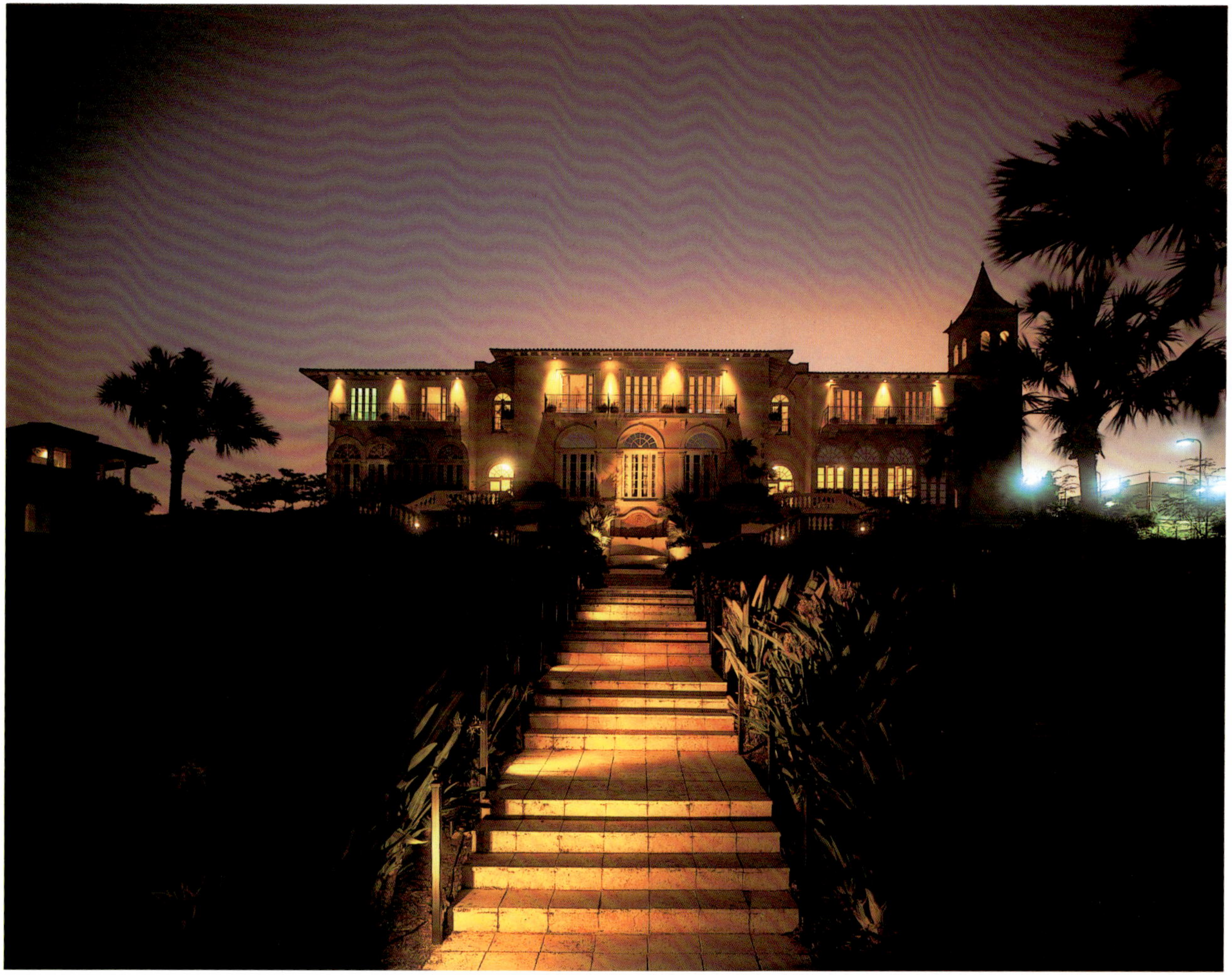

GRAND PALAZZO HOTEL (ST. THOMAS)

VILLA SANTANA (ST. THOMAS)

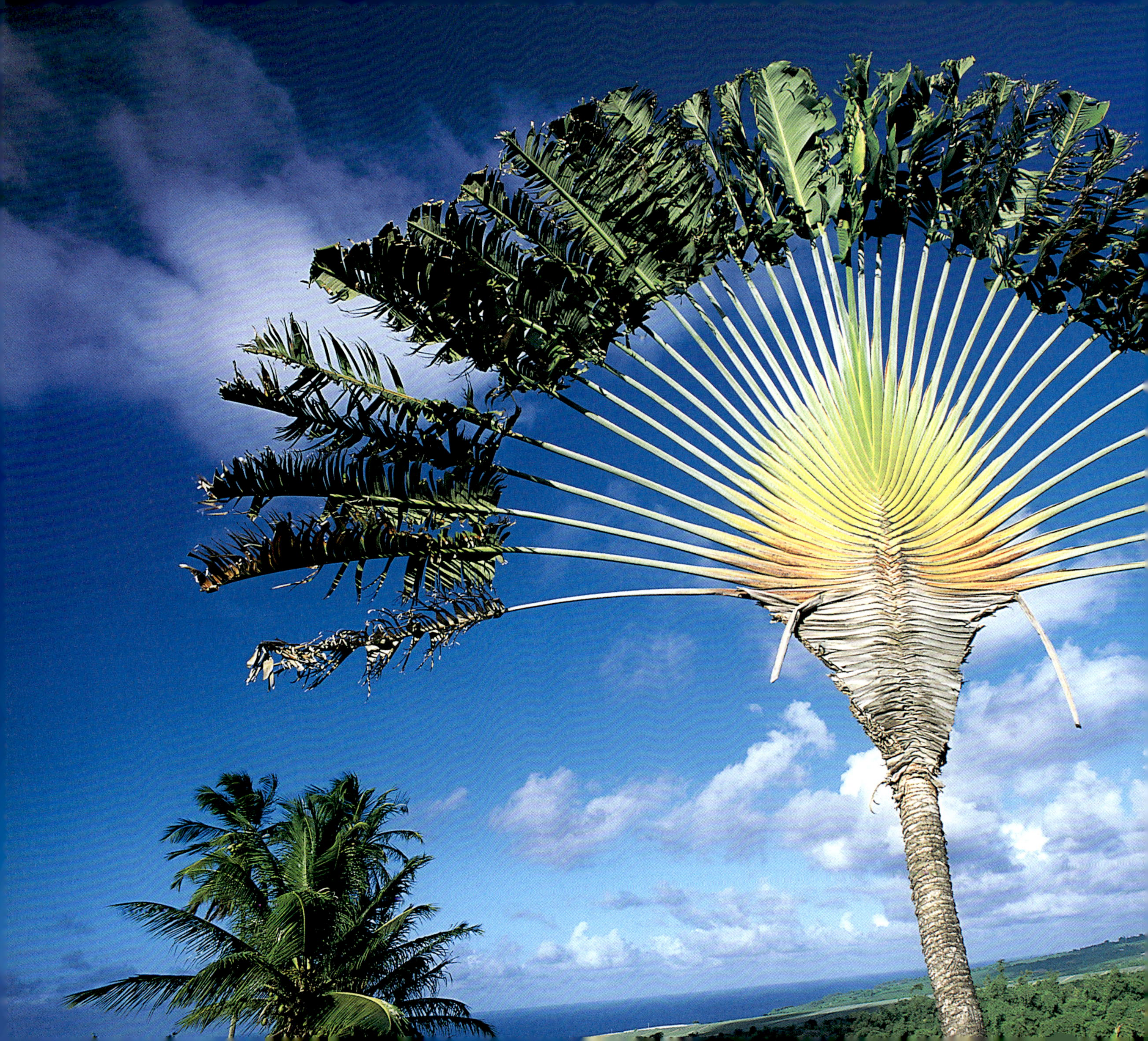

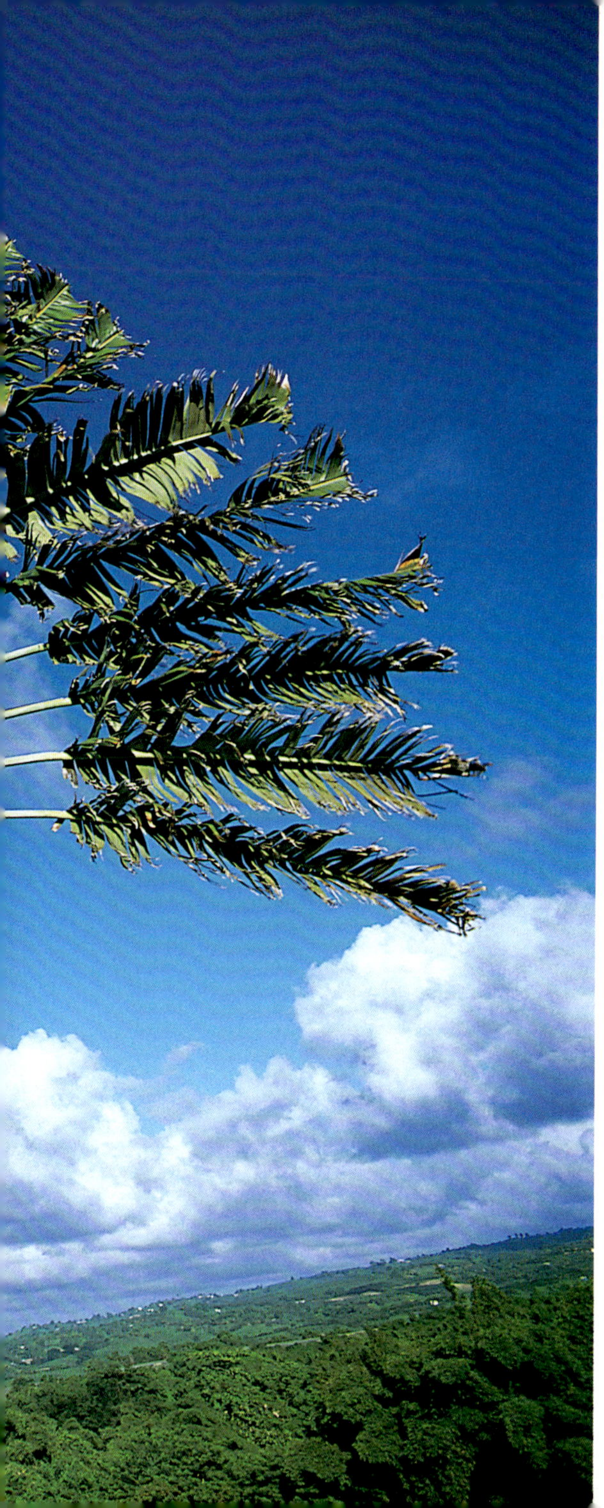

HOTEL PLANTATION DE LEYRITZ (BASSE POINTE)

MARTINIQUE

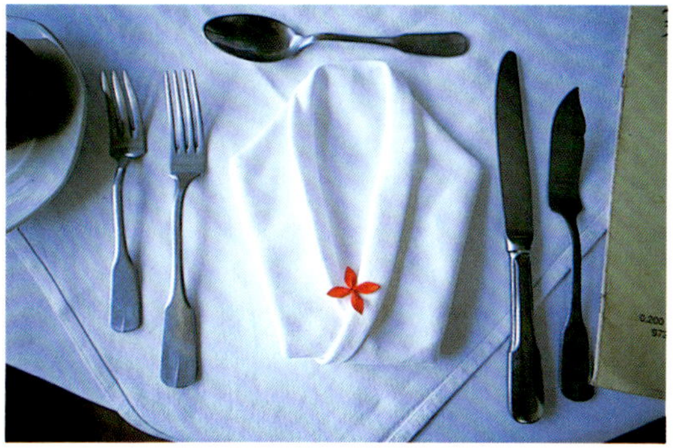

LE BRISTOL (FORT-DE-FRANCE)

62

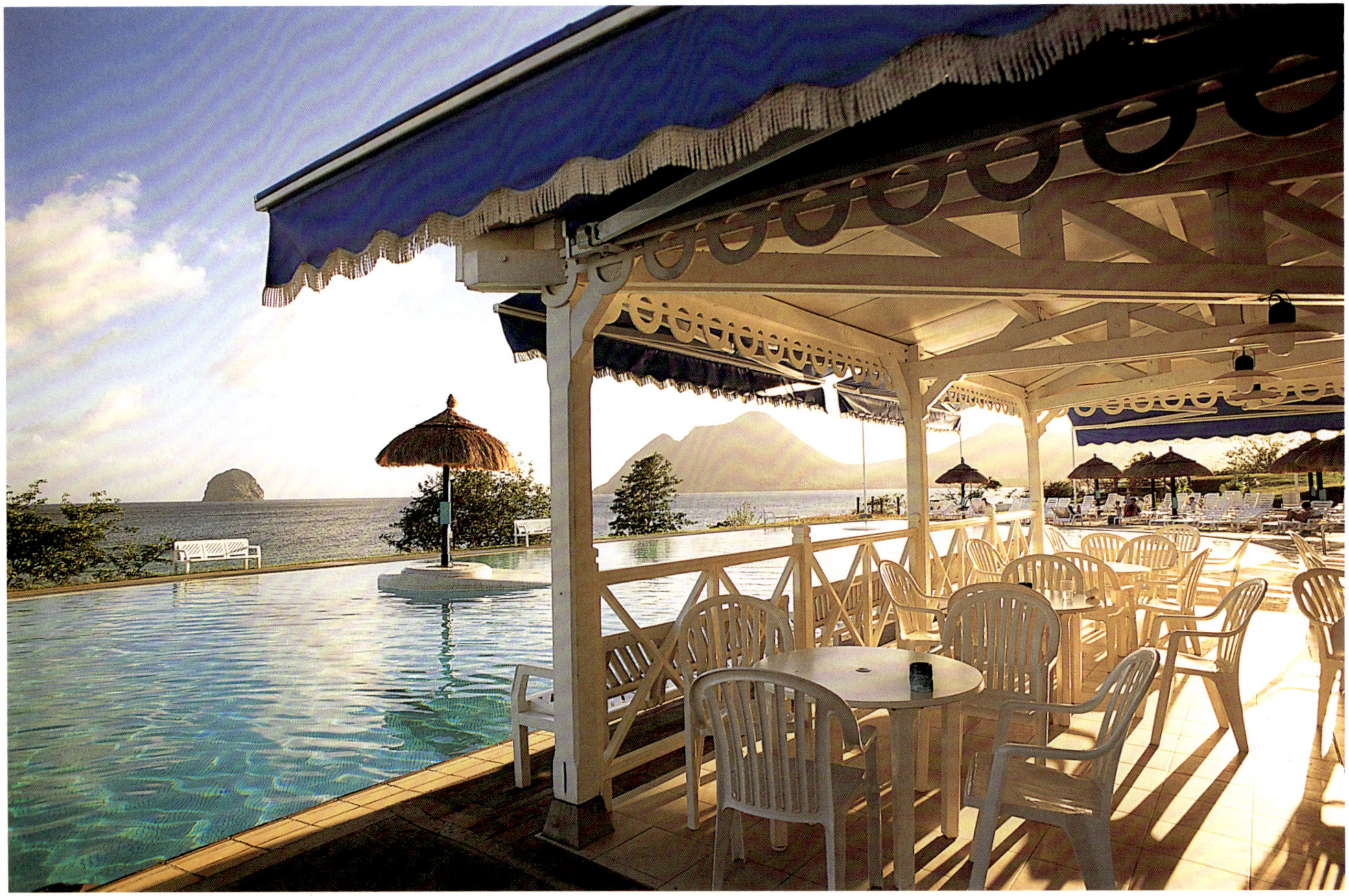

MARINE HOTEL (DIAMANT)

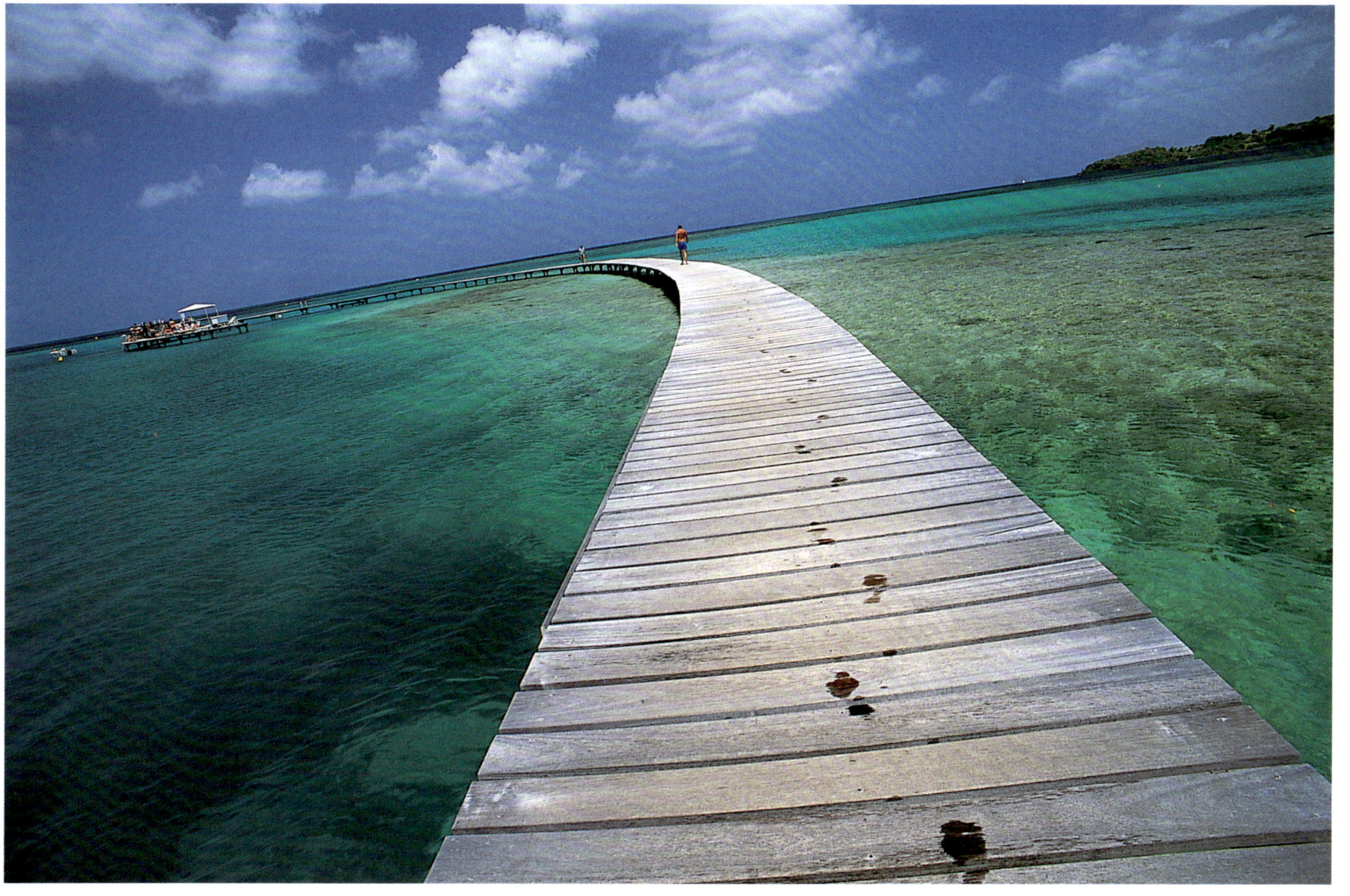

HOTEL LE BAKOUA (LES TROIS-ÎLETS)

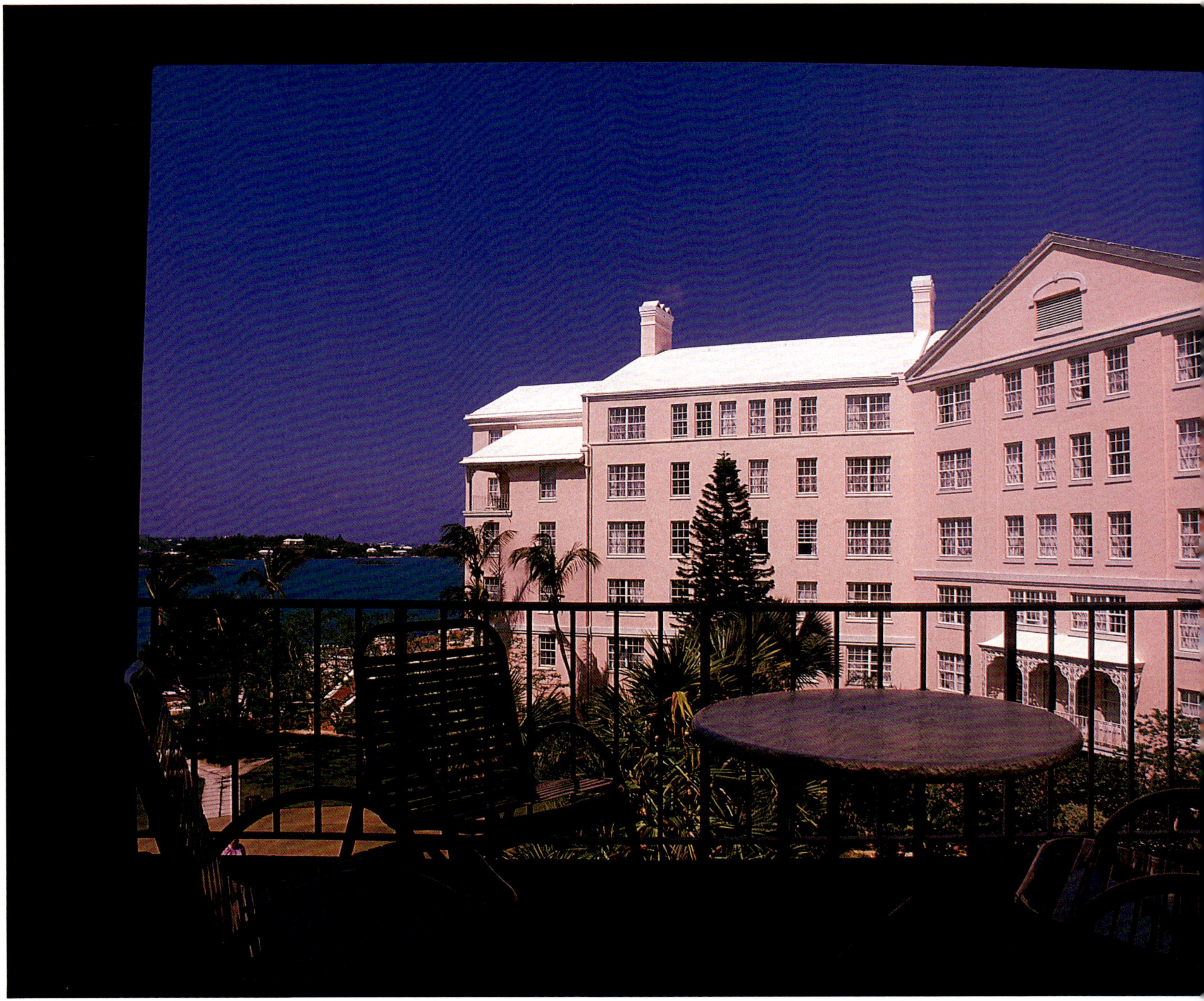

THE PRINCESS HOTEL (PEMBROKE PARISH)

BERMUDA ISLANDS

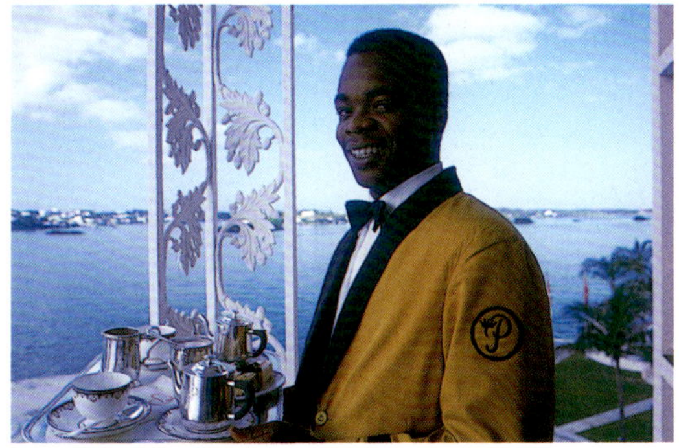

THE PRINCESS HOTEL (PEMBROKE PARISH)

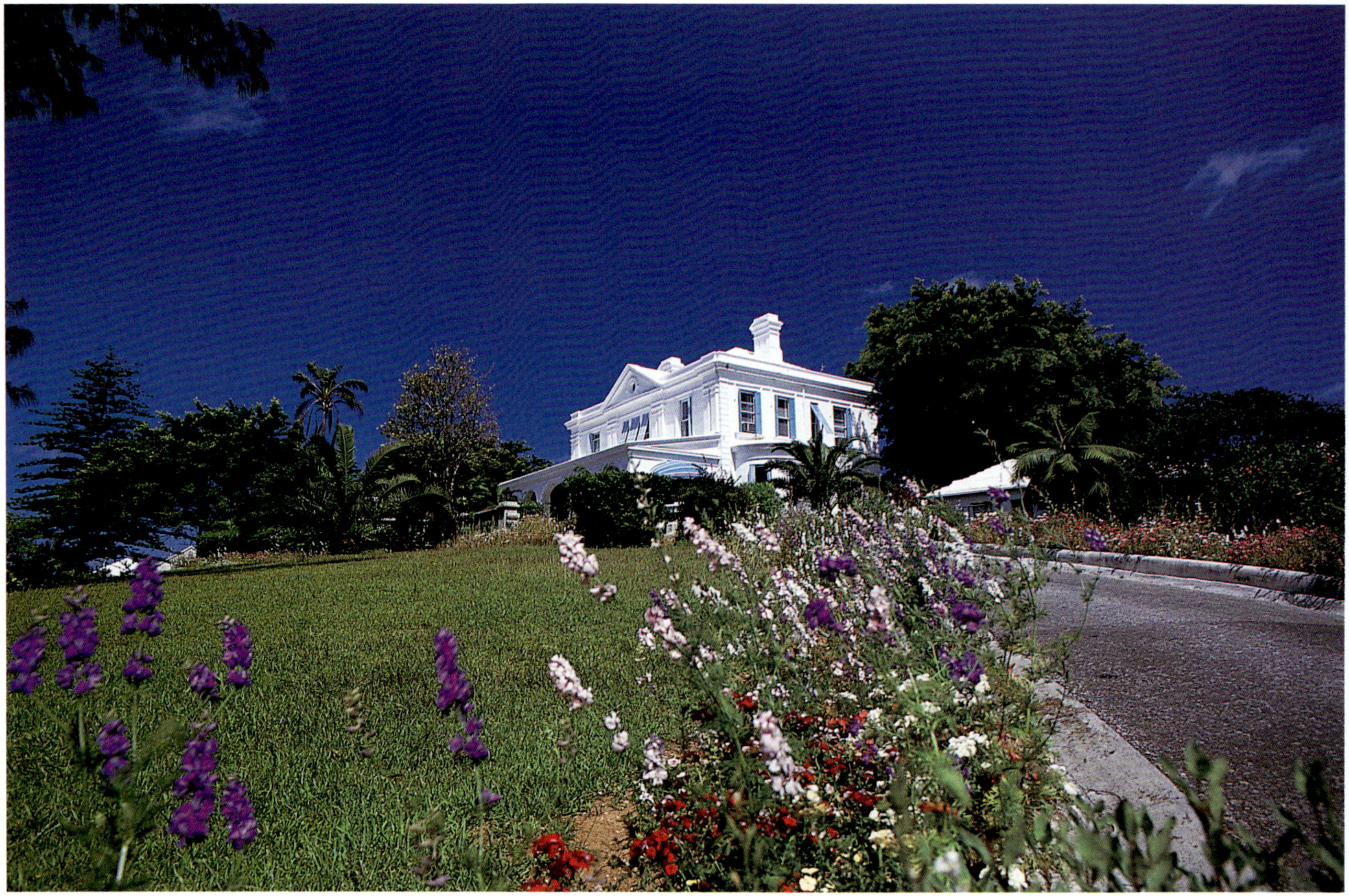

ROSEDON (HAMILTON)

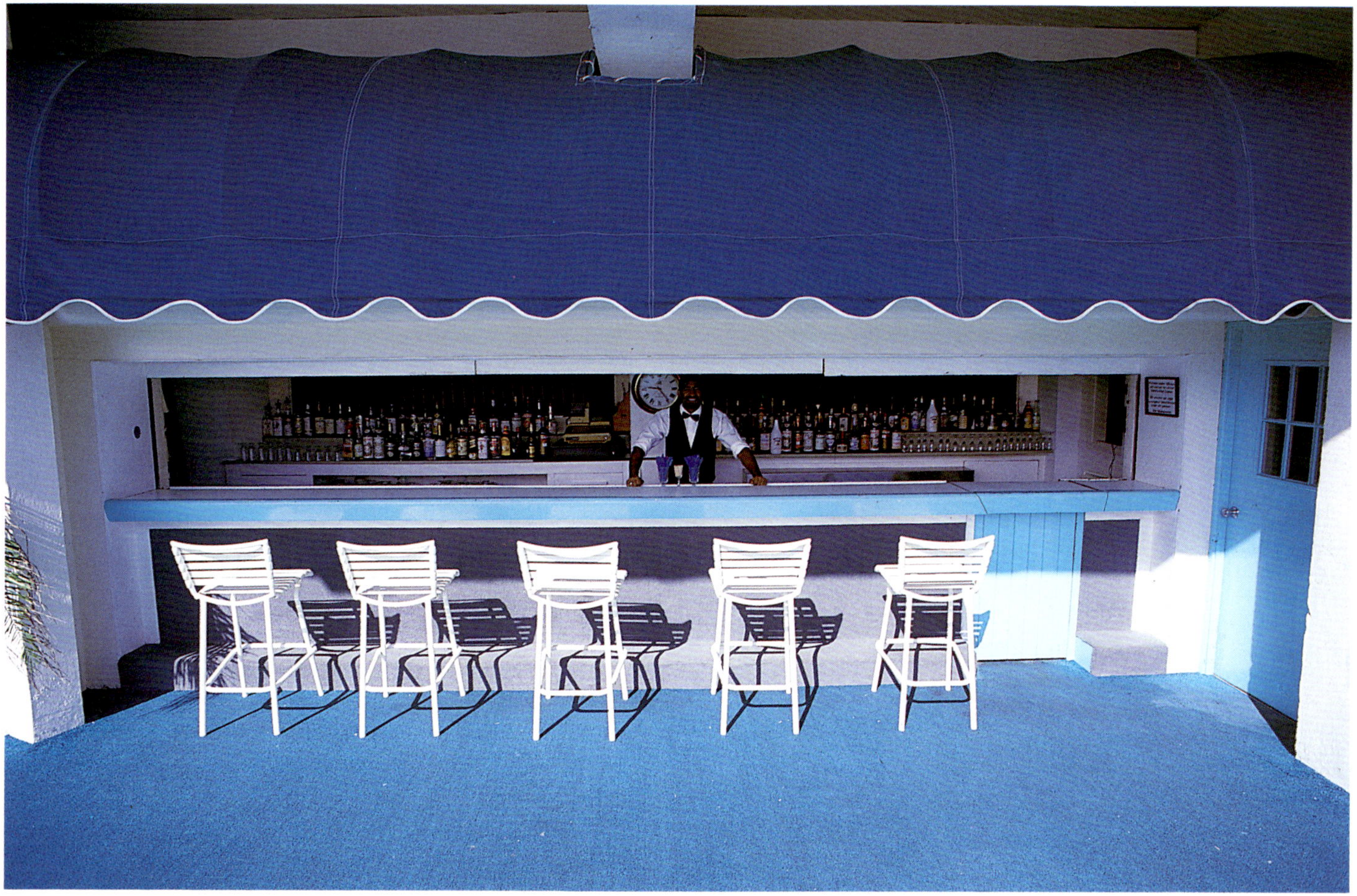

ELBOW BEACH HOTEL (PAGET)

MIAMI

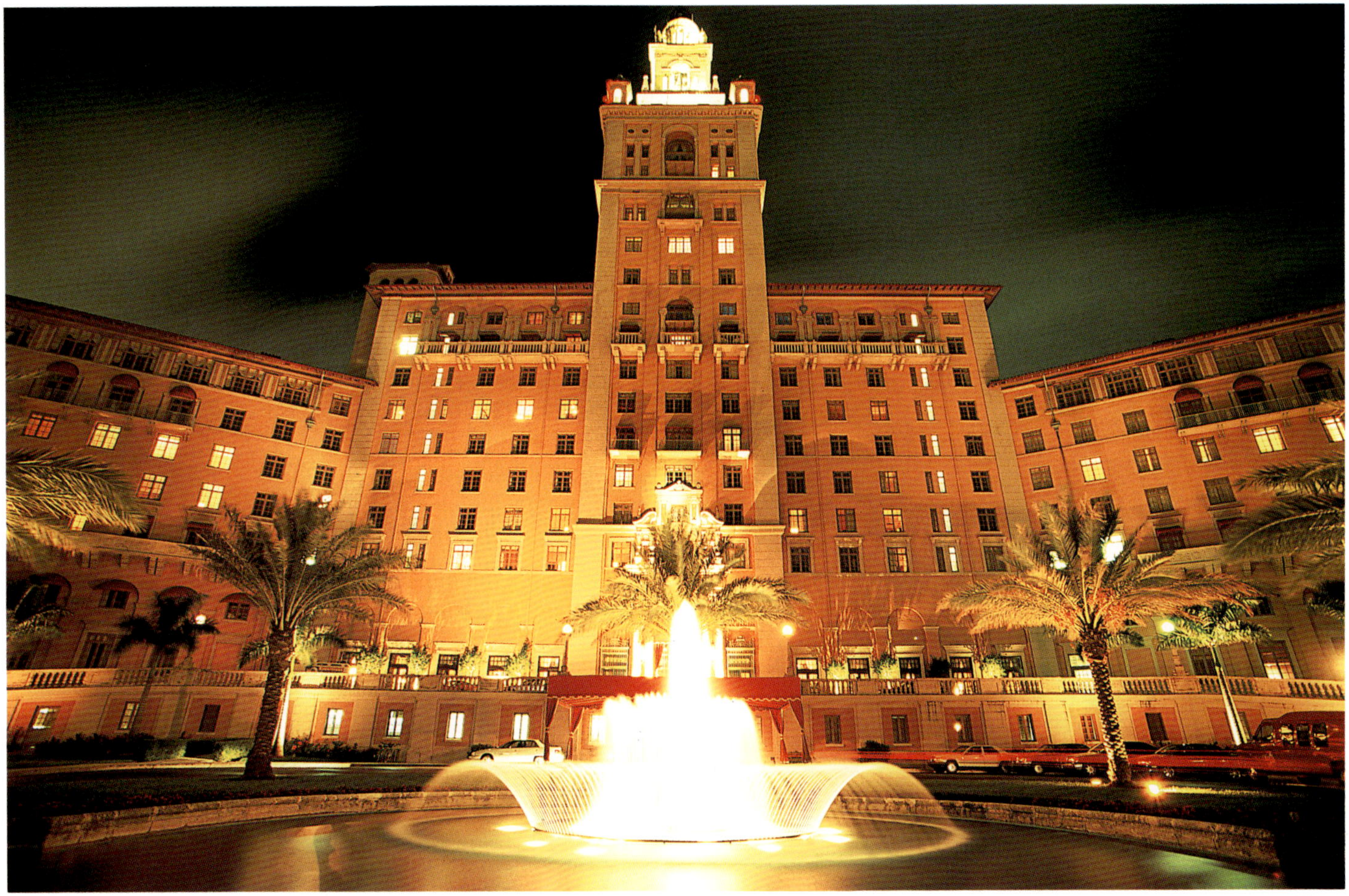

THE BILTMORE HOTEL (CORAL GABLES)

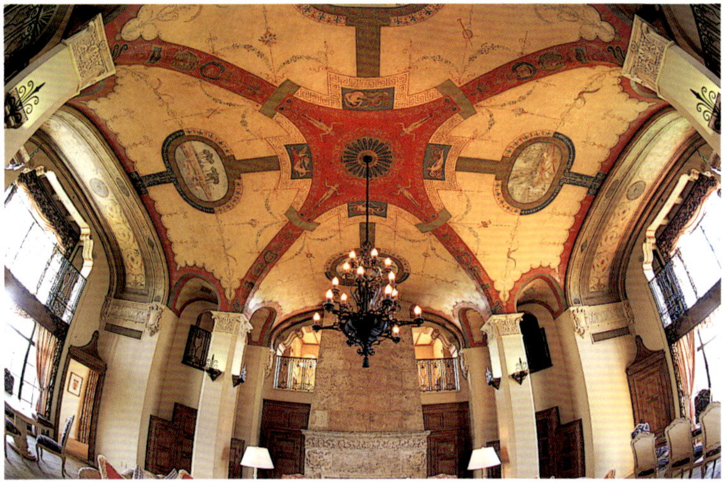

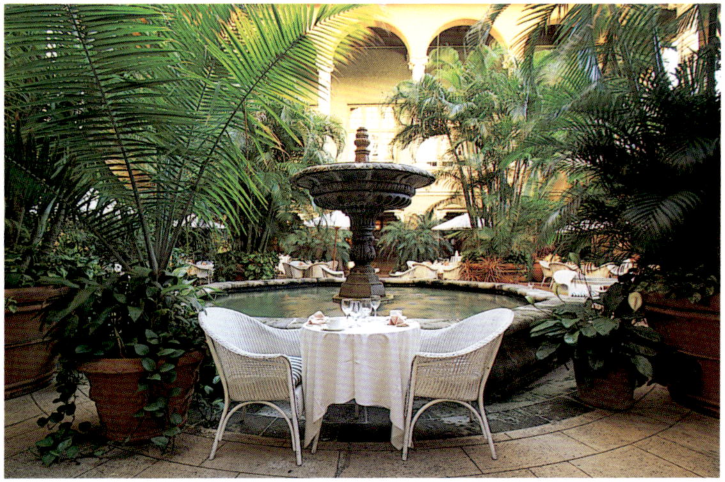

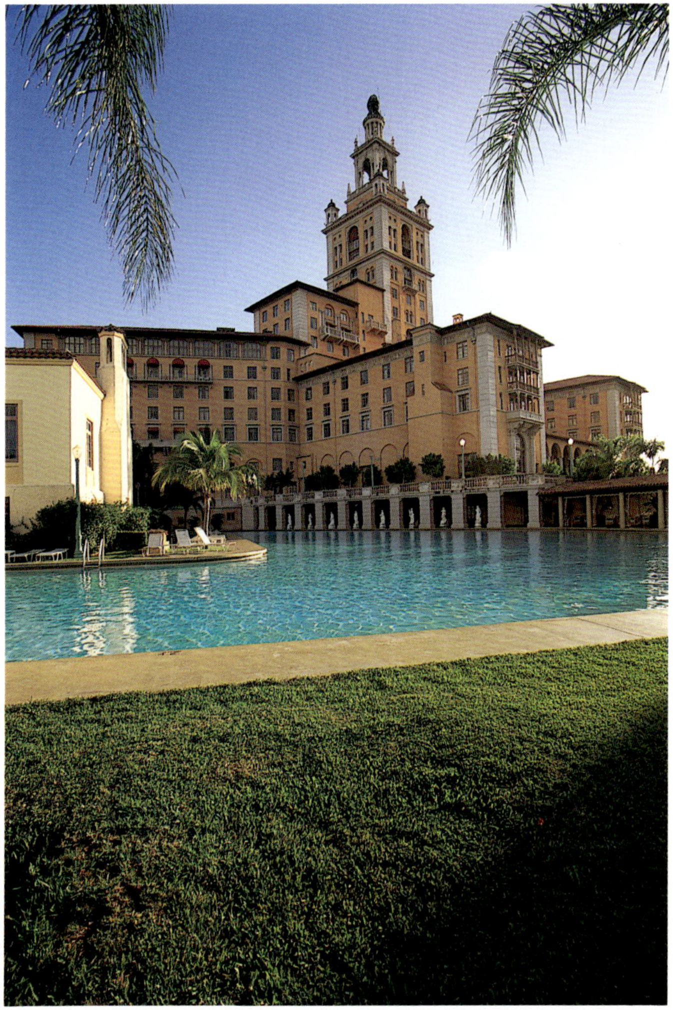

THE BILTMORE HOTEL (CORAL GABLES)

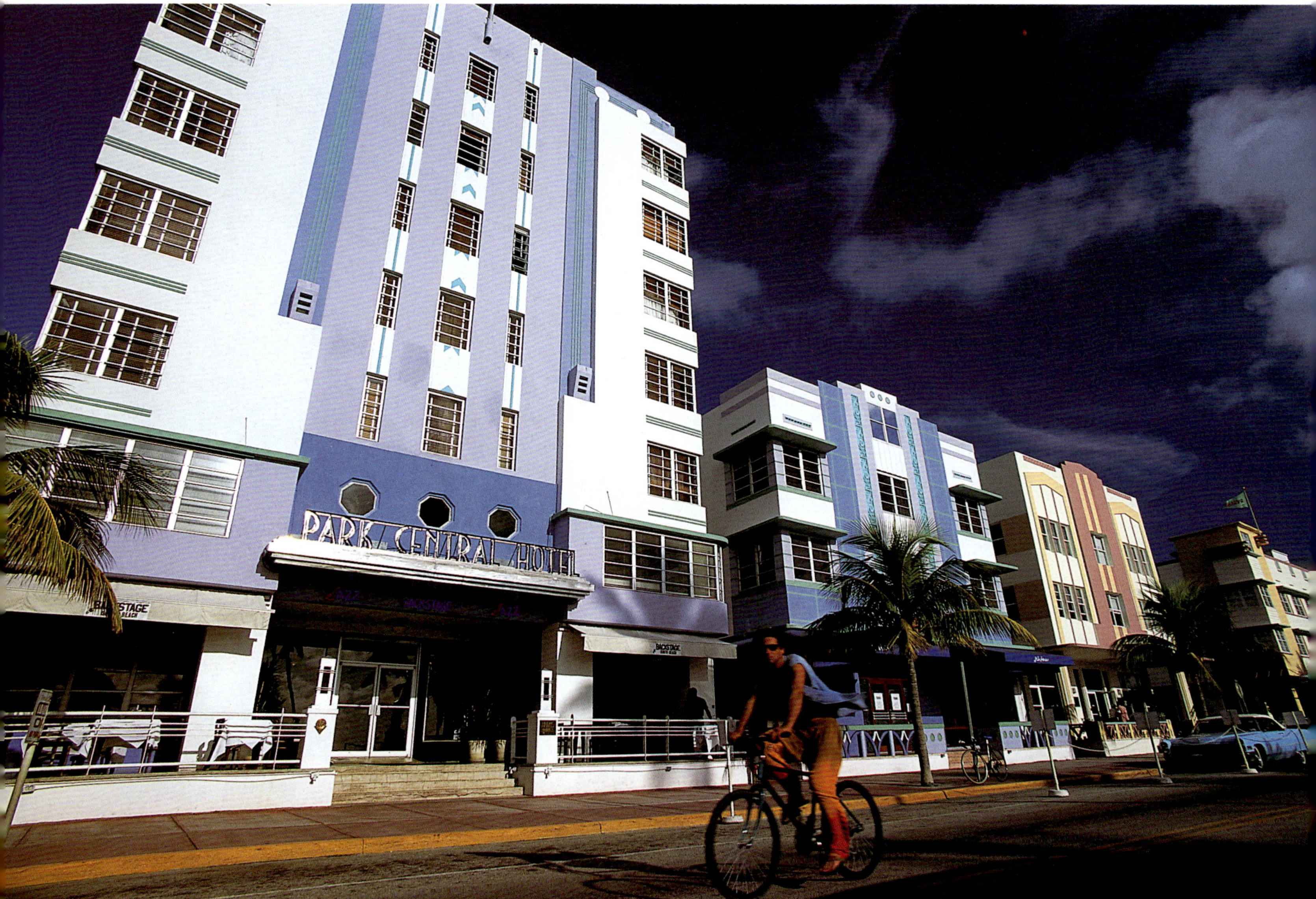

ART DECO HOTELS (MIAMI BEACH)

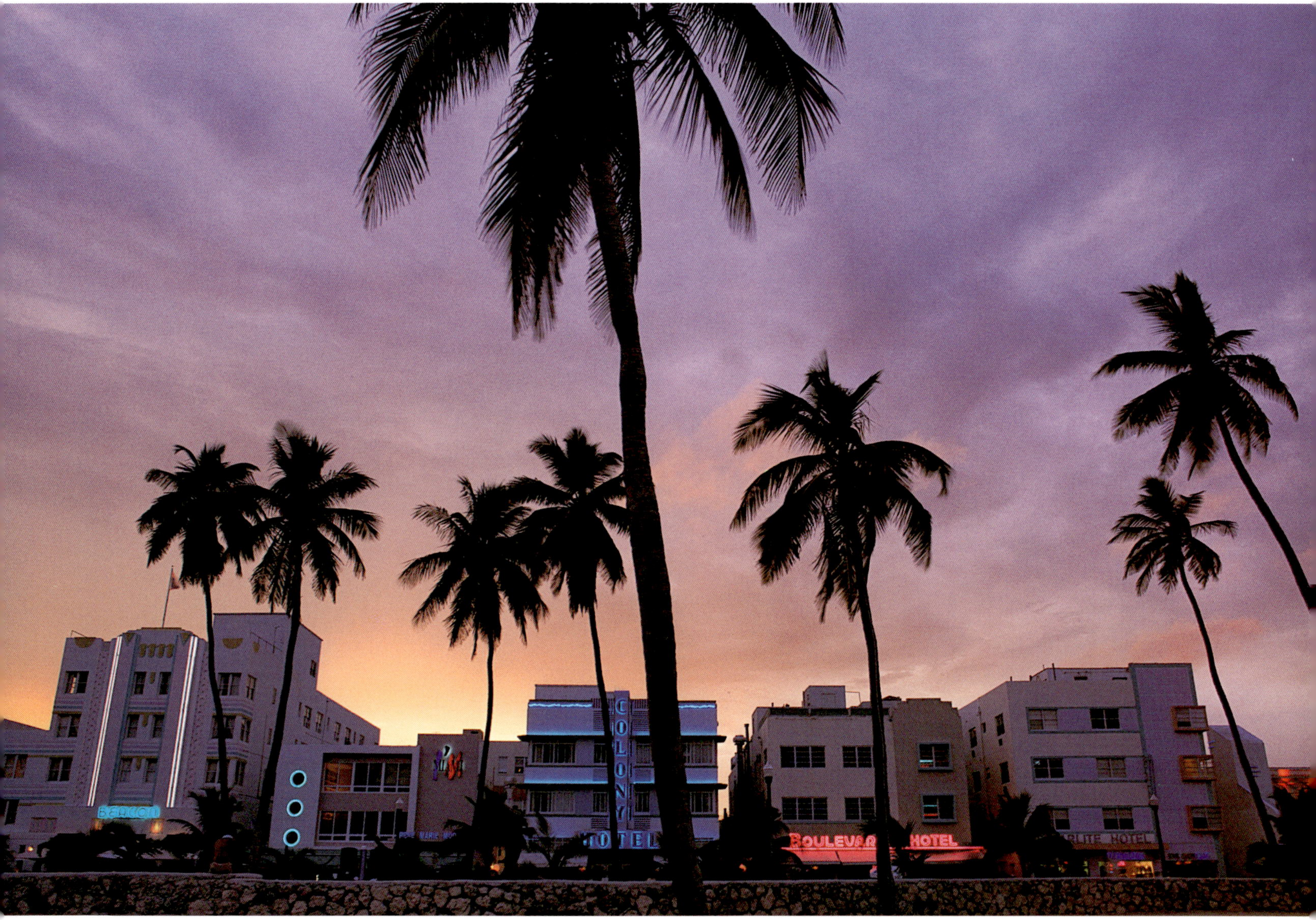

ART DECO HOTELS (MIAMI BEACH)

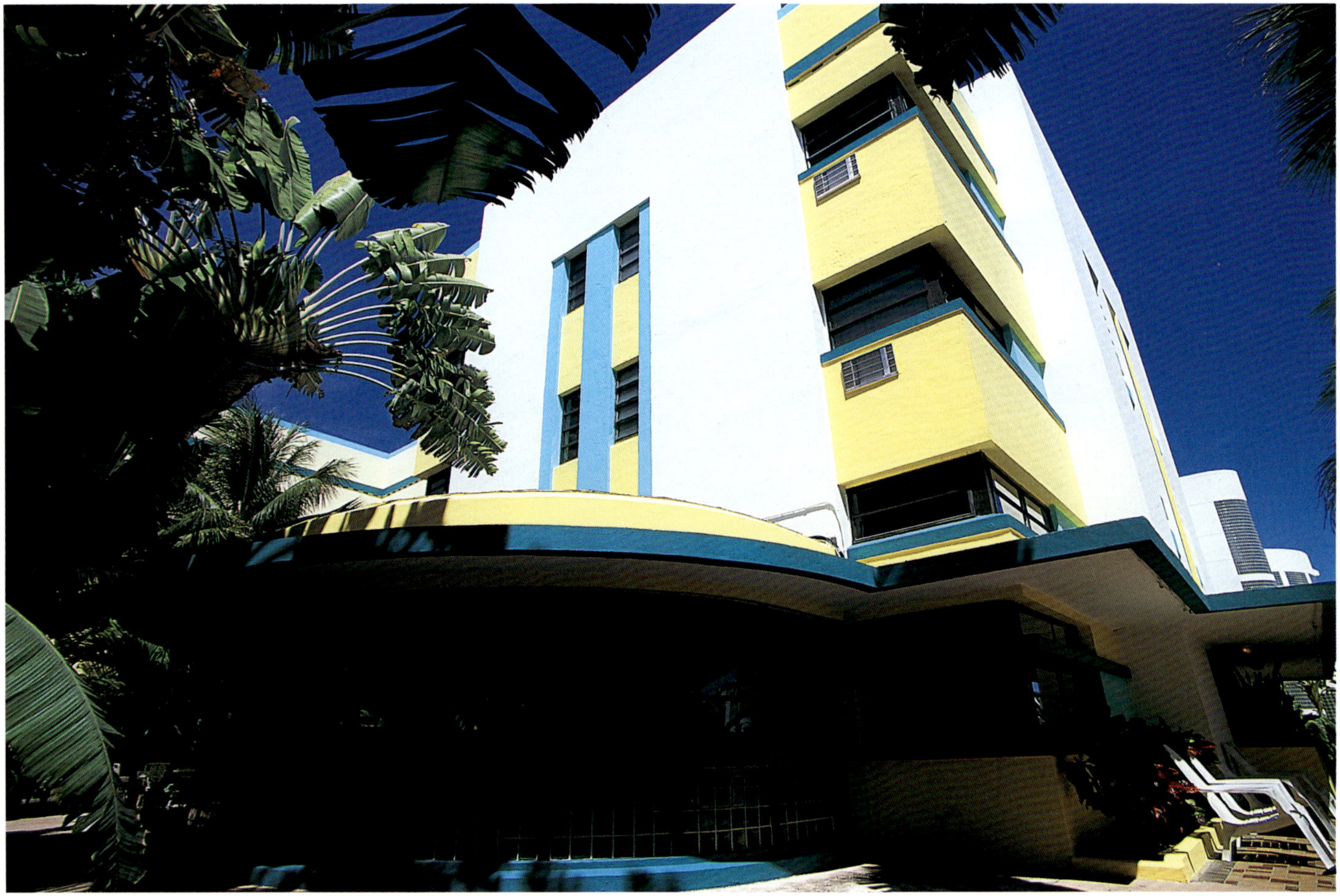

KENMORE HOTEL (OLD MIAMI BEACH)

72

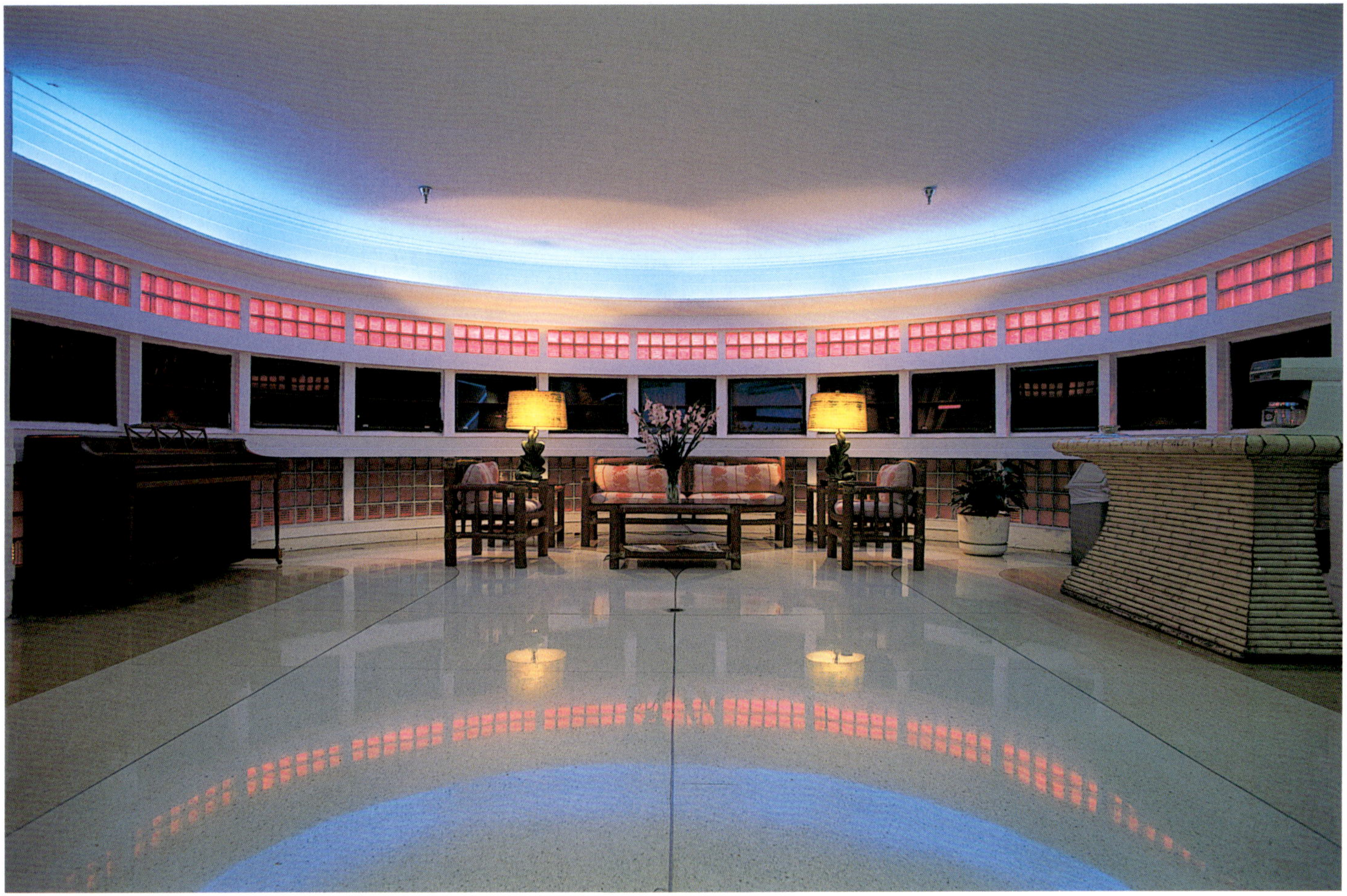

KENMORE HOTEL (OLD MIAMI BEACH)

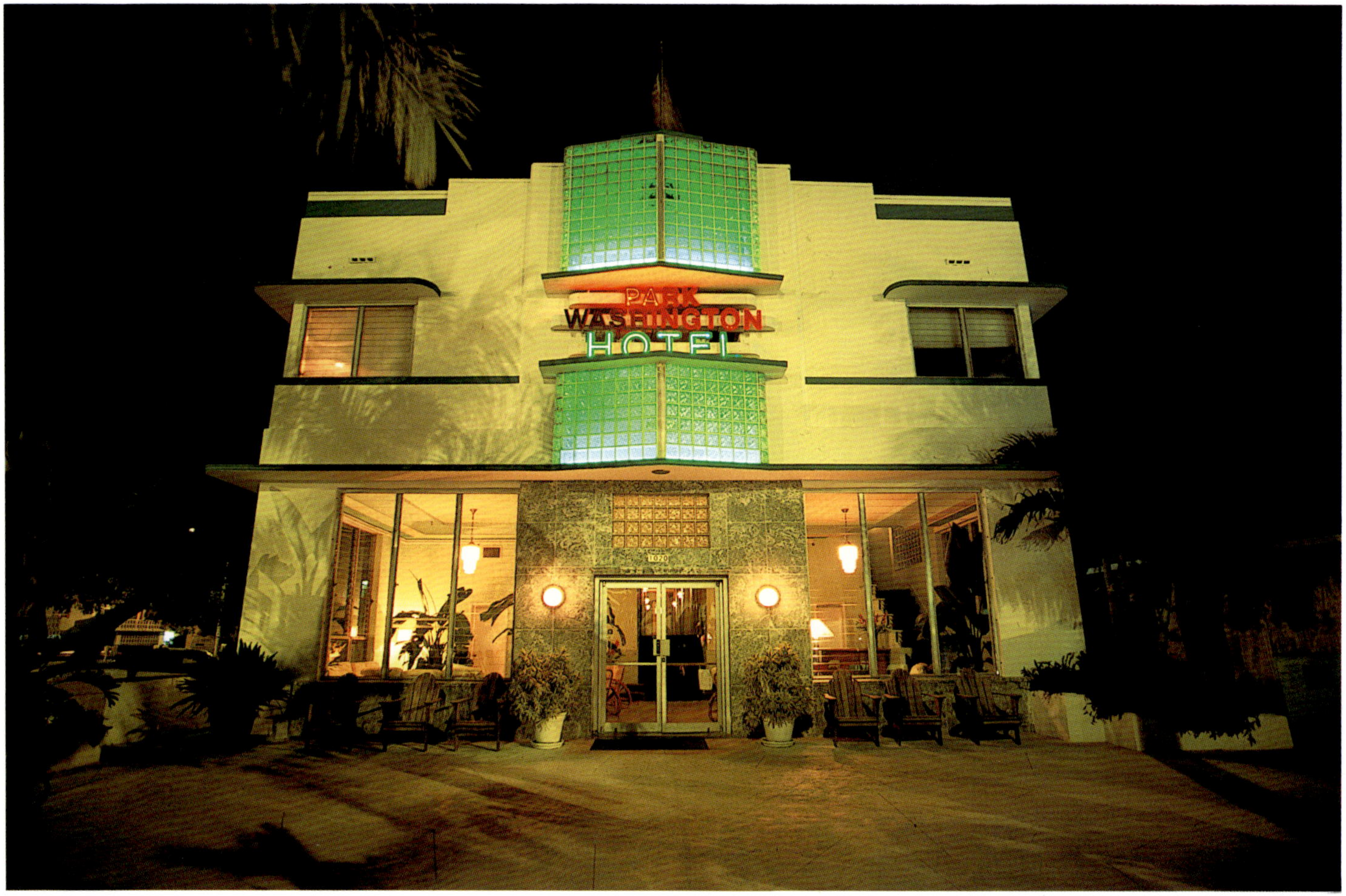

PARK WASHINGTON HOTEL (OLD MIAMI BEACH)

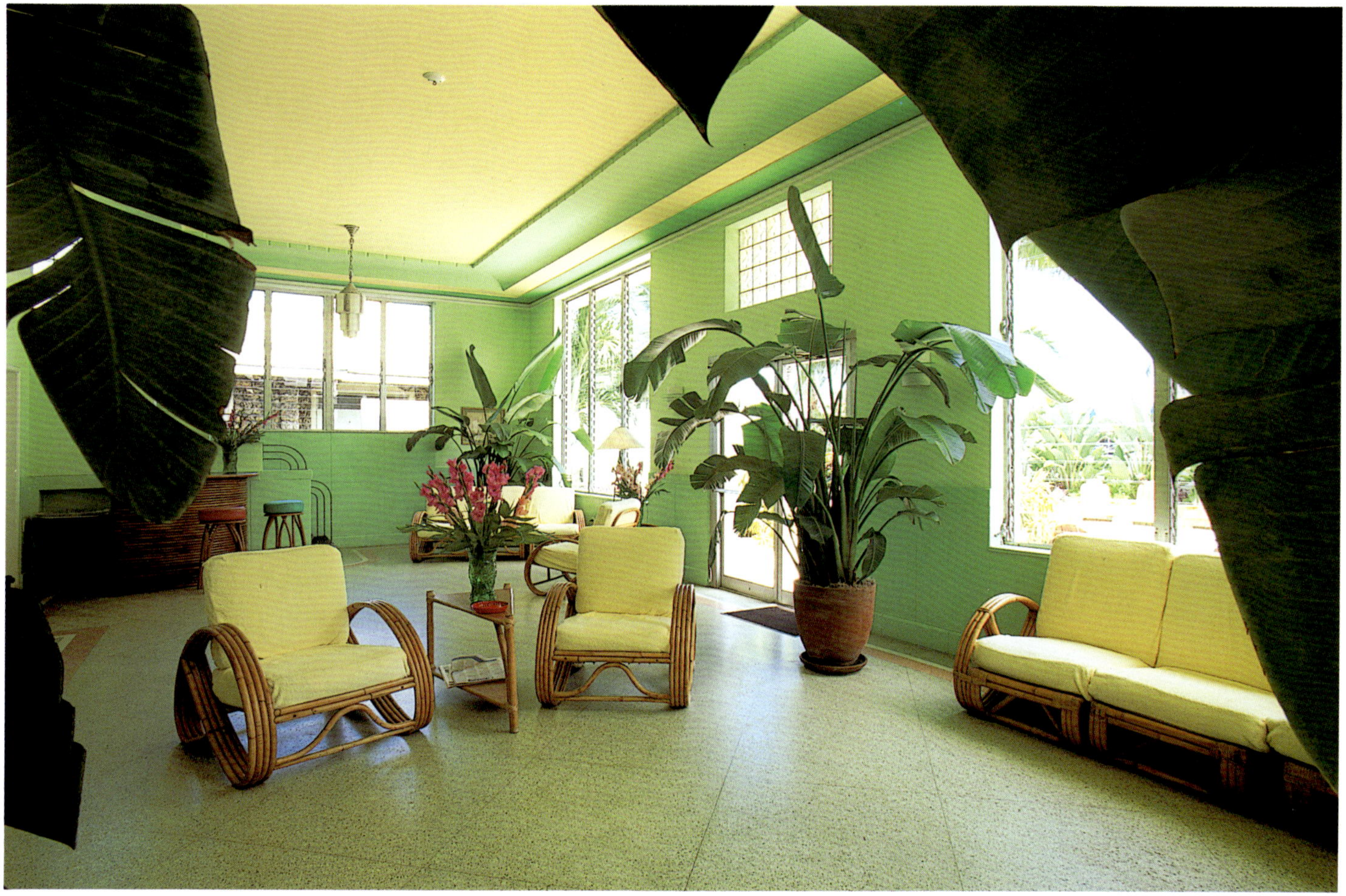

PARK WASHINGTON HOTEL (OLD MIAMI BEACH)

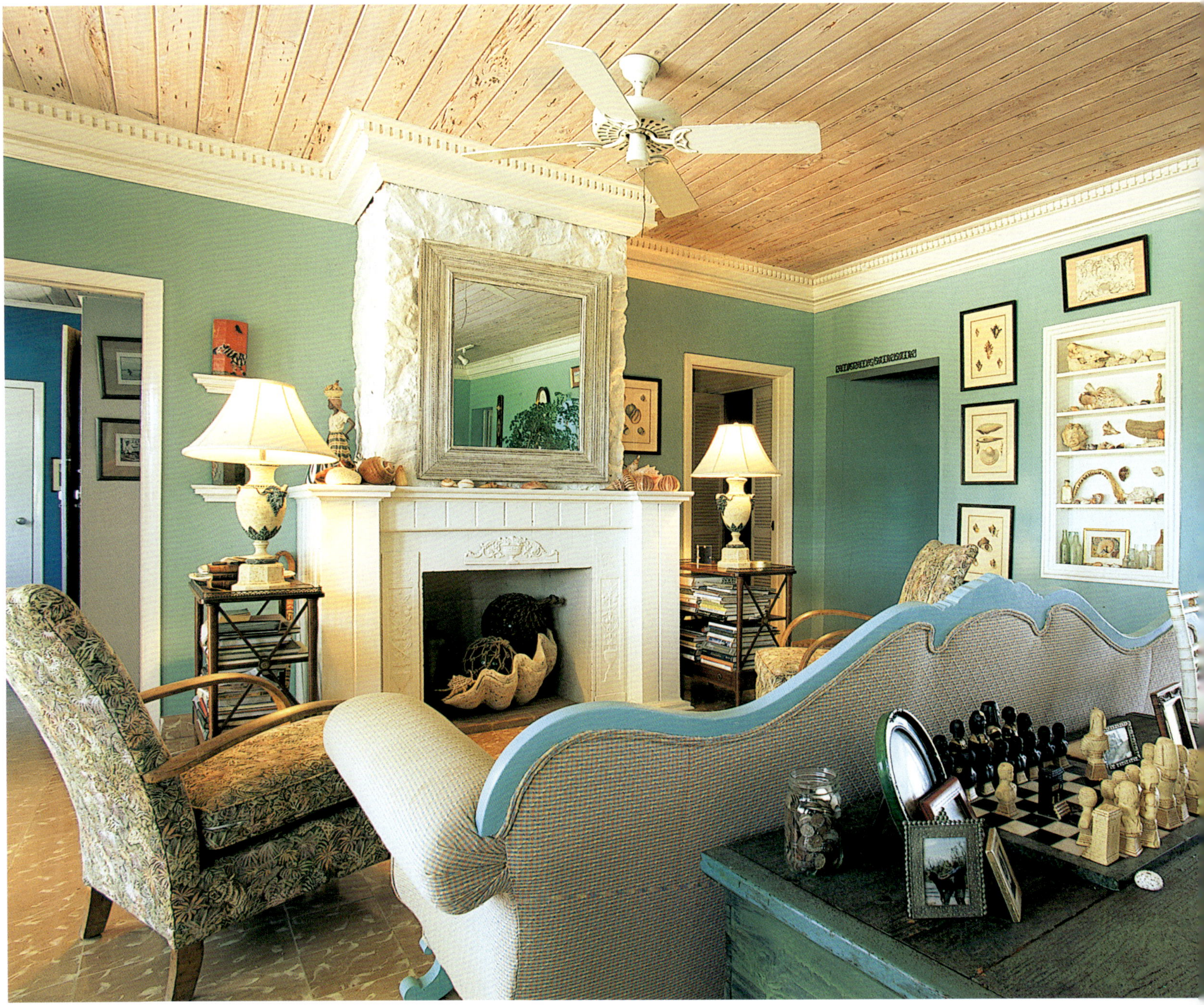

OCEAN VIEW CLUB (HARBOUR ISLAND)

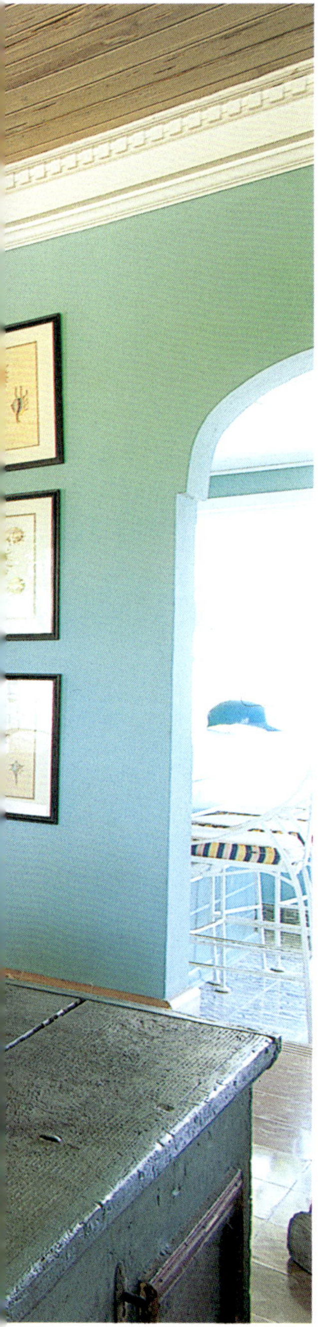

BAHAMAS

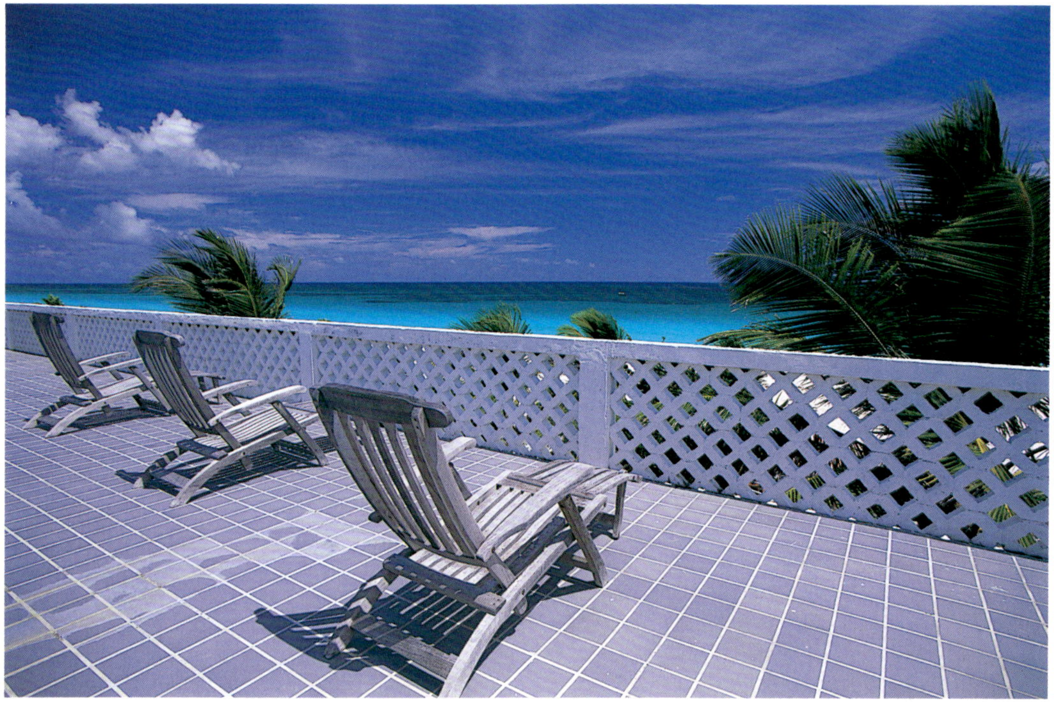

OCEAN VIEW CLUB (HARBOUR ISLAND)

MEXICO

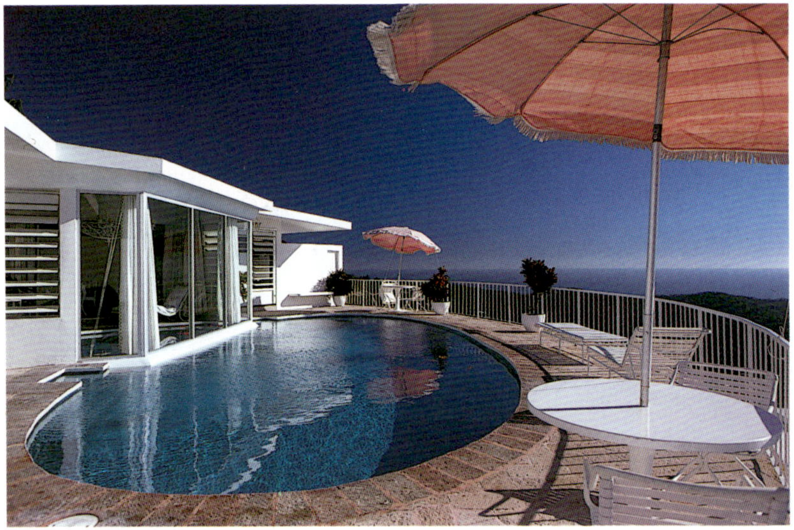

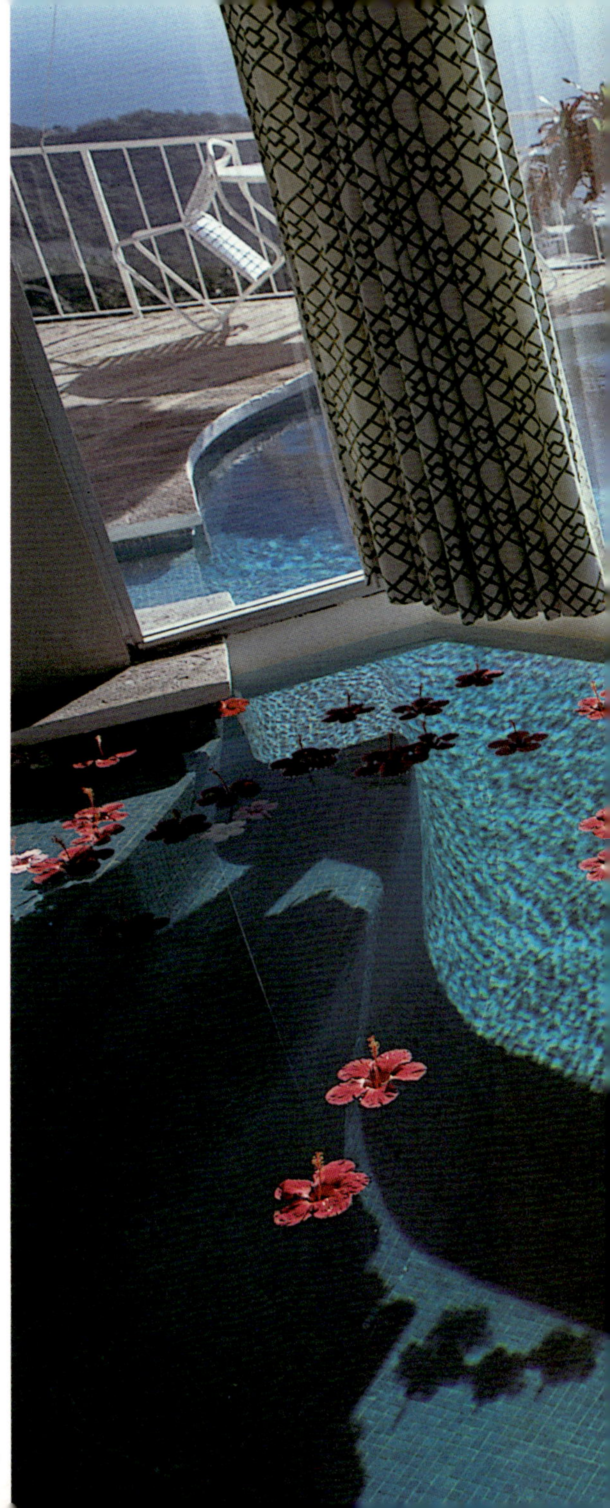

LAS BRISAS (ACAPULCO)

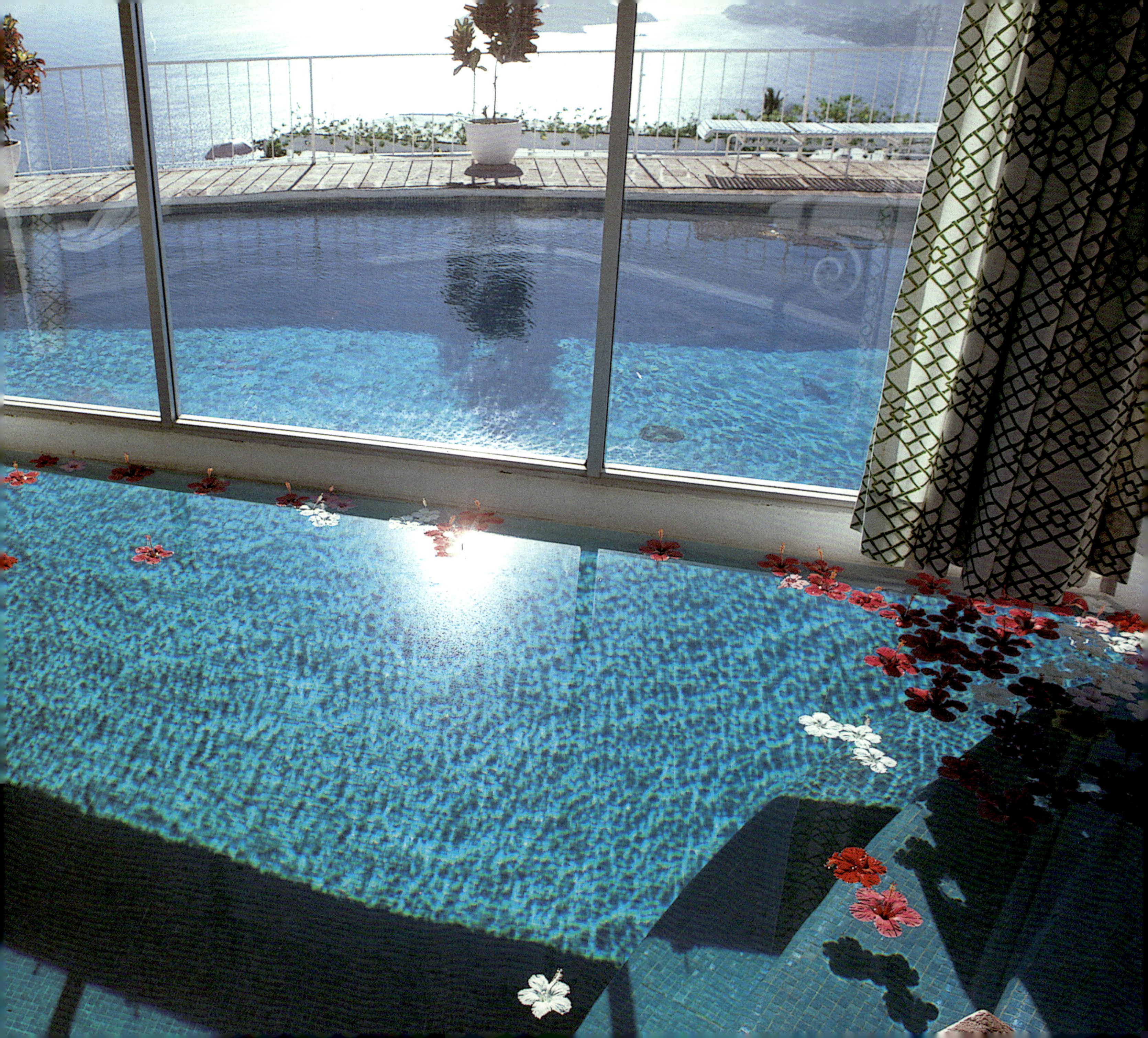

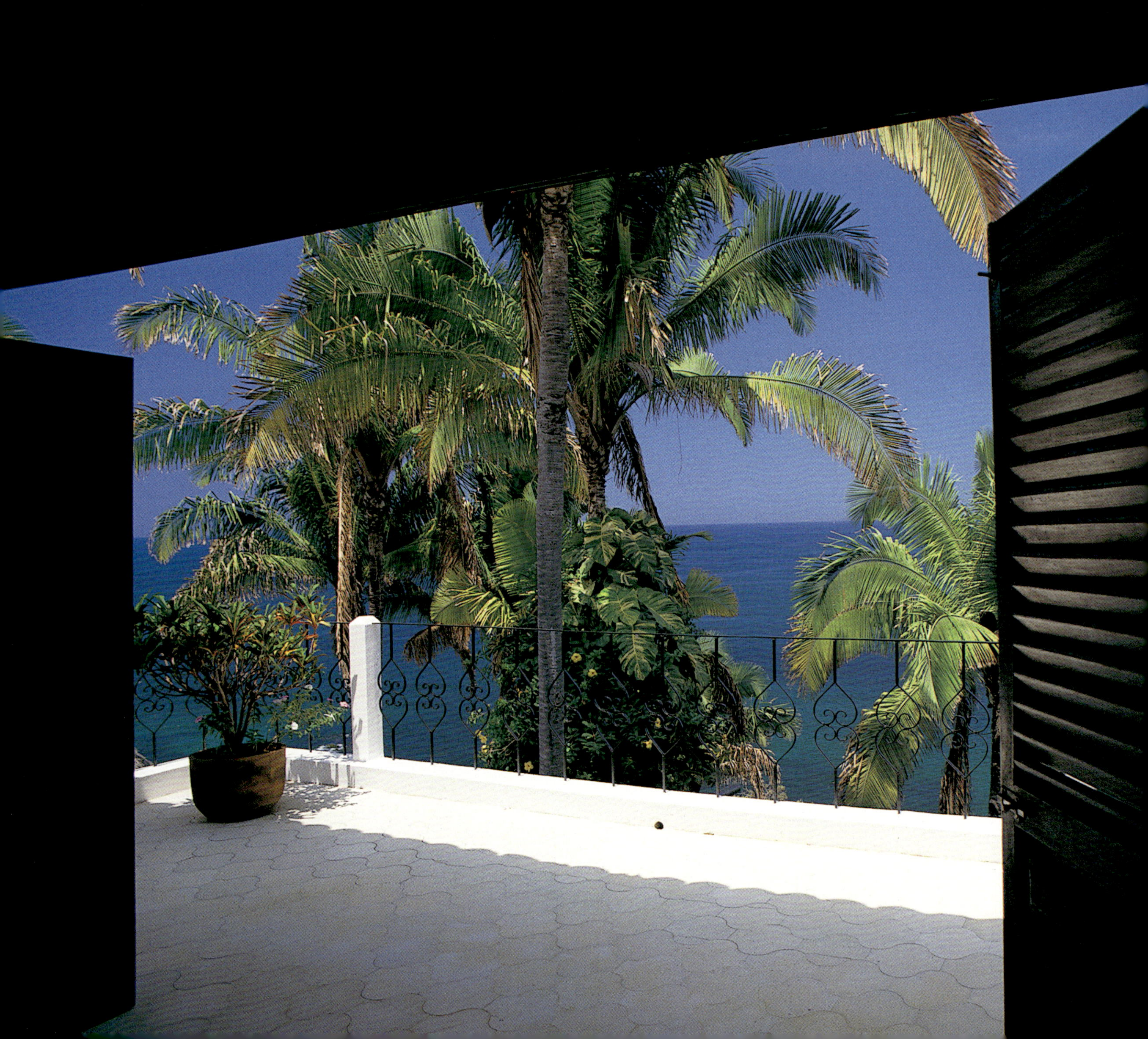

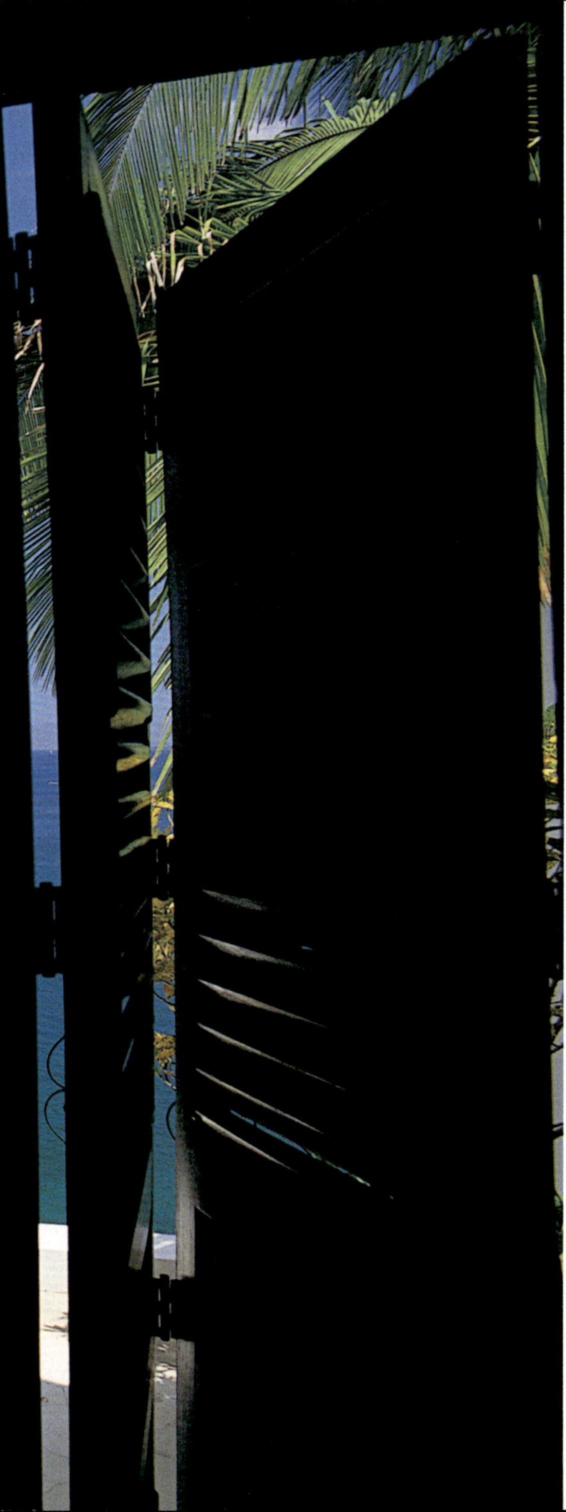

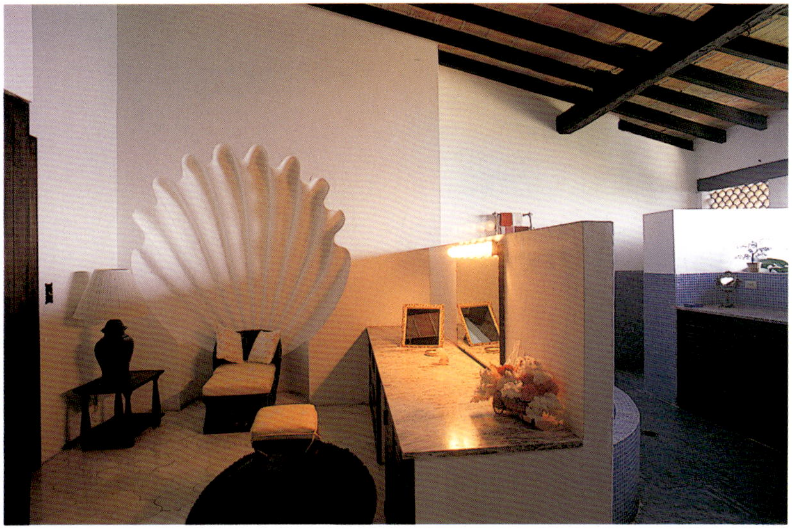

QUINTA LAURA (PUERTO VALLARTA)

QUINTA LAURA (PUERTO VALLARTA)

82

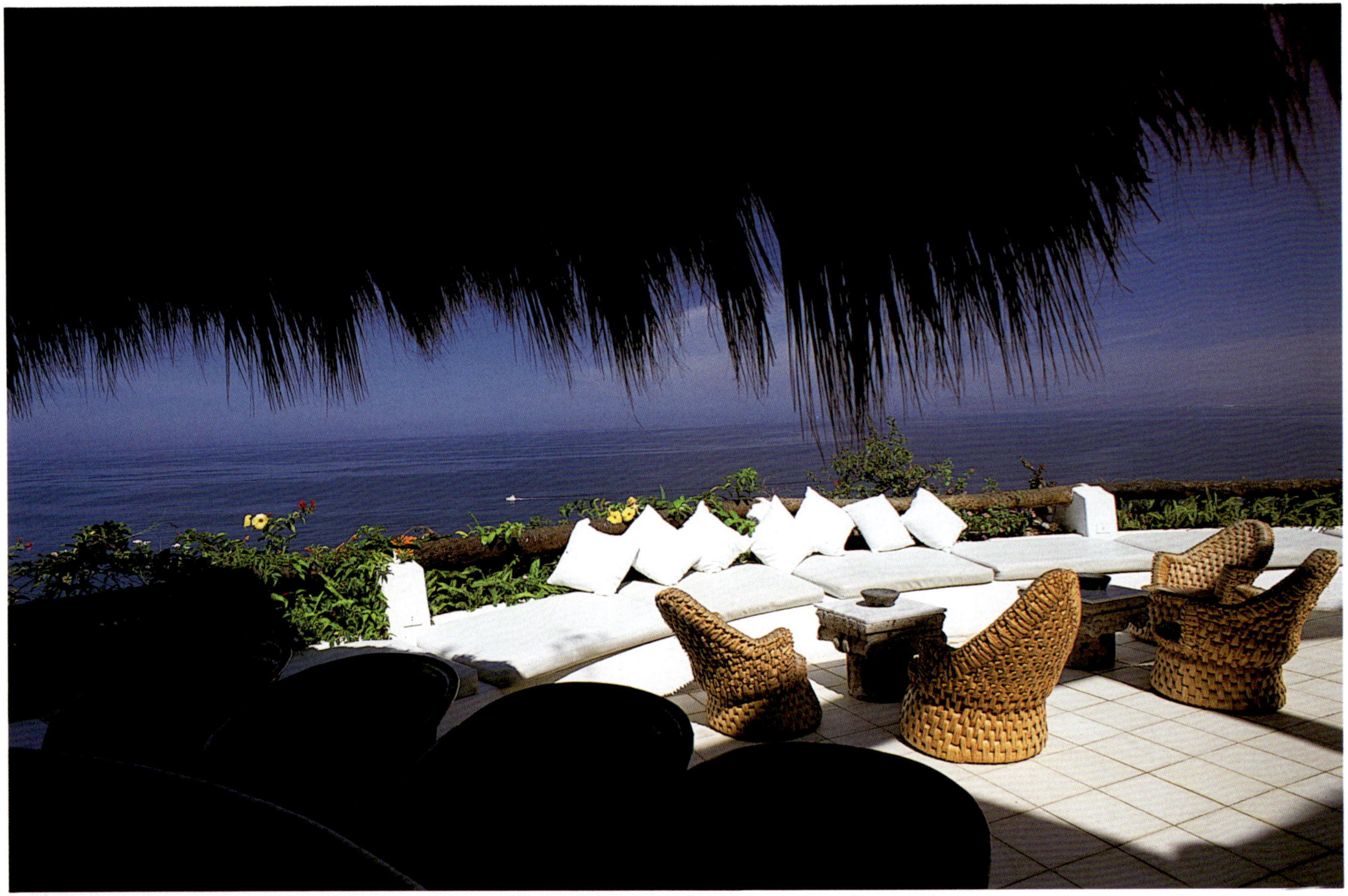

OCHO CASCADAS (PUERTO VALLARTA)

OCHO CASCADAS (PUERTO VALLARTA

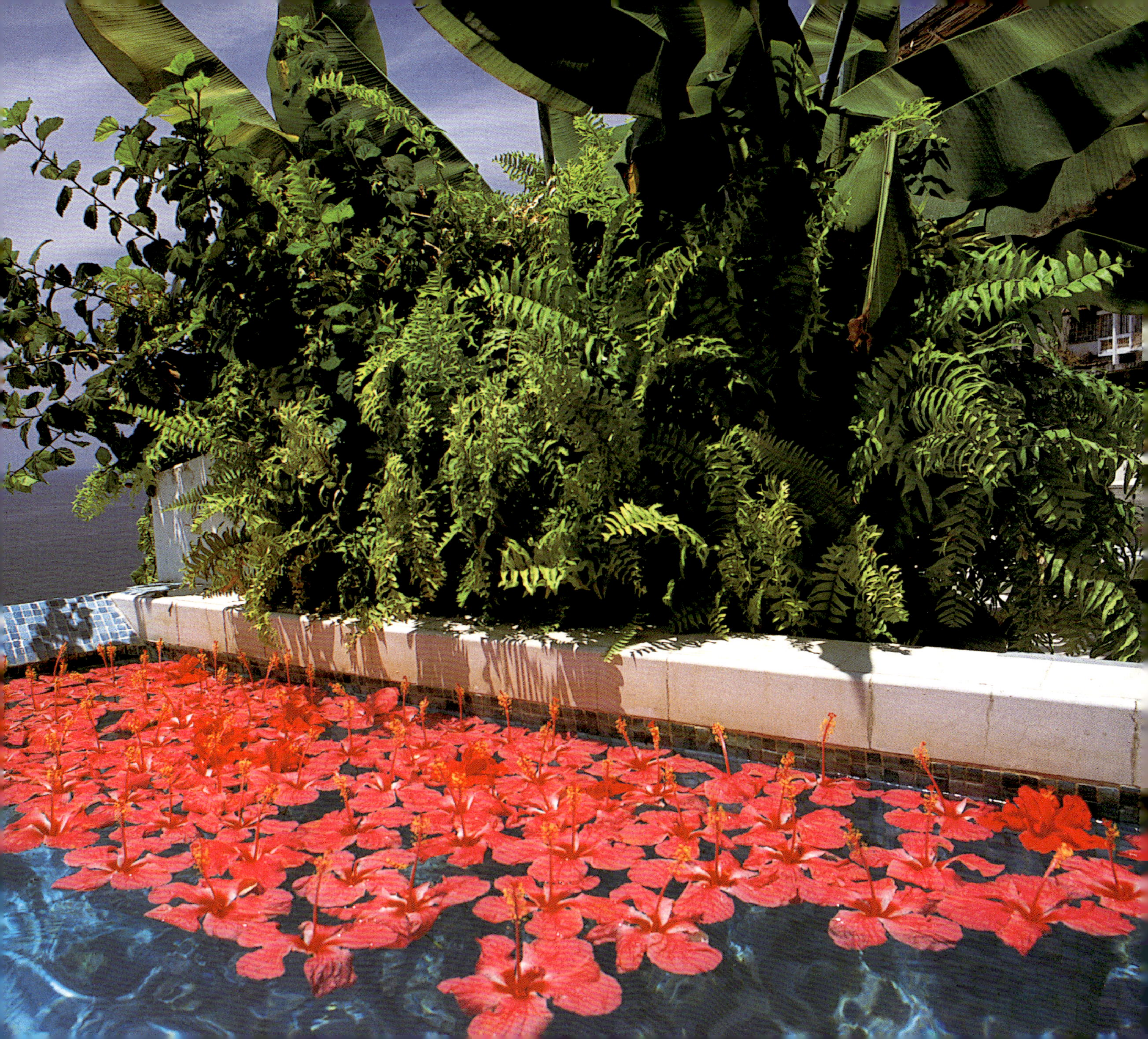

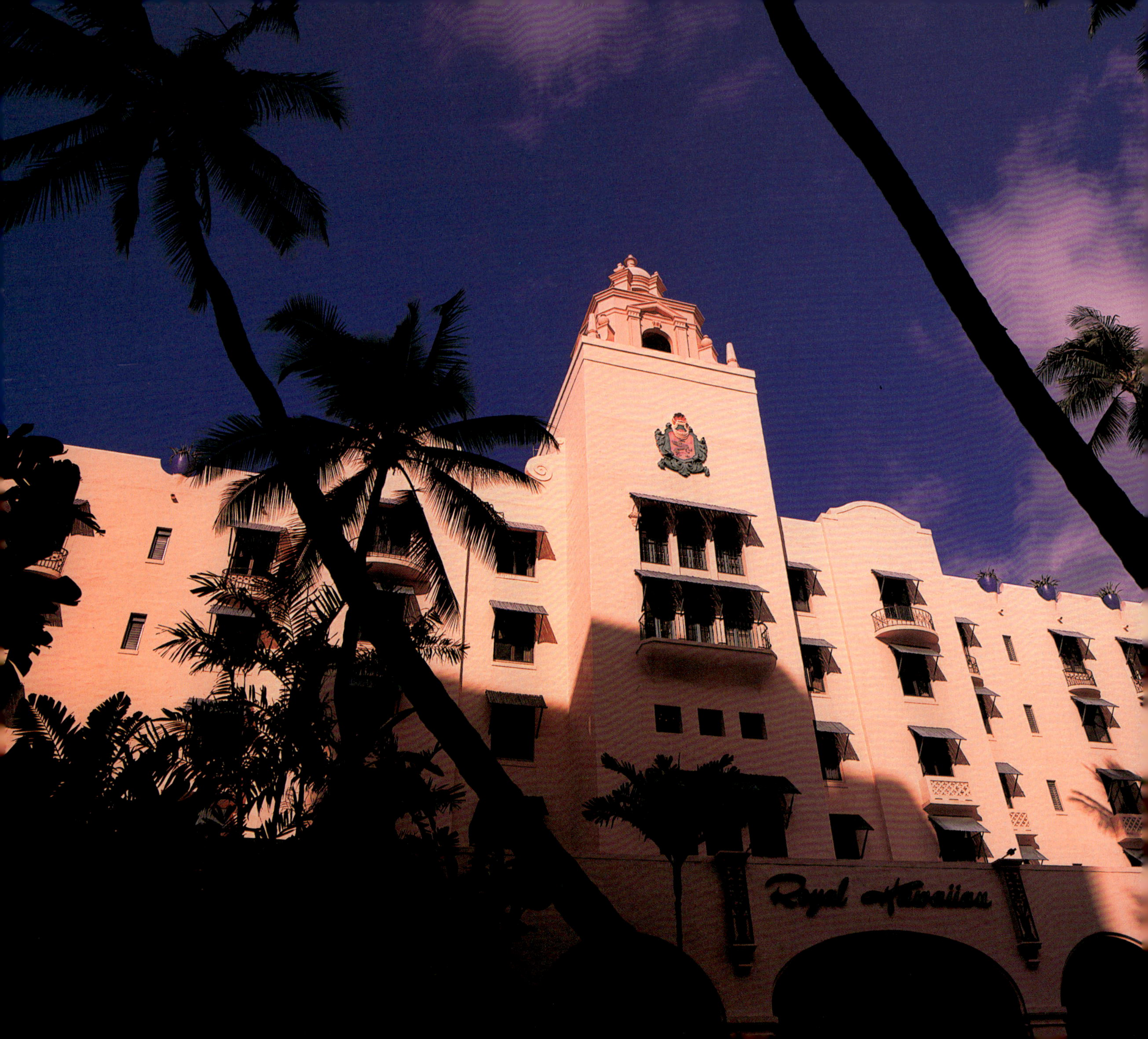
Royal Hawaiian

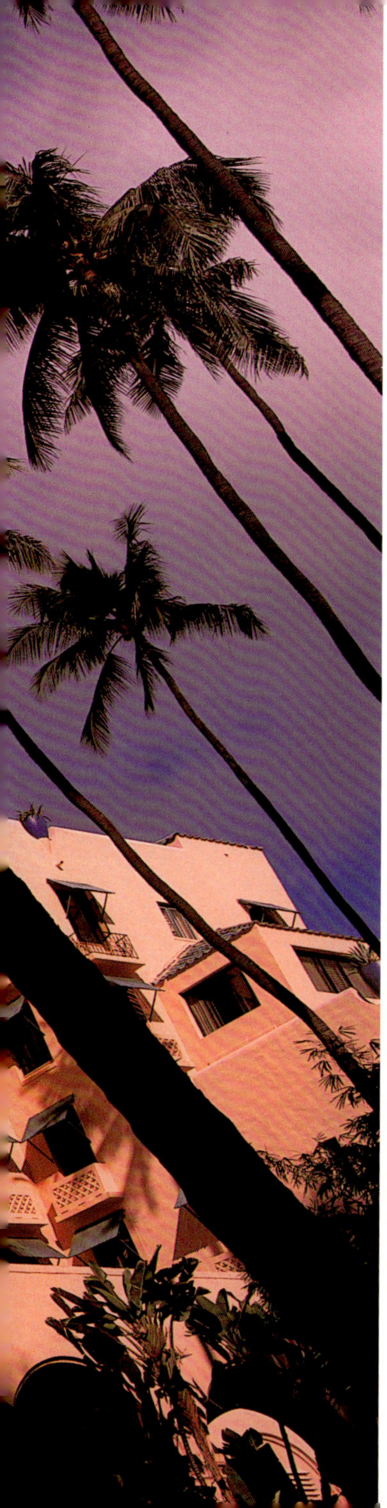

HAWAII

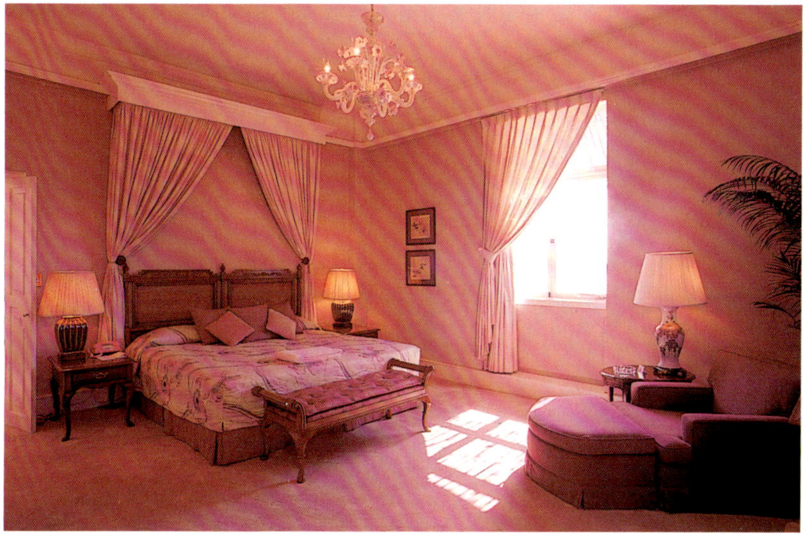

ROYAL HAWAIIAN HOTEL (HONOLULU)

ROYAL HAWAIIAN HOTEL (HONOLULU)

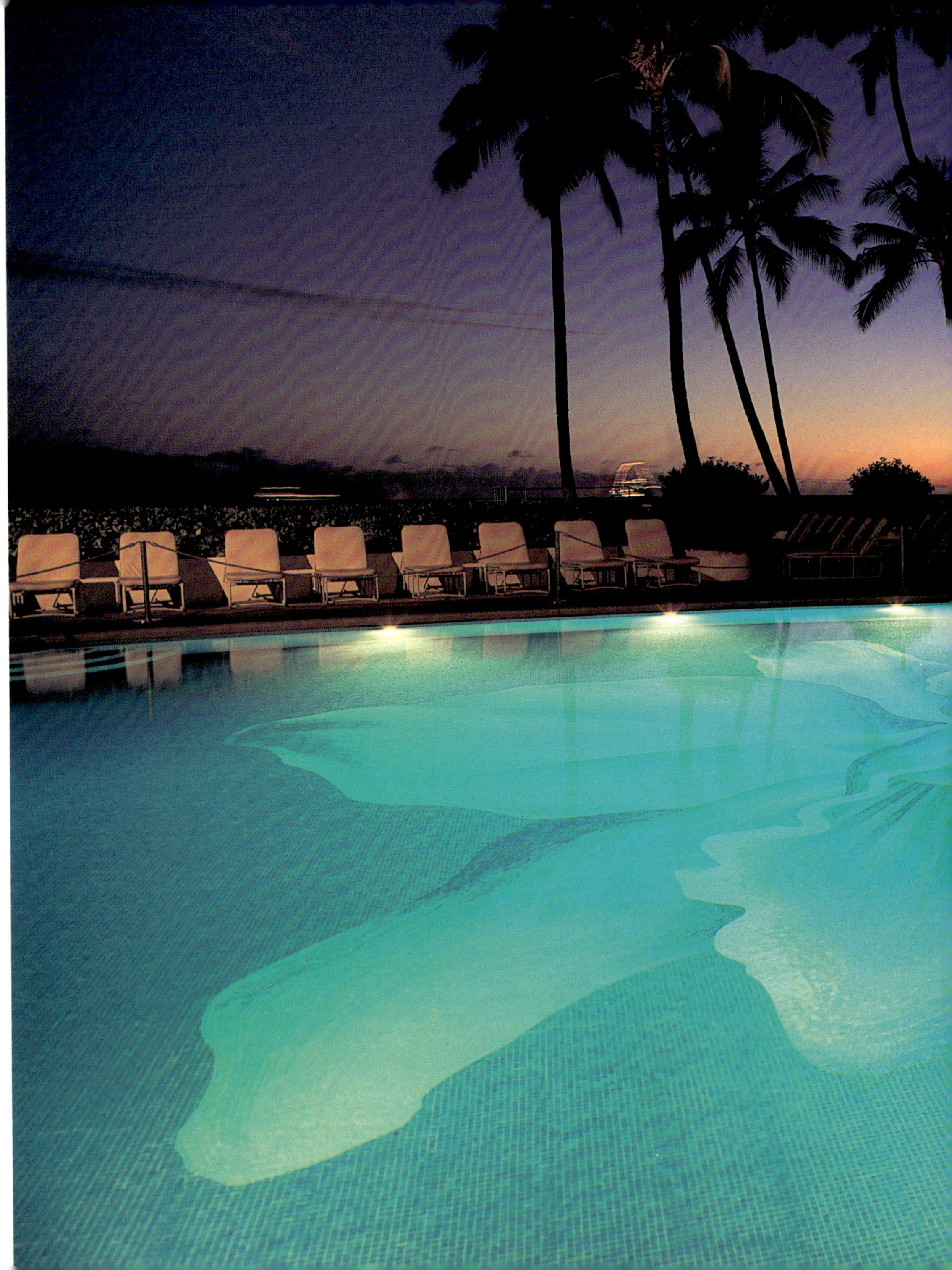

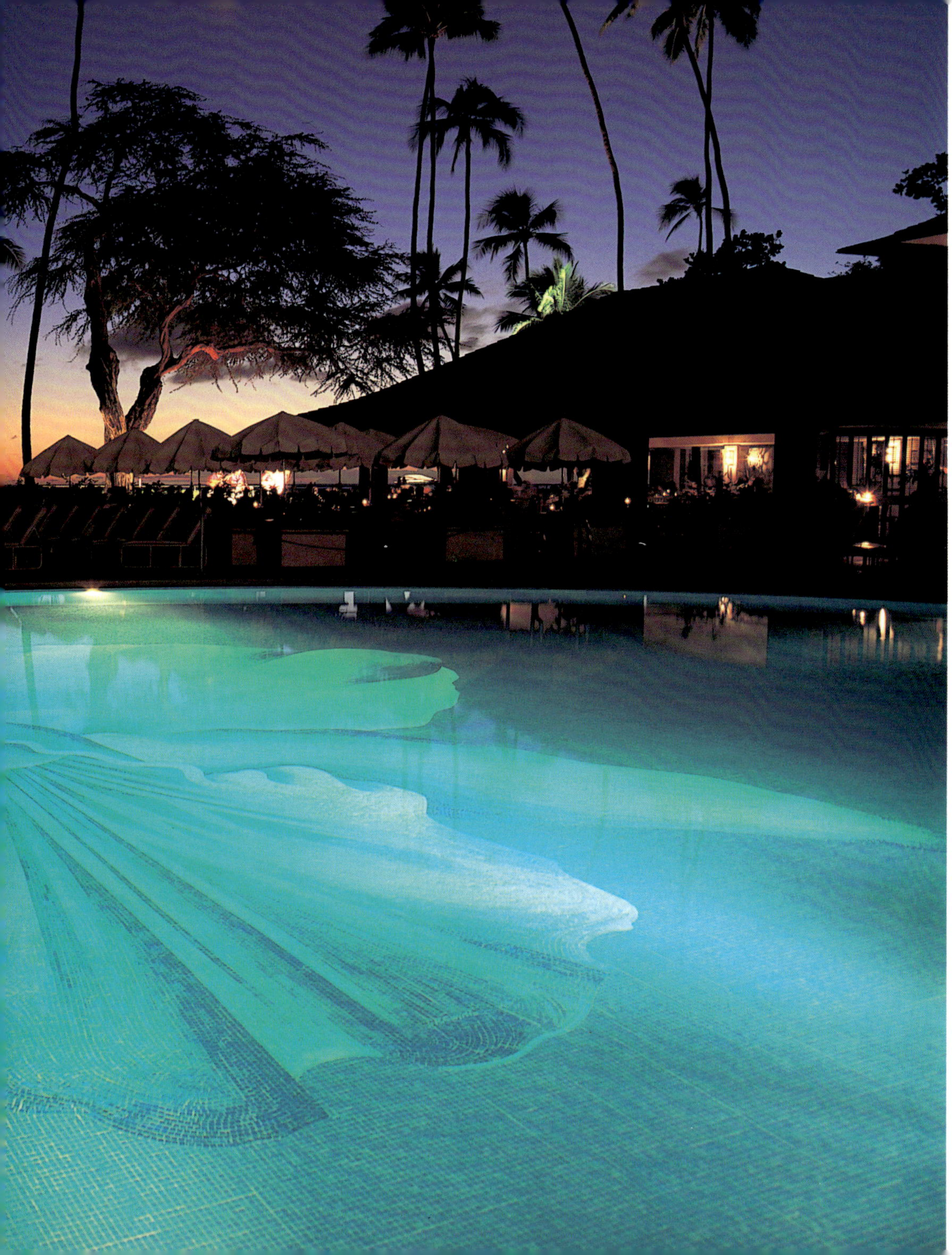

HALEKULANI (HONOLULU)

88

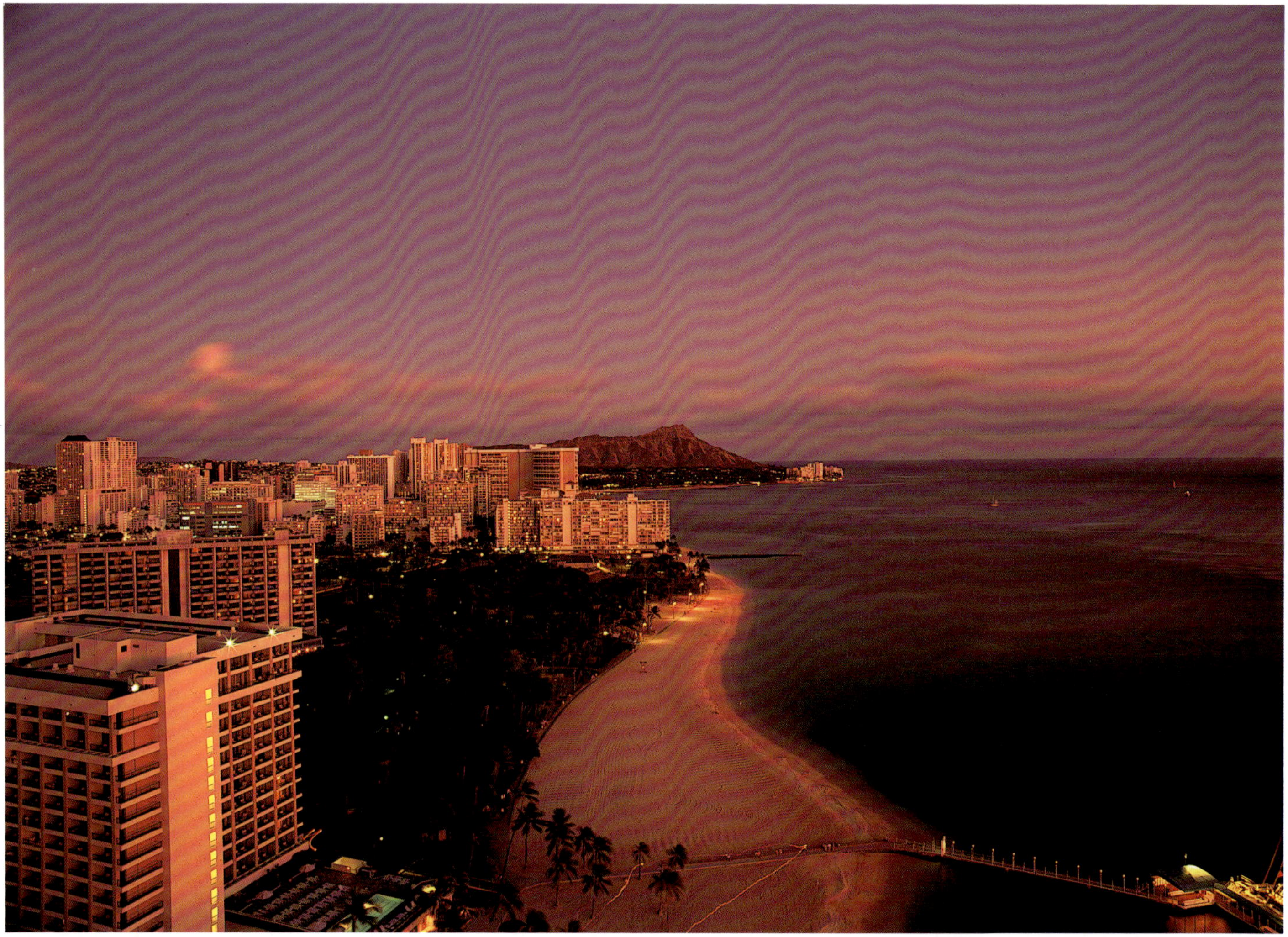

HILTON HAWAIIAN VILLAGE (HONOLULU)

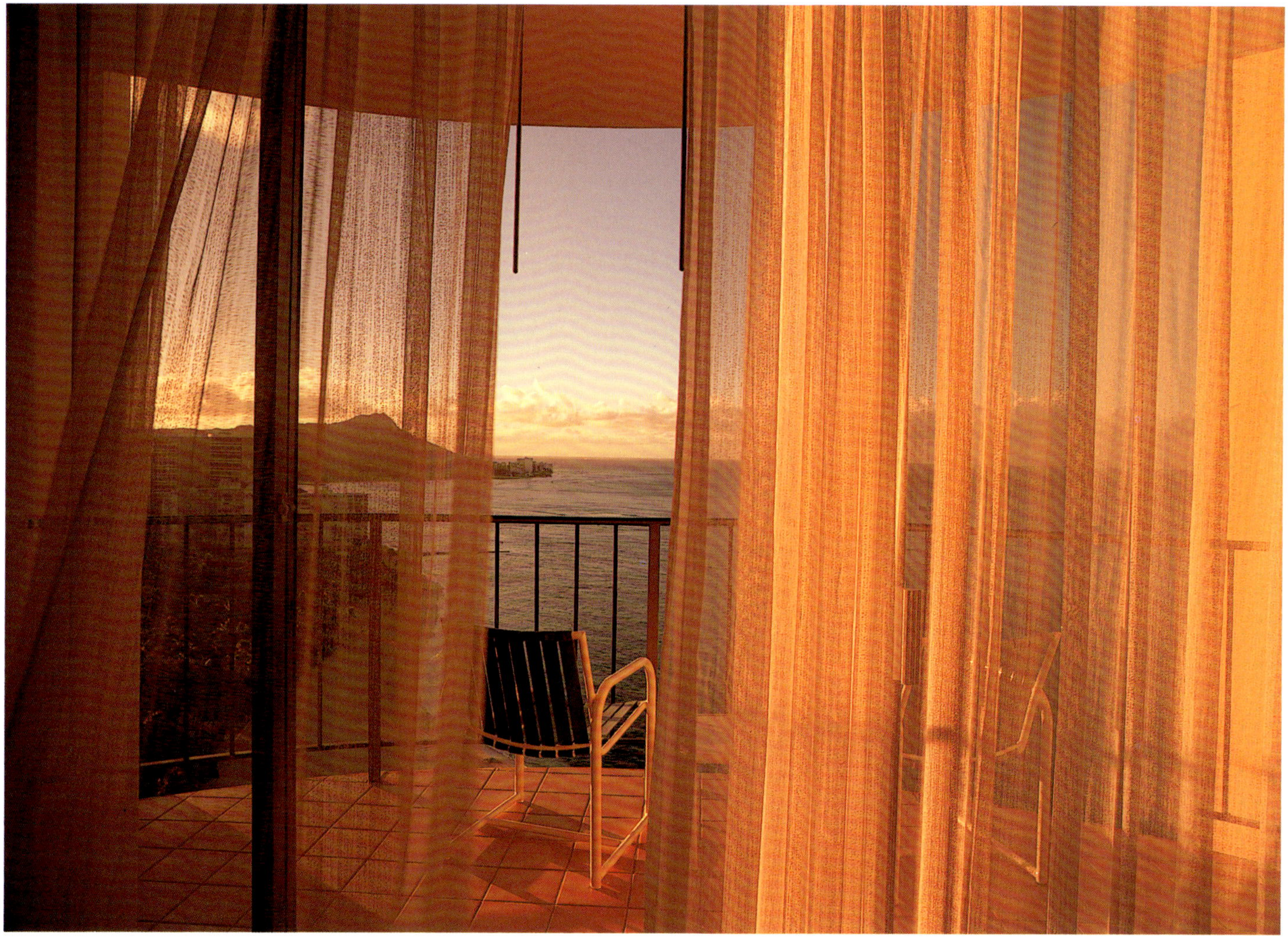

HILTON HAWAIIAN VILLAGE (HONOLULU)

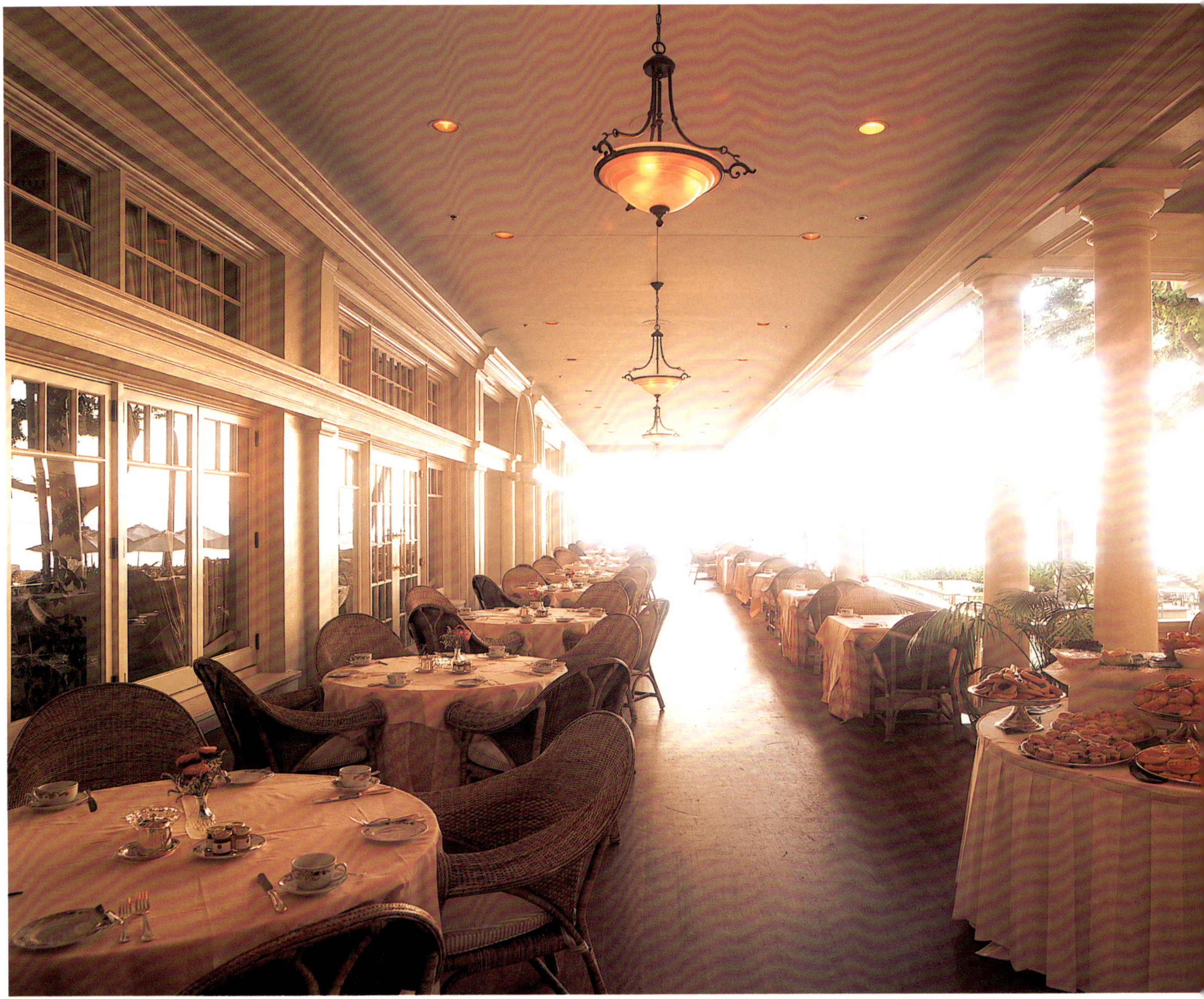

SHERATON MOANA SURFRIDER (HONOLULU)

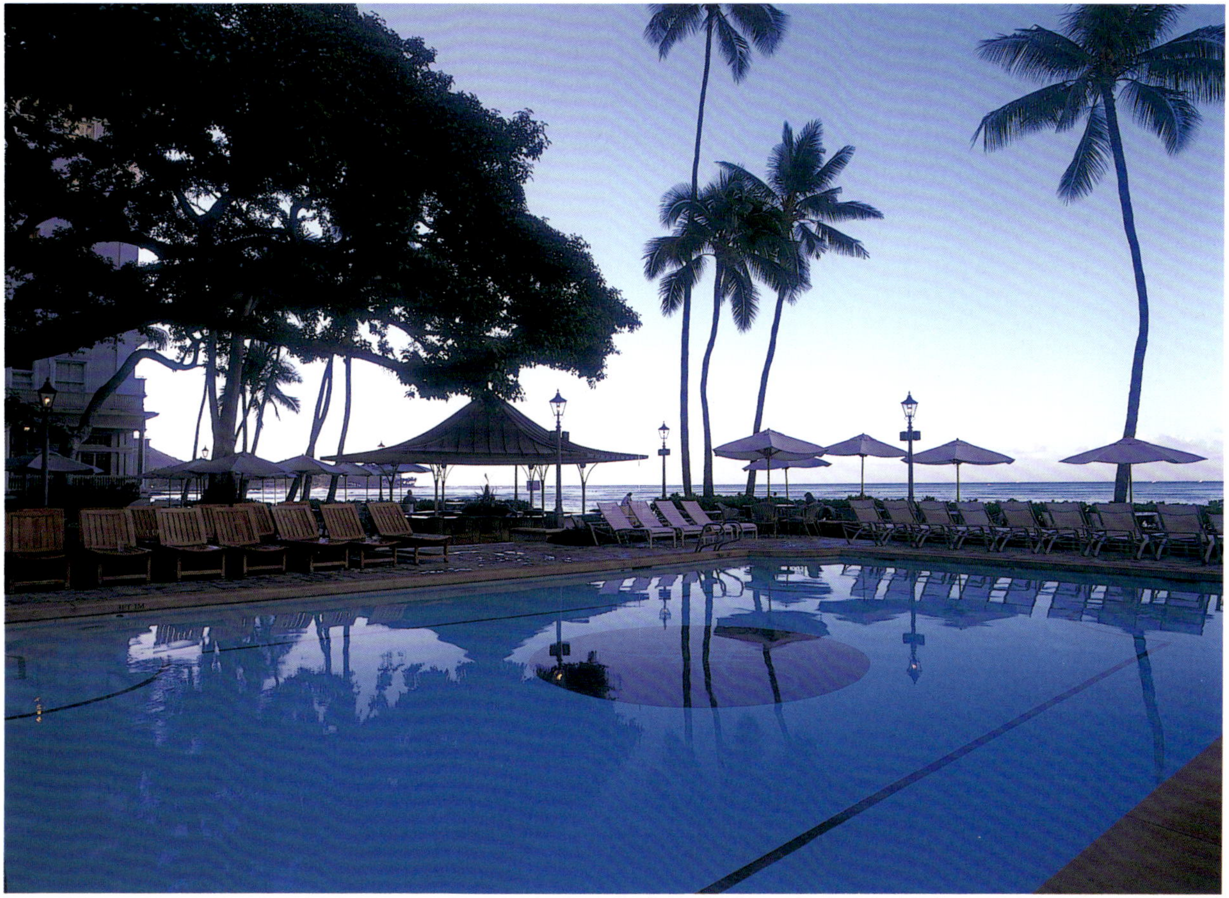

SHERATON MOANA SURFRIDER (HONOLULU)

TAHITI

92

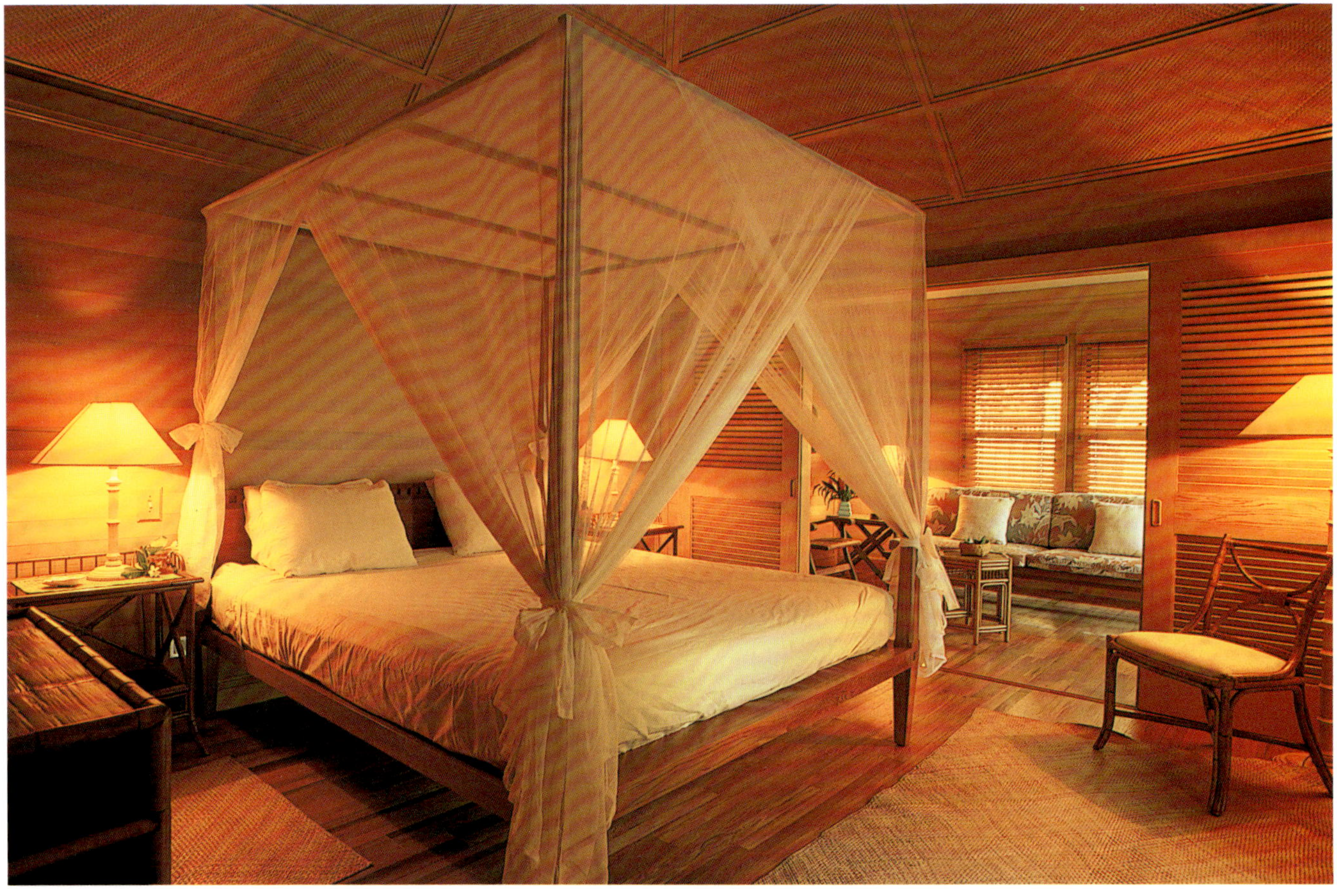

HOTEL BORA BORA (BORA BORA)

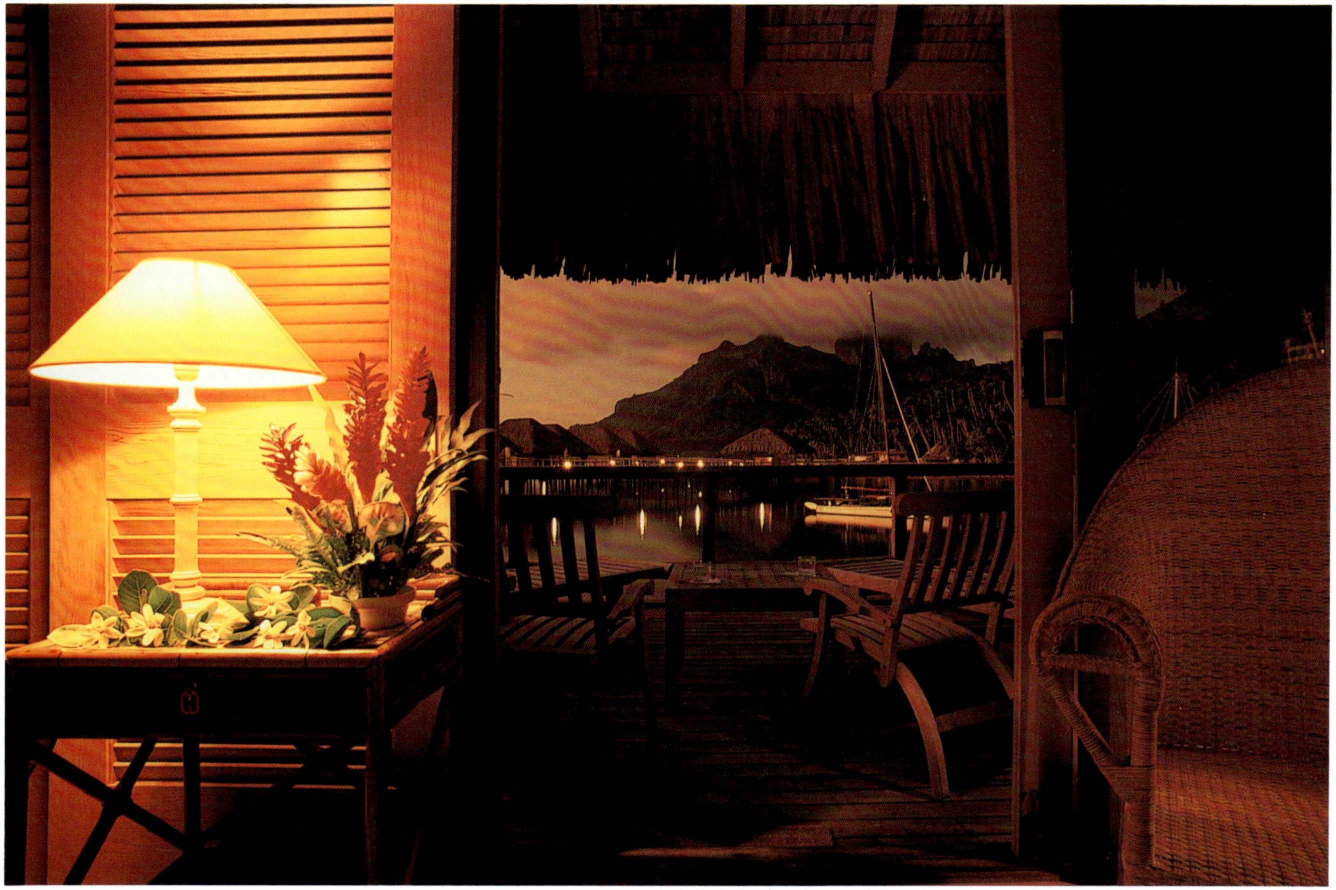

HOTEL BORA BORA (BORA BORA)

94

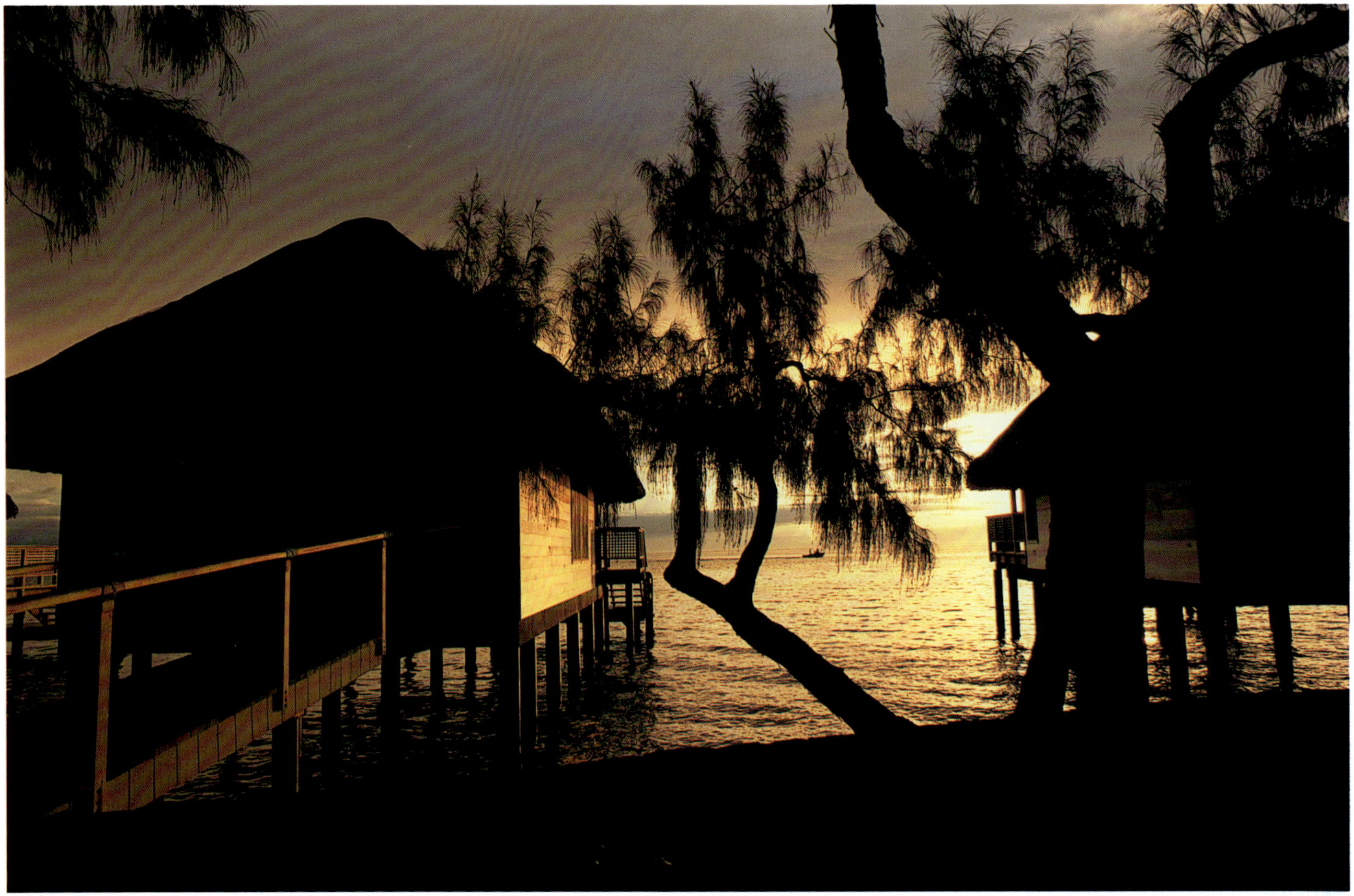

HOTEL BORA BORA (BORA BORA)

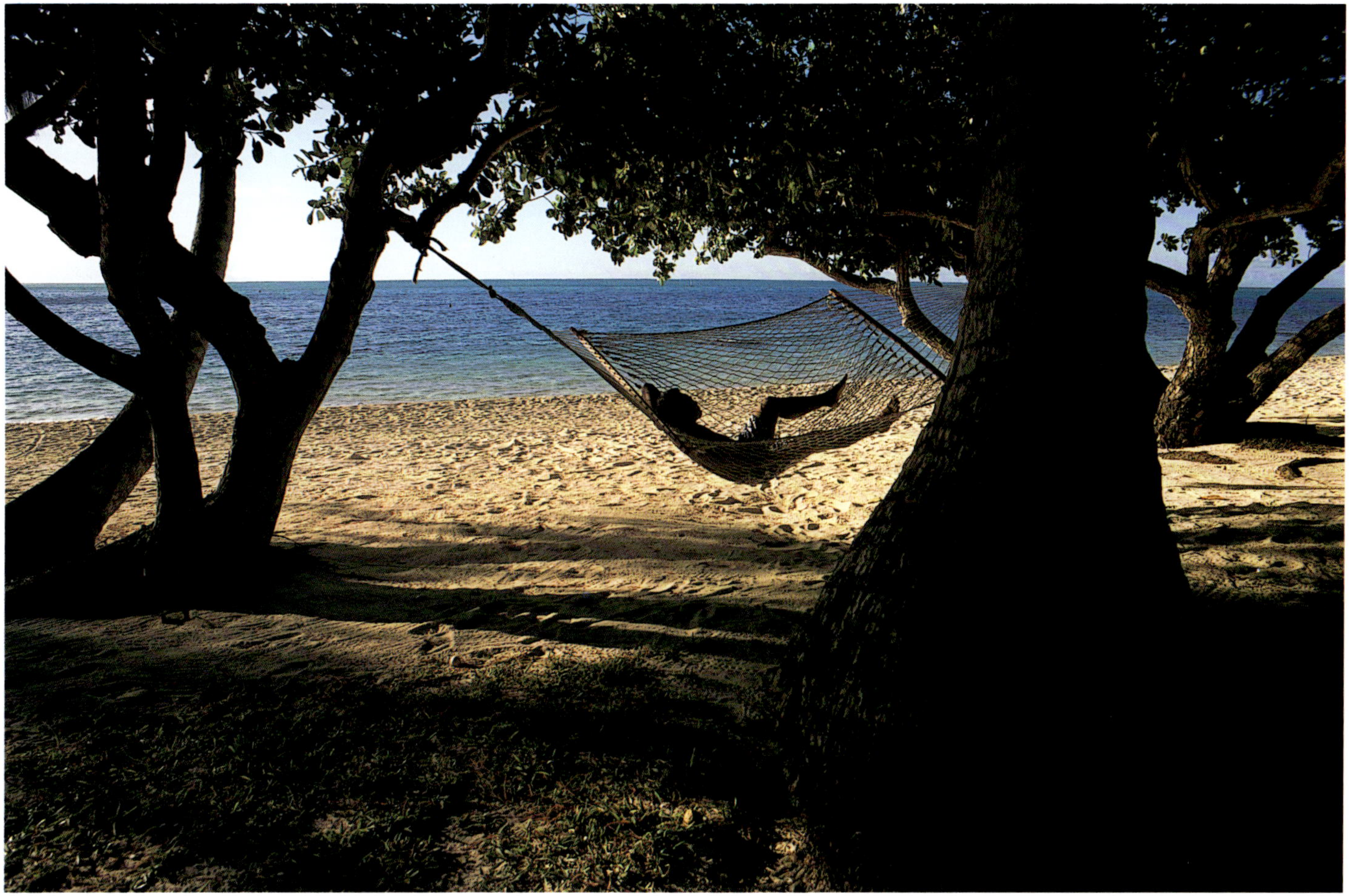

HOTEL BORA BORA (BORA BORA)

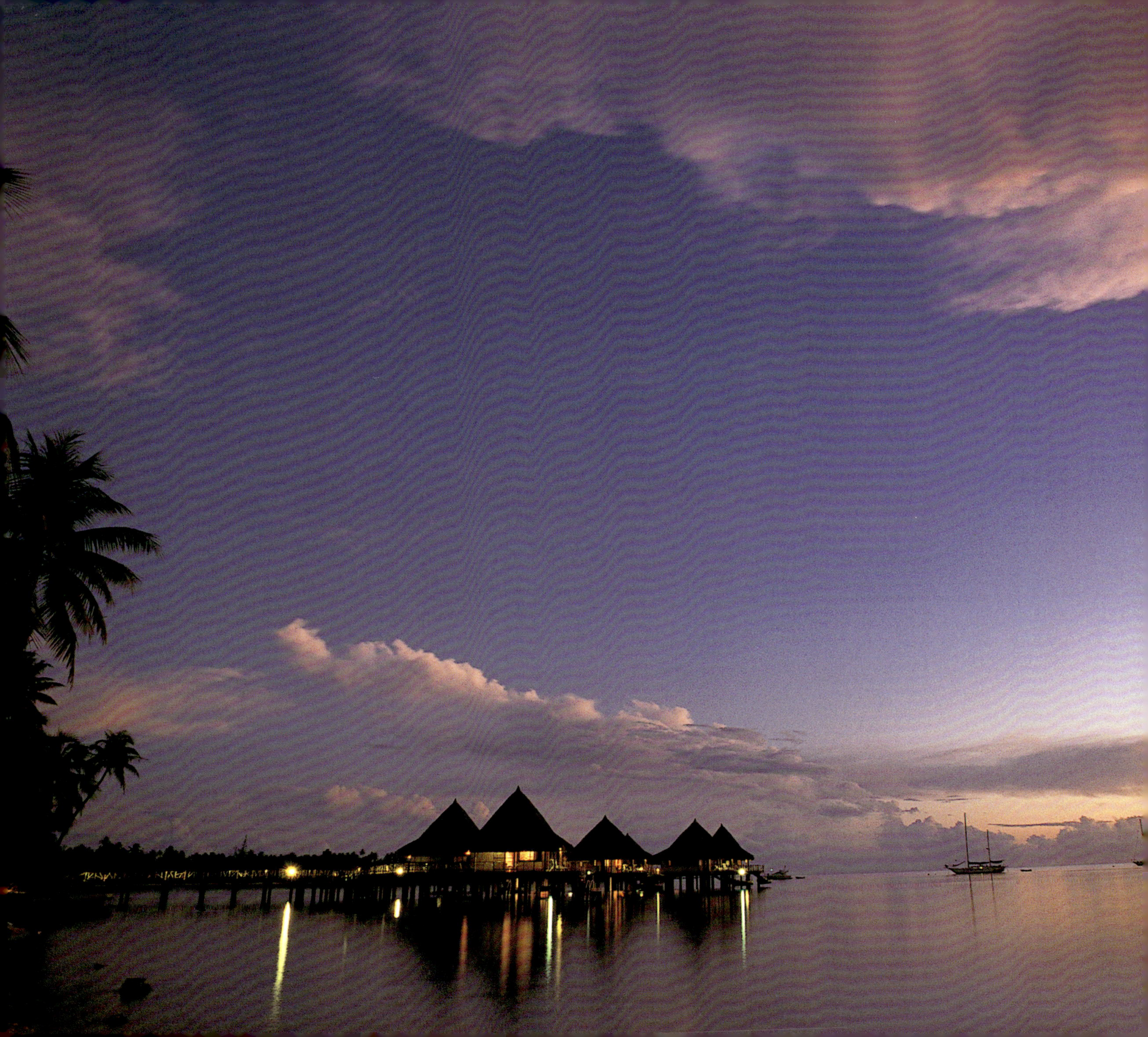

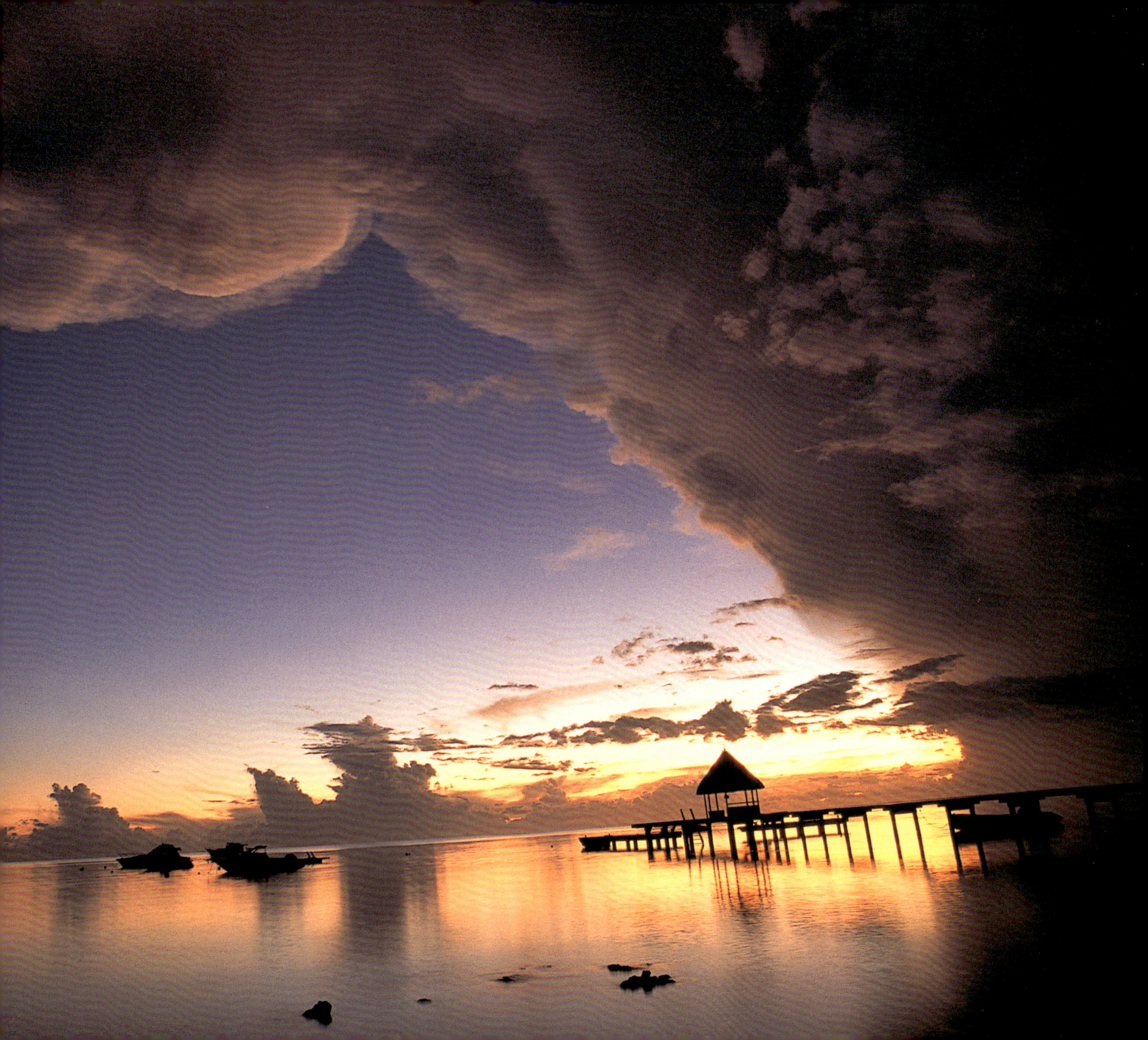

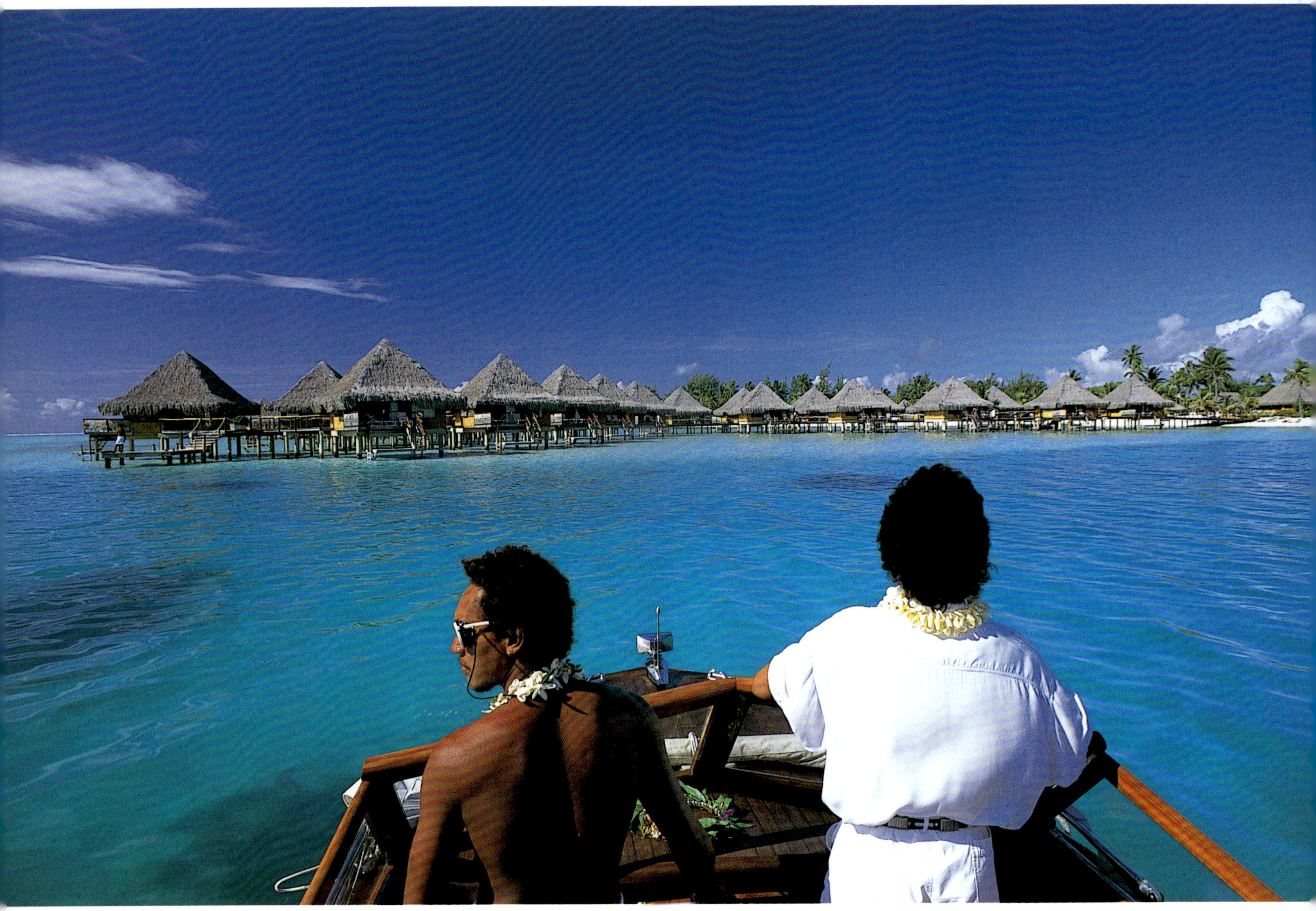

MOANA BEACH PARK ROYAL (BORA BORA)

PRECEDING PAGES/KIA ORA VILLAGE (RANGIROA)

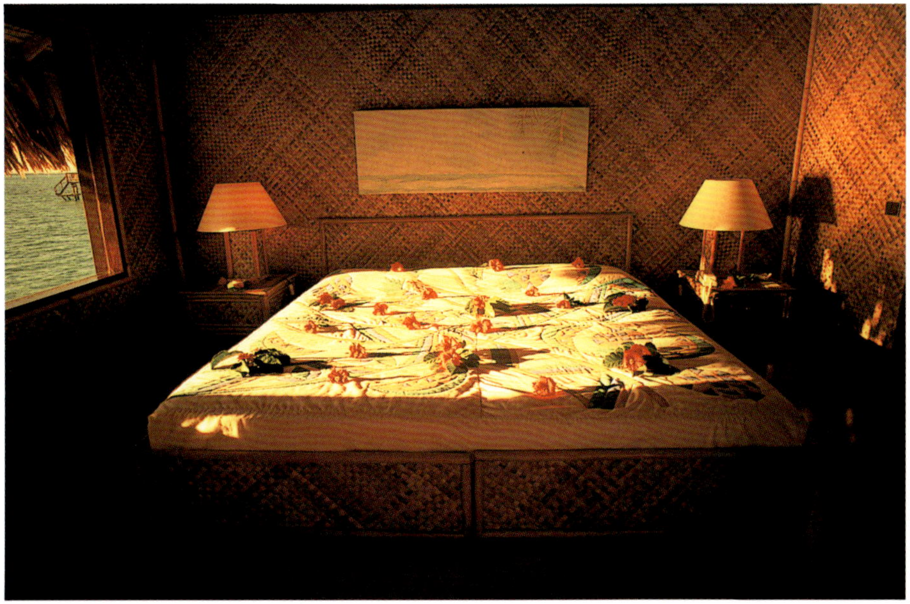

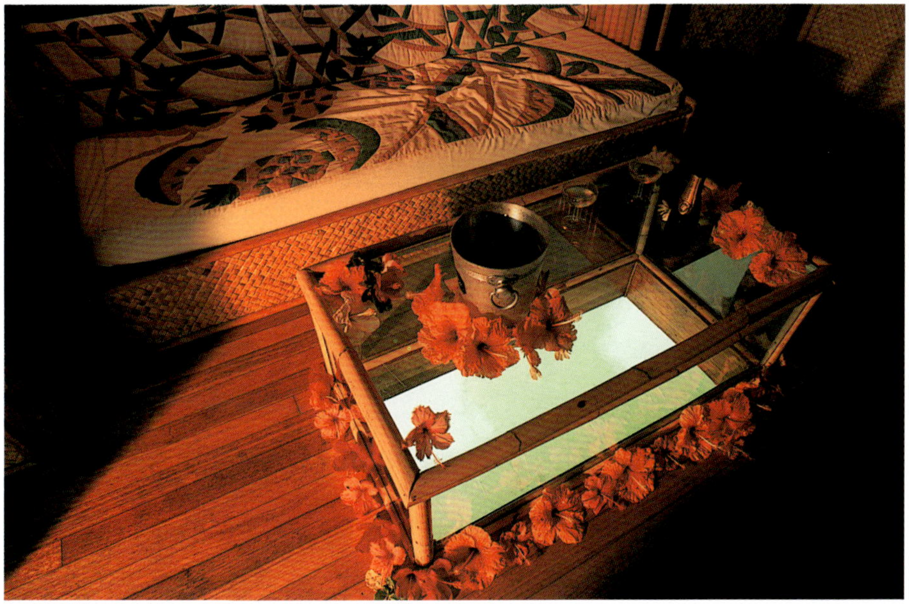

MOANA BEACH PARK ROYAL (BORA BORA)/ALSO FOLLOWING PAGES

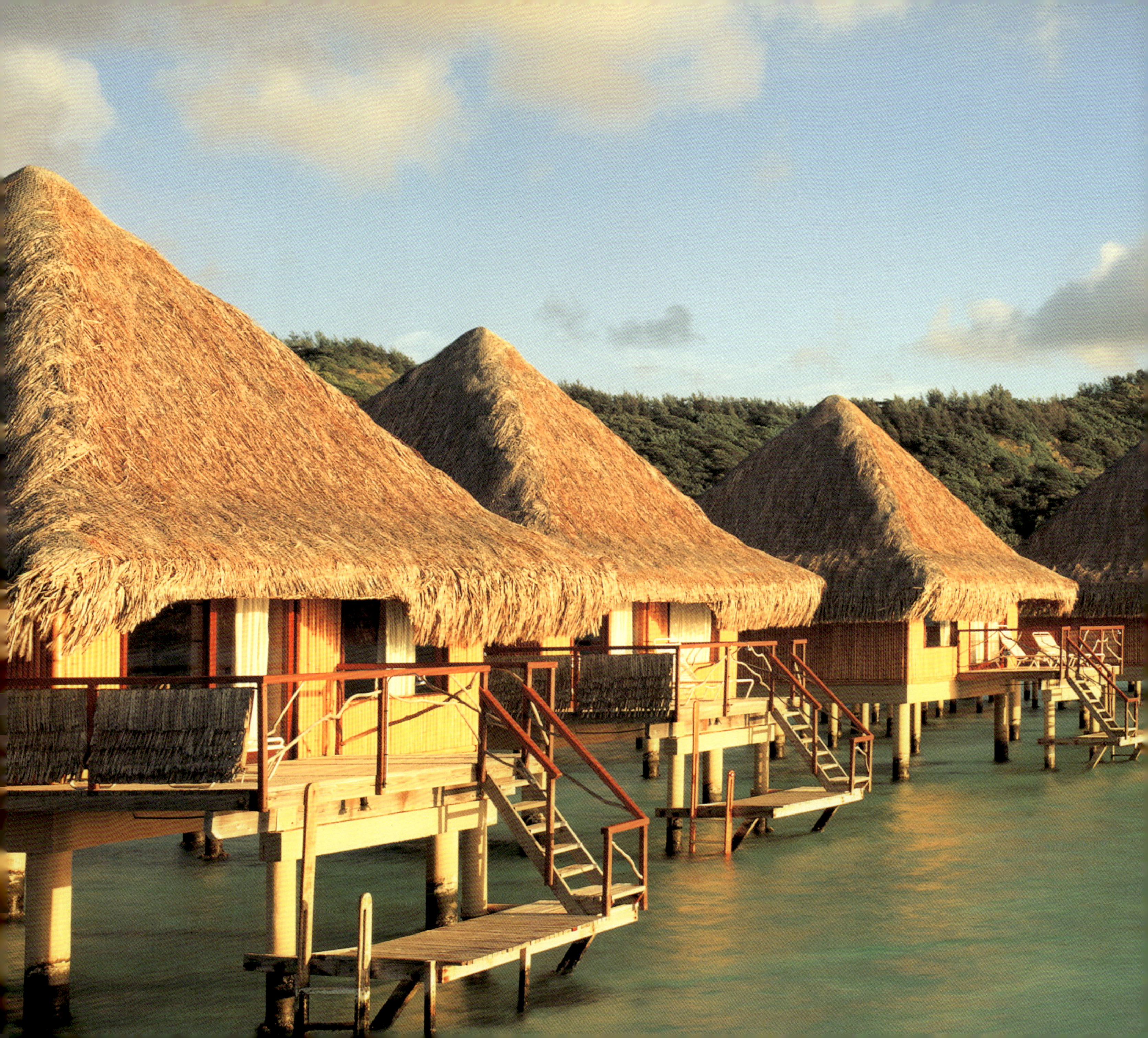

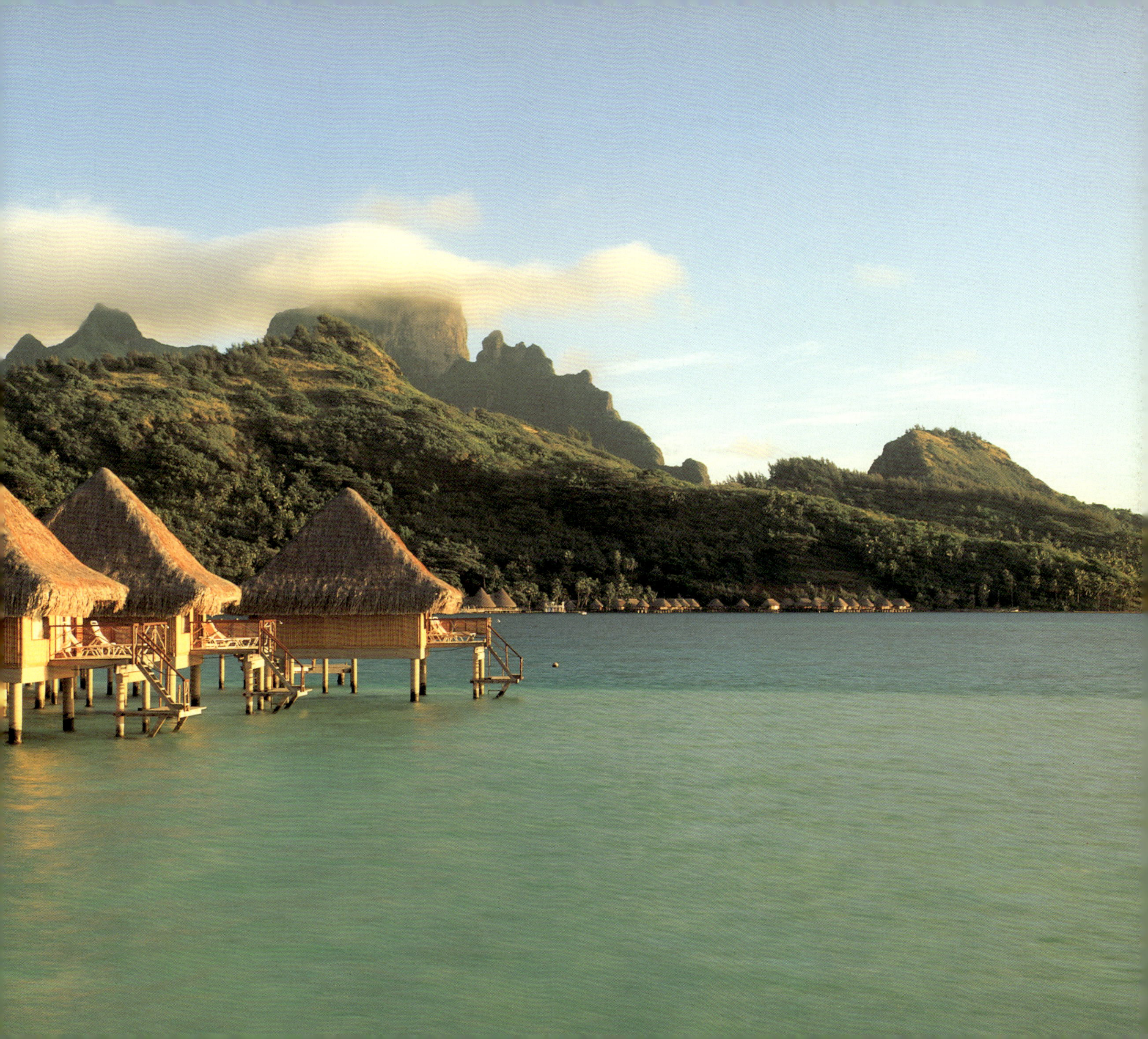

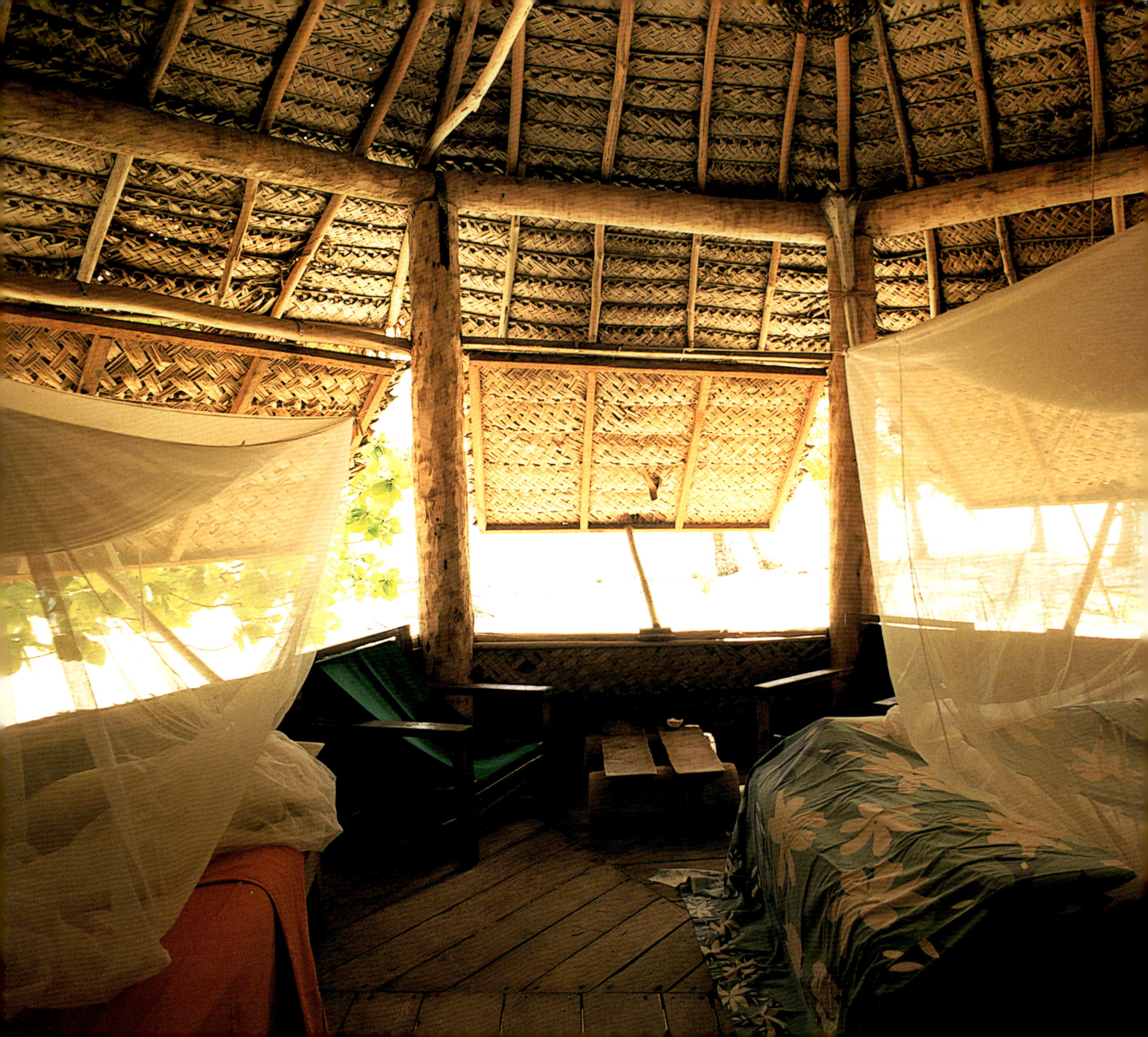

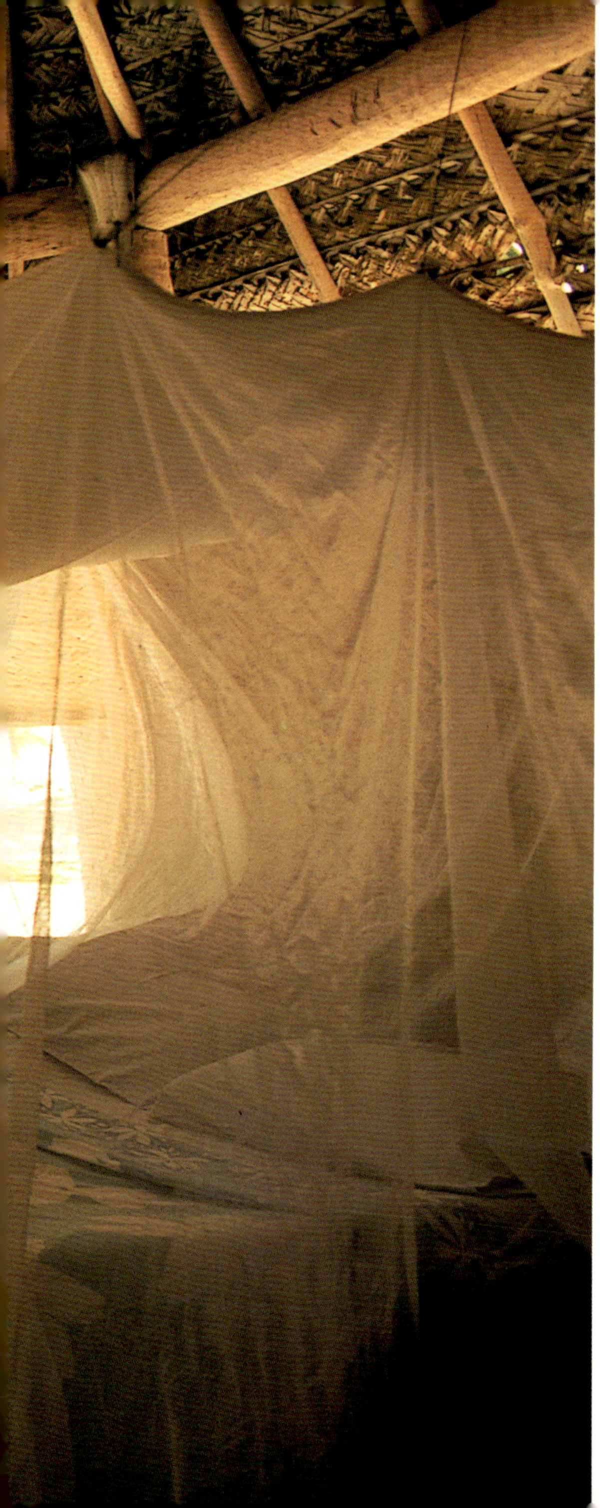

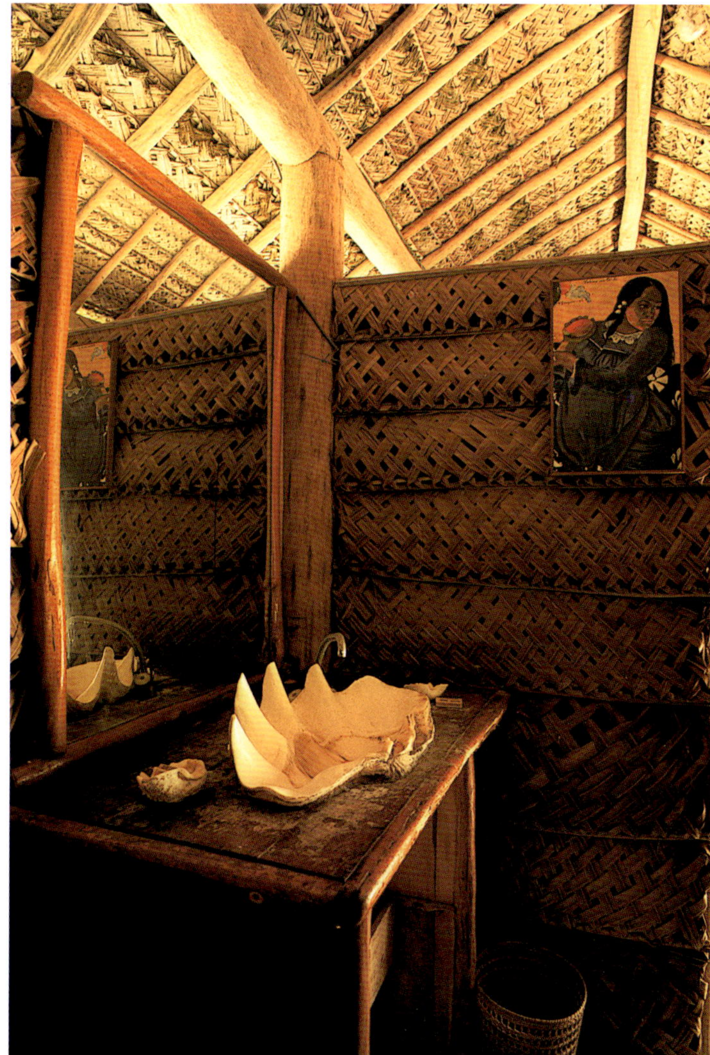

TETIAROA VILLAGE (TETIAROA)

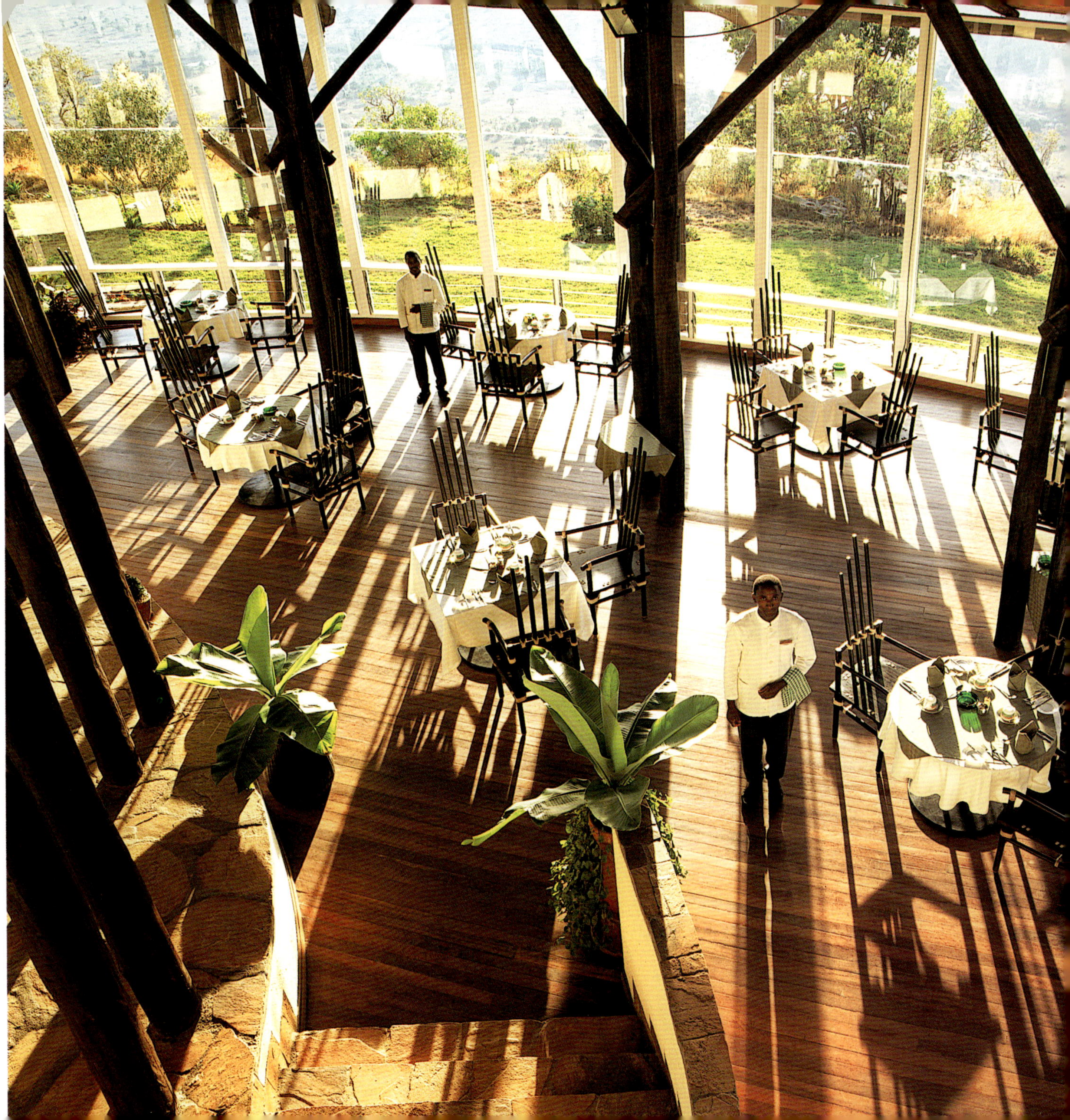

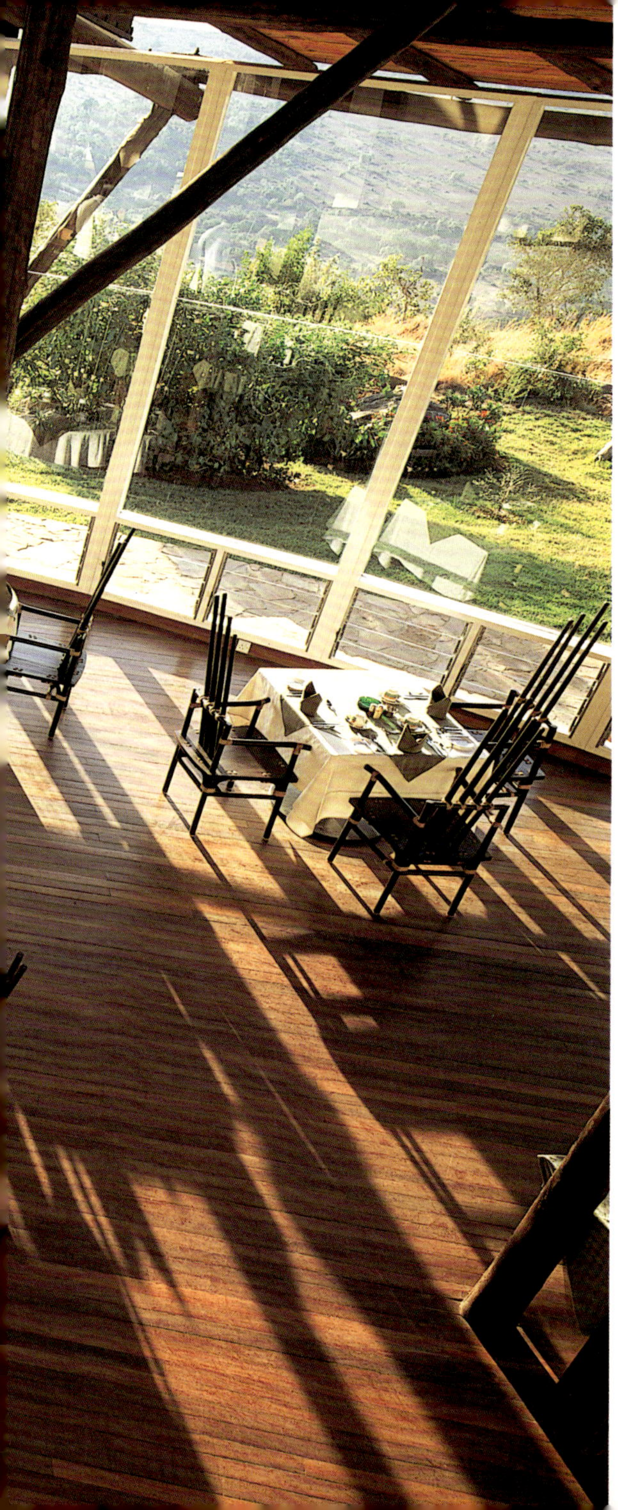

MPATA SAFARI CLUB (MASAI MARA)

KENYA

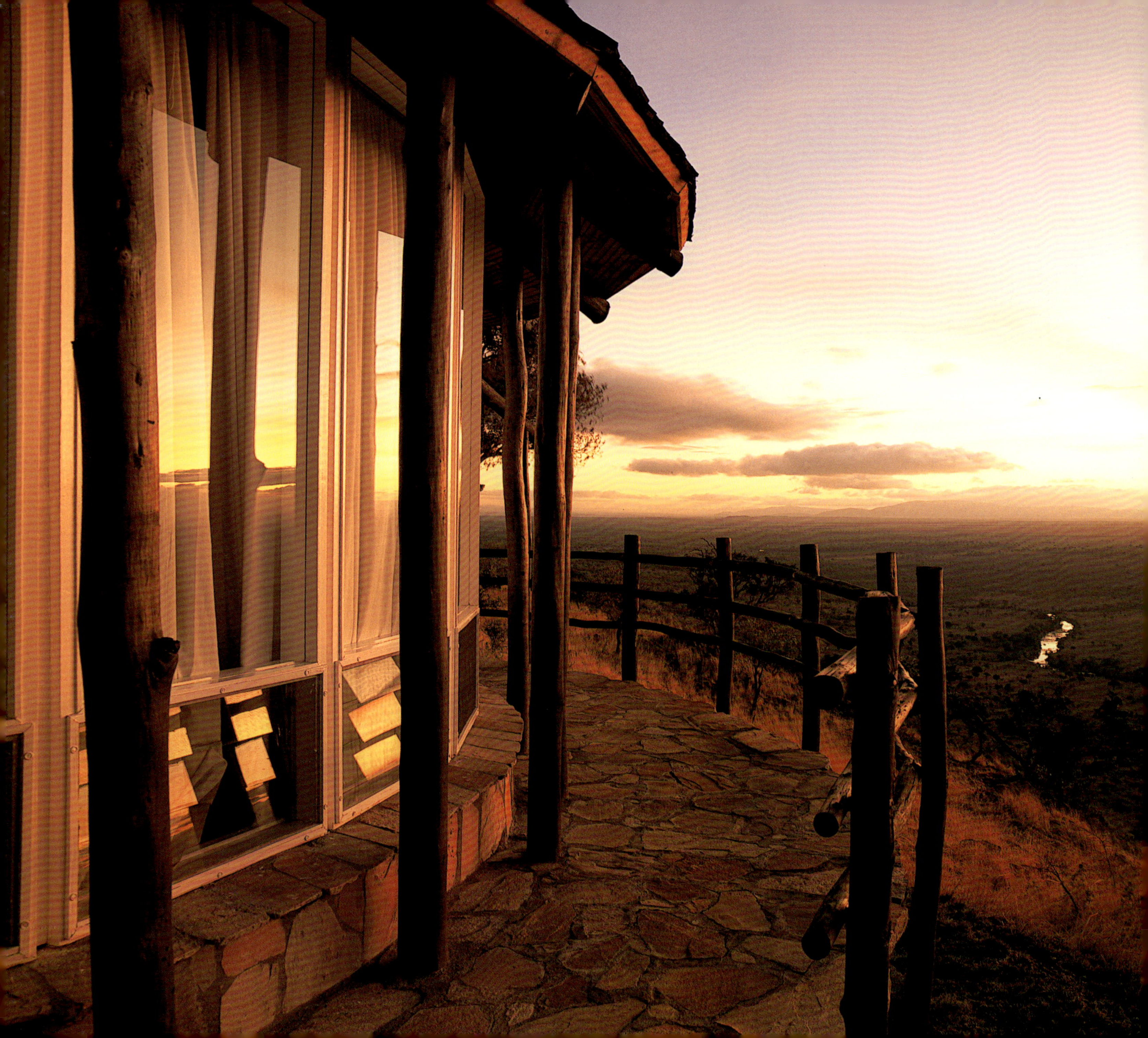

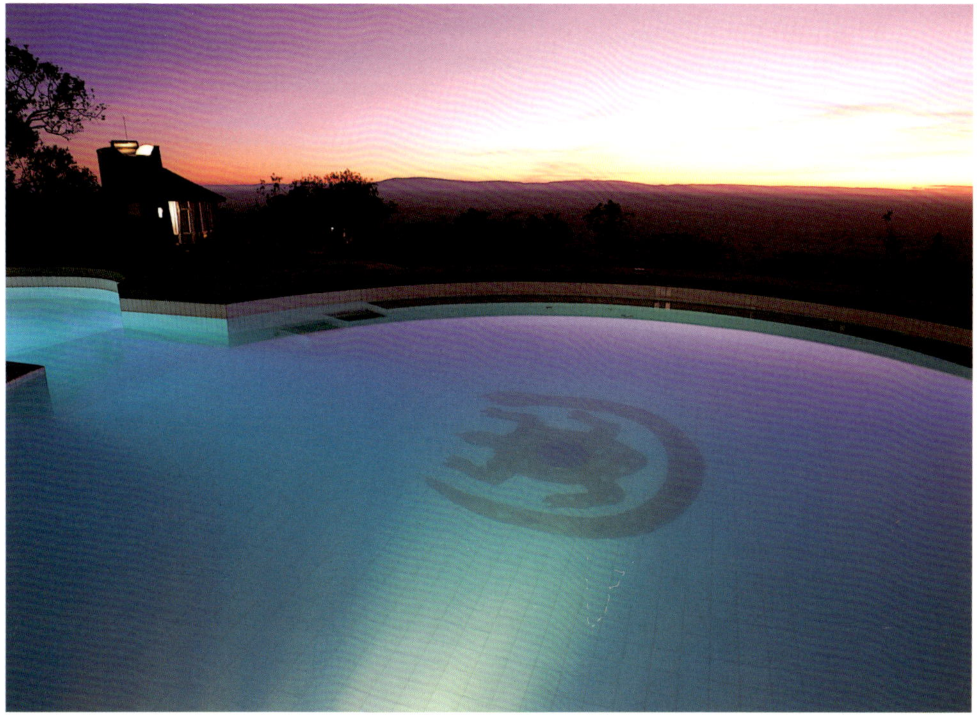

MPATA SAFARI CLUB (MASAI MARA)

Hotel Information
by Kazuyoshi Miyoshi

Note: Room rates are per day unless otherwise specified, include seasonal variations, do not include taxes and gratuities, and are subject to change. Although the contact information for each hotel is the most recent available, the photographs were taken over a period of several years and may not accurately depict current accommodations.

● INDIA

Lake Palace Hotel

▸4-5, 10-13

P.O. Box No. 5, Udaipur 313 001, India
Mailing Address: The Taj Group of Hotels,
511 Lexington Ave., New York, NY 10017
Phone (91) (294) 527961 ext. 73/U.S. (212) 755-4400
Fax (91) (294) 527974/U.S. (212) 751-4091
84 rooms, $160-$600

Udaipur, in the state of Rajasthan, is a two-day drive south from New Delhi. Udaipur is in a harsh desert region, but in the seventeenth century, over a period of thirty years, Maharani Jagat Singh I erected this small palace in the middle of Pichola Lake, creating a personal Shangri-La. It was turned into a hotel in 1971. As you drink tea beside the marble-tiled pool, the view of the surrounding lake makes you feel as if you're on the deck of a ship. The Venetian glass swords on the roof gleam. If you're lucky enough to stay in the Khush Mahal Suite (pp. 4-5) you'll see something incredible: in the morning, the sunlight reflecting off the surface of the lake shines through the seven stained-glass windows, making the entire room shimmer gently. Half-awake, you'll lose track of who and where you are. The Lake Palace is reputed to have mesmerized both Queen Elizabeth II and Jacqueline Onassis.

Rambagh Palace

▸14-17

Bhawani Singh Rd., Jaipur 302 005, India
Phone (91) (141) 381919
Fax (91) (141) 381098
106 rooms, $37-$300

The city of Jaipur, located in northwestern India, was built by Maharaja Sawai Jai Singh II in 1727. Often referred to as the "Pink City," it is entirely constructed of red sandstone. The white Rambagh Palace is on the outskirts. The maharaja lived here until it was converted into a hotel thirty years ago. The pool was built indoors for the maharani. The bathrooms are made of pink marble, and each room has a fountain! The bar was designed around the motif of the Maharaja's favorite sport, polo. Hints of a luxurious past can be found here and there. No one seems to notice the large, broken fountain in the garden. As you take an early morning stroll through the magnificent garden, you may even encounter a wild peacock. Oh, to lead a leisurely life like the maharaja or the maharani!

●SRI LANKA

GALLE FACE HOTEL

▸18-21

P.O. Box 63 or 330, Kooupitja Rd., Colombo, Sri Lanka
Phone (94) 15-41010 ext. 6
Fax (94) 15-41072
21 suites, $55-$170

This hotel, located in Sri Lanka's capital, faces the Indian Ocean. Built in 1864 in the classic colonial style popular during British rule, the traditions of service remain intact, making a stay here very pleasant.

THE HILL CLUB

▸19

Grand Hotel Road, Hill Country, Nuwara Eliya, Sri Lanka
Phone (94) 52-2653, (94) 52-2231
Fax (94) 52-2654
36 rooms, $31-$75

It takes an entire day to get to Nuwara Eliya, 170 kilometers east of Colombo. At an altitude of 1,889 meters, the area is known for its cool weather and high-grade Ceylon tea. British aristocrats built this mountain Shangri-La, which includes the oldest golf course in Asia, over 100 years ago. The Hill Club and horse racetracks were constructed for social occasions.

●MALDIVES

KUDAHITI TOURIST RESORT

▸22-25

North Male Atoll, Maldives
Mailing Address: Safari Tours, SEK, No. 1, Chandhani Magu, Male, Maldives
Phone (960) 44-4613
Fax (960) 44-1992
6 rooms, $200 plus

Maldives consists of over 1,200 islands in the Indian Ocean, studded with seventy resort hotels, one per island. Kudahiti, an island of seven cottages, is so tiny you can walk its perimeter in four minutes. The Italian owner has themes for each cottage: Safari, Maldives, Ship Captain's Room, and so on. Each bright room is meticulously decorated. The furniture is tasteful—the best in Maldives—and both the wine and the wine glasses are of the finest makes. Famous European designers reserve the entire island for their friends.

COCOA ISLAND

▸26

South Male Atoll, Maldives
Phone (960) 44-3713
Fax (960) 44-1919
8 bungalows, $305-$490

A *Playboy* photographer owns this island, which has only eight rooms. The island's size changes according to the tide. The bar in the photo is located on the beach within earshot of the waves below. The buildings are all built out of palm trees and palm leaves. Room interiors are minimal, but tasteful.

IHURU TOURIST RESORT

▸27

North Male Atoll, Maldives
Mailing Address: c/o Ihuru Investments Pvt. Ltd., H. Bodukosheege,
Ameer Ahmed Magu, Male 20-05, Maldives
Phone (960) 44-3502
Fax (960) 44-5933
44 rooms, $120-$260

Ihuru is one of the more established hotels in Maldives. It takes only fifteen minutes to walk around this island. A weekly buffet dinner is served on the white beach under beautiful palm trees. Eating by the shore is a rare experience. The other day, a school of dolphins passed near the island during the meal, causing an uproar.

Angaga Resort

▸ 28-29

Wahoo Enterprise, Ari Atoll, Maldives
Phone (960) 45-0520
Fax (960) 45-0520
50 rooms, $100-$160

You have to fly forty minutes by hydroplane or helicopter from the Maldives Airport to get to this island. Because it's located on the outskirts of Maldives, its natural environment is well preserved. Fish swimming through the coral reefs ignore human intruders. In the photo, taken at sunset, the birds near the bar are snatching up small sardines swept onto the beach. The floor of the restaurant and bar is made of white sand, so you can remain barefoot. It makes me feel like I've returned to nature.

●NEPAL

Hotel Everest View

▸ 30-33

Near Shyangboche Airport and Namche Bazaar
12 rooms, $120-$150
No further information available

To get here, you have to take a one-hour flight from Katmandu on an eight-passenger Cessna and then walk one hour uphill from the airport. In the past, you had to trek two weeks from the closest bus stop. Miyahara, a Japanese, built this resort, which sets the record for the hotel at the highest altitude: 3,800 meters. From any of the rooms, Mount Everest appears to be within hand's reach. The Himalayas are a moving sight during the day, but at night, the sight of the mountain peaks reflecting the stars above is truly an awesome, spiritual experience. The meals—Japanese, Western, and Chinese—are comparable with those served at hotels at lower altitudes. From the dining room (pp. 30-31), Mount Everest is visible slightly left of center.

●SINGAPORE

Raffles Hotel

▸ 34-37

1 Beach Road, Singapore 189673
Phone (65) 337-1886
Fax (65) 339-7650
104 rooms, $460-$2,850 and "price upon request"

This legendary hotel was established in 1887, and the exotic atmosphere that fascinated English writer Somerset Maugham hasn't changed at all. Three traveler's palms grace the Palm Court, the courtyard where Maugham wrote his masterpiece, *Rain*. A soft light filters through the skylight three stories above, suffusing the atmosphere inside. Nearly three years of renovations, begun in 1991, have transformed the Raffles into a very modern, upscale establishment. I photographed the Palm Court (p. 35) in November of 1988 to record the hotel's antique qualities. Page 37 (upper right) depicts the Somerset Maugham Suite.

Goodwood Park Hotel

▸ 38-39

22 Scotts Road, Singapore 228221
Phone (65) 737-7411/U.S (800) 772-3890
Fax (65) 732-8558
235 rooms and suites, $270-$2,130

This historic hotel, honored as a national treasure, is located slightly above the skyscrapers of Singapore. Built in 1900 as a German clubhouse, it was modeled after German castles. In 1926 it became a hotel, but during World War II the Japanese Army assumed ownership. Now it's an ideal place to have a luxurious afternoon tea. The Brunei Suite—where the king of Brunei often stayed—is equipped with a personal elevator.

●BALI

AMANDARI ▶ 40-43

Kedewatan, Ubud, Bali, Indonesia
Phone 62 (361) 771267/N.A. (800) 447-7462
Fax 62 (361) 771266
29 garden suites, $430-$800

The rooms at this resort, in a village renowned for its arts and crafts, are built in the style of traditional huts. Amandari just opened in 1989, but already presidents of nations and VIPs have stayed here. The excellent staff know the names of all the guests. The main pool leads into the ravine, blending perfectly into the natural surroundings. At night you can gaze up at the stars while swimming. In this serene setting, you'll feel the spirits drifting around you.

TANDJUNG SARI ▶ 44-45

P.O. Box 3025 Denpasar, Tandjung Sari,
Jl. Danau Tamblingan 41, Sanur, Denpasar 80228, Bali, Indonesia
Phone 62 (361) 288441/N.A. (804) 739-0002
Fax 62 (361) 287930
28 bungalows, $220-$448

This villa-style beach hotel is so low-key it's like a hideaway resort. In fact, many famous people come here to get away from it all. The bungalows are scattered about a dense forest. Tandjung Sari means "Cape of Flowers." Countless tropical blossoms bloom here, giving off the rarefied scent of Bali. Suite twenty-three has a bathtub in front of the bed. It's slightly embarrassing.

●THAILAND

THE ORIENTAL BANGKOK ▶ 46-48

48 Oriental Avenue, Bangkok 10500, Thailand
Phone (662) 2360400
Fax (662) 2361937 ext. 9
361 rooms, 35 suites, $250-$3,490

Established in 1876 in a prime location on the banks of the Chaopuraya River, this hotel began with only twelve rooms. Consistently ranking high in hotel guides, the Oriental Bangkok's secret has less to do with interesting interiors or conspicuous luxury than with incredible service. A variety of fresh fruits are delivered to your room every morning, and if you step out for even a moment, you come back to a freshly cleaned room. A personal butler is assigned to each suite. To put it simply, no other establishment offers service like this hotel. Page 47 depicts the Somerset Maugham Suite, in the original wing. The interiors are a perfect blend of East and West.

HOTEL SOFITEL CENTRAL HUA-HIN ▶ 49-51

1 Damnernkasem Road, Hua-Hin 77110, Thailand
Phone (66-32) 512 021/N.A. (800) 221-4542
Fax (66-32) 511 014/N.A. (914) 472-0451
154 rooms and suites, 64 Thai-style villas, $140-$910

This beach resort is a two-hour express-train ride south of Bangkok. Established in 1923, it is occasionally visited by royalty. All the floors are made of teak, making it pleasant to walk barefoot. The tea room is now an exhibit, so you can catch a glimpse of history while enjoying the sea breezes. The room was used as a set in the film *The Killing Fields*.

●U.S. VIRGIN ISLANDS

VILLA SANTANA ▶ 52-53, 58

Denmark Hill, St. Thomas, USVI 00802
Phone & Fax (809) 776-1311
5 rooms, $95-$195

St. Thomas is the most cosmopolitan of the three U.S. Virgin Islands, located in the middle of the Caribbean Ocean. Previously owned by the Dutch, the islands became a United States territory in 1917. When Columbus discovered them in 1493, the islands were, as the name indicates, virginal and uninhabited. The Villa Santana is located on a hilltop above the beautiful harbor. The original early-nineteenth-century structure, a cosy villa with a kitchen, has been kept intact. If you take your breakfast on the veranda, little birds will approach you for bread.

Safari

▸ 54-55

Tropical Properties, P.O. Box 135,
Cruz Bay, St. John, USVI 00831
Phone (809) 776-6862
Fax (809) 693-7395
vacation villa, $3,500-$7,000 weekly

This tiny three-room resort is built on a coral reef inlet in a national park, so the sights are truly incredible. From the Great Room (pp. 54-55) you can see not only tropical fish but whales and sea turtles as well. There are no glass windows, and the breeze blows pleasantly through the rooms. But don't worry about bad weather—you can close the shutters if need be.

Hilty House Inn

▸ 55

#2 Herman Hill (off Questa Verde Road),
P.O. Box 26077, Gallows Bay,
St. Croix, USVI 00824
Phone & Fax (809) 773-2594
5 suites, $60-$165

Located on the largest U.S. Virgin Island, in the small town of Christiansted, this nineteenth-century plantation home, with its large Mediterranean-style living room and Florentine tiles, has been kept intact. Due to its historical status, it has been featured in many magazines, including *National Geographic.*

Sprat Hall Plantation

▸ 56-57

P.O. Box 695, Route 63 U., Frederiksted,
St. Croix, USVI 00841
Phone (809) 772-0305/U.S. (800) 843-3504
6 rooms, 2 cottages, $90-$350

This small inn, once a plantation owner's residence, looks like a museum exhibit or a movie set. Sometimes I prefer this kind of old-fashioned place to a modern hotel. It's fun to travel through history.

Grand Palazzo Hotel

▸ 59

6900 Great Bay, Saint Thomas, USVI 00802
Phone (809) 775-3333/N.A. (800) 545-0509
Fax (809) 775-4444
152 suites (ADA accommodations available),
$250-$1,425

The Grand Palazzo, well placed on an inlet facing the sea, is at the end of a long, winding mountain road. Renowned in Europe, this romantic resort is modeled after Venetian palaces and featured in fashion magazines such as *Vogue* and *ELLE.* You'll want to dress up for dinner.

●MARTINIQUE

Hotel Plantation De Leyritz

▸ 60-61

Basse Pointe 97218, Martinique
Phone (596) 78-53-92
Fax (596) 78-92-44
68 rooms, $90-$120

The Martinique Islands are located in the eastern Caribbean Sea. The French painter Gauguin spent time on this island of flowers, still ruled by the French, who call it "Tropical Paris." Originally a large eighteenth-century plantation, this hotel is now well-equipped with modern facilities and comforts. Outbuildings scattered across a large field have been converted into guest houses. The restaurant, originally a sugar refinery, has a maximum capacity of 800 persons.

Le Bristol ▸61

Rue Martin Luther King, Fort-de-France, Martinique
Closed

This petite hotel is located at the top of a steep road above Fort-de-France, the largest city in Martinique. Outside the hustle and bustle of the city, this quiet place seems like another world. The ground-floor restaurant has an incredible view of the bay and city. Even the napkins are intricately folded, adding to the harmonious atmosphere.

Marine Hotel ▸62

Pointe de la Chéry, Diamant 97223, Martinique
Phone (596) 76-46-00
Fax (596) 76-25-99
149 rooms, \$77-\$165

This hotel is built on a hill with a great view of the famous Diamant Rock. The pool bar (where I ate an excellent sandwich) offers an unobstructed 180-degree view.

Hotel le Bakoua ▸63

Pointe du Bout, Les Trois-Îlets 97229, Martinique
Phone (596) 66-02-02/U.S. (800) 221-4542
Fax (596) 66-00-41
140 rooms, 2 suites, \$26-\$665

Located on the opposite side of the bay from Fort-de-France, all of this hotel's rooms face the ocean. The nightly performances are elaborate. Learn dances like the *beguine*, which originated on this island.

●BERMUDA ISLANDS

The Princess Hotel ▸64-65

Pitts Bay Road, Pembroke Parish, Bermuda
Phone (212) 715-7000
Fax (212) 752-4915
450 rooms, \$150-\$1150

Bermuda, located in the northern Caribbean—just a two-hour flight from New York City—consists of over fifty islands, still ruled by the British. All the buildings are painted in pastel colors. The luxurious Princess was established in 1884 near the capital, Hamilton. The oldest resort in Bermuda, it has a great reputation for service. A freshwater and saltwater pool face the bay, where passenger liners glide in and out.

Rosedon ▸66

P.O. Box HM 290, Hamilton HM AX, Bermuda
Phone (809) 295-1640/U.S. (800) 742-5008
Fax (809) 295-5904/U.S. (441) 295-5904
43 rooms, \$176-\$244

This cozy hotel across from the Princess is relatively small. Every day at four o'clock, an English tea is brought to each guest.

Elbow Beach Hotel ▸67

60 South Shore Road, Paget PG04, Bermuda
Phone (441) 236-3535/U.S. (800) 223-7434
Fax (441) 236-5882
295 rooms and suites, \$135-\$550

A ten-minute drive from Hamilton, this beach hotel has spacious rooms and a large pool.

●MIAMI

THE BILTMORE HOTEL ▸ 68-69

1200 Anastasia Avenue,
Coral Gables, Florida 33134
Phone (305) 445-1926/U.S. (800) 727-1926
Fax (305) 448-9976
275 rooms and suites, $159-$1,800

Located on the outskirts of Miami, one of the United States most popular winter resorts, the Biltmore, established in 1926, now has the largest hotel pool in the country, an eighteen-hole golf course, and ten tennis courts. The Spanish Tower (modeled after the Giralda Tower in Seville) is impressive, and the interior decoration luxurious. Al Capone's favorite suite can be found here. (p. 69, top left).

KENMORE HOTEL ▸ 72-73

1050 Washington Avenue,
Old Miami Beach, Florida 33139
Phone (305) 674-1930
Fax (305) 534-6591
60 rooms, $39-$119

PARK WASHINGTON HOTEL ▸ 74-75

1020 Washington Avenue,
Old Miami Beach, Florida 33139
Phone (305) 532-1930
Fax (305) 672-6706
30 rooms, $39-$119

Art deco buildings line up along the southern end of Old Miami Beach. This architectural style, called "surf deco" or "tropical deco," was fashionable in Miami from the 1910s through the 1930s. Both the Kenmore and the Park Washington were built during this era.

●BAHAMAS

OCEAN VIEW CLUB ▸ 76-77

P.O. Box 134, Harbour Island,
North Eleuthera, Bahamas
9 rooms, $295-$325
No further information available

Harbour Island is a thirty-minute drive from the capital, Nassau, and North Eleuthera is only an eight-minute motorboat ride from there. The pink beach is tinted with red coral grains mixed with powdery sand. The interiors of the Ocean View reflect the owner's appealing personal taste.

●MEXICO

LAS BRISAS ▸ 78-79

Carretera Escenica, Clemente Mejía #5255,
Acapulco, Guerrero 39868, Mexico
Phone (52) 74-841580/N.A. (800) 228-3000
Fax (52) 74-842269
300 rooms and suites, $165-$465

This high-class resort sits on a hilltop overlooking the entire Acapulco Bay. Each room has an indoor pool that extends out beneath the window, so you can exit your room by diving through! Fresh hibiscus flowers float in the water every day. Rent one of the hotel's 150 pink-and-white jeeps to explore this tropical paradise.

QUINTA LAURA ▸ 80-81

#466 Calle Santa Barbara, Colonia Conchas Chinas, Puerto Vallarta, Jalisco 48300, Mexico
Phone (800) 681-5777
Fax (805) 565-1420
7 rooms, $107-$194

Puerto Vallarta is a seaside resort with a quaint, relaxing air. U.S. presidents have stayed at the Quinta Laura, located on a hilltop outside the city. There is, of course, a large pool, and the transparent blue sea is all yours.

Ocho Cascadas

▸ 82-83

Paseo de Los Delfines 116, Residencial Conchas Chinas, Puerto Vallarta, Mexico
Phone (800) 999-8455
Fax (505) 275-2882
10 villas, $500-$4,000 weekly

These time-share villas, built one above the other down the incline of a ravine, are occasionally available for sublet. Ocho Cascadas means "eight waterfalls" in Spanish. The water in the villas' pools spills down from one to the next in dramatic waterfalls. The rooms have no glass windows; they're all open air. It's very pleasant here—dry, not humid.

●HAWAII

Royal Hawaiian Hotel

▸ 84-85

2259 Kalakaua Avenue, Honolulu; Hawaii 96815-2578
Phone (808) 923-7311/N.A. (800) 782-9488
Fax (808) 931-7840
572 rooms and suites, $275-$2,800

This pink palace, now a Waikiki landmark, was built in 1927 where the Hawaiian royal family's resort used to be. When you finally reach the hotel after weaving your way between the city's skyscrapers, you enter a different world. The rooms have thick pink carpets, high ceilings, and large oriental vases filled with bright flowers.

Halekulani

▸ 86-87

2199 Kalia Road, Honolulu, Hawaii 96815-1988
Phone (808) 923-2311/N.A. (800) 367-2343
Fax (808) 922-5111
456 rooms, $290-$1,770

Halekulani means "house befitting heaven" in Hawaiian. This hotel has consistently received five star ratings in prominent hotel guides. A beautiful pool with a tile floor in the pattern of an orchid, Hawaiian music and *hula* dances in the evenings, the view of Diamond Head from your bathroom window, breakfast on the veranda while soaking up the morning sun... It's all fabulous!

Hilton Hawaiian Village

▸ 88-89

2005 Kalia Road, Honolulu, Hawaii 96815
Phone (808) 949-4321/U.S. (800) HILTONS
Fax (808) 947-7914
2,545 rooms, 368 suites, 31 ADA rooms, $175-$3,250

This is one of the hugest hotels on Waikiki Beach. As the name indicates, the premises accommodate an entire resort village, including four high-rise buildings, three pools, over one hundred shops, and nine restaurants. The photos were taken from a standard room on the twenty-eighth floor. Page 88 is an evening view, page 89 a morning.

Sheraton Moana Surfrider

▸ 90-91

2365 Kalakaua Avenue, Honolulu, Hawaii 96815-2943
Phone (808) 922-3111/U.S. (800) 325-3535
Fax (808) 923-0308
746 rooms, 45 suites, $230-$800 plus

The oldest hotel in Hawaii, the Sheraton was built in 1901 and renovated in 1989, reproducing all its original features. The banyan trees in the garden, over 100 years old, shade the veranda and pool.

●TAHITI

Hotel Bora Bora

▸ 92-95

Point Raititi, B.P.1, Bora Bora, French Polynesia
Phone (689) 60-44-11/U.S. (800) 421-1490

Fax (689) 60-44-22

55 bungalows and villas, $395-$700

Opened in 1961, this prestigious hotel—part of the Amanresorts luxury resort chain—was entirely renovated in 1994. The appealing new wooden interiors gleam. There are all kind of rooms: floating bungalows, beach cottages, garden suites, and so on.

KIA ORA VILLAGE

▸ 96-97

P.O. Box 4607, Papeete, Tahiti, French Polynesia
Phone (689) 96-02-22
Fax (689) 96-02-20
45 bungalows, $320-$490

Rangiroa is a diver's mecca. Kia Ora is the best resort on the island. In 1994, floating bungalows were added. The butterfly fish near the bridge over the shallows love french bread, and are delighted when you feed them your leftovers from breakfast.

MOANA BEACH PARK ROYAL

▸ front cover, 98-101

Point Matira, B.P. 156, Nunue, 98730, Bora Bora, French Polynesia
Phone (689) 60-49-00/U.S. (800) 835-7742
Fax (689) 60-44-99
41 bungalows, $508-$657

This hotel, the most famous in Tahiti, has been featured in television commercials. The emerald-green lagoon surrounding it is truly one-of-a-kind, and the interiors are cosy and cute. Through the glass tables in the floating bungalows, you can see fish swimming in the coral reef below you (p. 99).

TETIAROA VILLAGE

▸ 102-103

Tetiaroa Island, B.P. 2418, Papeete, Tahiti, French Polynesia
Phone (689) 82-63-03
Fax (689) 85-00-51
several bungalows, $350-$740

A local king had a resort here, and now this lagoon island—a thirty-minute flight from Tahiti—is privately owned by actor Marlon Brando. The beautiful bungalows, fashioned from palm trees and palm leaves, are primitive, yet cozy. You can live like Robinson Crusoe here.

●KENYA

MPATA SAFARI CLUB

▸ 104-107

Masai Mara
Mailing Address: c/o Mpata Investments, 20th Floor, Anniversary Towers, University Way, P.O. Box 58402, Nairobi, Kenya
Phone (2542) 217015
Fax (2542) 217016
23 cottages, $145-$560

A forty-minute plane ride from Nairobi, this hotel, boasting a five star rating, is located in the Masai Mara Wildlife Preserve. The lodge, built in 1992, is a members-only safari club. Located on a hilltop, the hotel overlooks the savanna, spreading out endlessly beneath like an ocean. With binoculars, you can see elephants and giraffes. The dining room is striking (pp. 104-105), and serves gourmet French meals. Free of background music, this place will make you forget life in the big city.